THIS IS HOW IT HAPPENED

Also by Paula Stokes

The Art of Lainey

Infinite Repeat (A Digital Novella)

Liars, Inc.

Girl Against the Universe

PAULA STOKES

THIS

IS

HOW

IT

HAPPENED

An Imprint of HarperCollinsPublishers

HarperTeen is an imprint of HarperCollins Publishers.

This Is How It Happened
Copyright © 2017 by Paula Stokes
All rights reserved. Printed in the United States of America.
No part of this book may be used or reproduced in any manner whatsoever without written
permission except in the case of brief quotations embodied in critical articles and reviews. For
information address HarperCollins Children's Books, a division of HarperCollins Publishers,
195 Broadway, New York, NY 10007.
www.epicreads.com
Library of Congress Control Number: 2016040465
ISBN 978-0-06-237993-1 (trade bdg.) — ISBN 978-0-06-268852-1 (special edition)
Typography by Sarah Nichole Kaufman
17 18 19 20 21 PC/LSCH 10 9 8 7 6 5 4 3 2 1

First Edition

In memory of Dallas

THE ST. LOUIS TIMES

Local YouTube Sensation and Fusion Recording Artist Killed in Car Accident

BY OLIVIA AHN, May 13, 6:00 a.m.

Early this morning, at approximately 1:15 a.m., seventeen-year-old Fusion Records recording artist and Ridgehaven Academy senior Dallas Kade was killed in a head-on collision on Highway Z in Wentzville. Kade was a passenger in his own car, which was being driven by his girlfriend, Genevieve Grace, another Ridgehaven Academy senior.

The two were returning home from a release party for Kade's debut album, *Try This at Home*. The first single, "Younity," a rock/rap anthem featuring Kade's label-mate Tyrell James, hit airwaves four weeks ago and is already racing up the Billboard charts.

Kade and Grace were hit by Bradley Freeman, 38, a former St. Charles County paramedic who now works as a cook at the Eight Ball Bar & Grill in New Melle. Freeman resigned from EMS duty two years ago after pleading guilty to a DWI charge. A Wentzville Police Department officer who was one of the first on the scene said he "smelled alcohol" on Freeman, but officials are awaiting the results of blood tests to determine if Freeman was indeed driving under the influence at the time of the accident.

Kade was pronounced dead upon arrival at Lake St. Louis Medical Center. Grace and Freeman remain in critical condition. More on this story as events unfold.

Comments 1–10 of 2,401

Kadet4Ever: This is a joke, right? Some sort of publicity stunt because the album just went on sale? Someone please tell me it's a joke.

Lila Ferrier: I think it's true. They're running the same article over at MTV and Tyrell James just tweeted condolences to the entire KadetKorps.

KickassKadet: OMG. I'm dying right now.

pxs1228: You know who should be dying? The guy who hit him. I hope that drunk SOB never wakes up. Brad Freeman is white trash garbage. Human waste.

fullgrownkademaniac: No way. He needs to take responsibility for what he did. The Scoop is reporting that a radar detector was found in the wreckage of Freeman's truck. You don't have one of those unless you're a habitual speeder or drunk driver. I hope he wakes up and then goes to jail for the rest of his life. Which is long. And painful.

pxs1228: Good point. I hope he gets sued for every penny he owns along the way. Can you imagine how much money Dallas Kade might have earned in a lifetime?

fullgrownkademaniac: #JusticeForDallas

Kadet4Ever: #Justice4Dallas And don't forget to #Pray4Genevieve too. Can you imagine how grief-stricken she's going to be when she wakes up and realizes Dallas is gone forever? I can't even!

fullgrownkademaniac: IF she wakes up :(

pxs1228: Freeman better hope she wakes up, or else that'll be two people he killed.

CHAPTER 1

When I open my eyes, my first thought is that I'm underwater. Everything is bright and out of focus. My instincts tell me I need to breathe, but I'm afraid that if I try to inhale the water will rush into my throat and I'll drown. As I push for the surface, I exhale a tiny breath of air and my teeth press hard against something plastic. Reaching my hand up to my mouth, I realize there's a tube in my throat. I gag violently as I pull on it. Some sort of machine starts beeping.

"No, no," a female voice says sharply. A strong hand grips my wrist and moves it away from my face. I blink hard. The whole world is still blurry. I try to ask what's happening but no words come out.

"Well, don't yell at her. I can only imagine how scary it is to wake up on a ventilator," a male voice says. "Page Derby and see if we can extubate." Someone places my hand down next to my hip. "Genevieve. You were in an accident," the male voice continues. "The tube in your throat is helping you breathe. If you pull it out, you could damage your larynx."

Ventilator. Extubate. Accident. I'm in the hospital, but that's as far as I get. The rest of the guy's words fall through the grates of my brain, lost in a current of blood. What if I have brain damage? I lift my hand again to make sure my skull is still intact, but my fingers get distracted by a bandage wrapped around my head.

My hand is quickly pinned against the soft mattress and held there. "Don't mess with your dressing, okay? Try to stay calm."

"He's coming." The female voice is back. "I brought you a warm blanket." Something cozy unfolds over my whole body, like slipping into pajamas fresh from the dryer. A soft cloth wipes across my eyes and suddenly I can see again. The forms are a little fuzzy, but I can make out a tall black guy and a shorter redheaded woman, both dressed in navy blue nursing scrubs.

A man in a white coat strides into the room. "Well, hello, young lady," he says in a booming voice. "I'm Dr. Derby from Neurosurgery. Let's see if you're ready to breathe on your own again." He shines a tiny flashlight into each of my eyes and then has me squeeze both of his hands. He hands me a whiteboard and a marker. "Can you write your name for me?"

My whole body aches and the marker feels awkward in my hand, like I'm back in preschool, learning how to write for the first time. And just like my four-year-old self probably did, I curse internally at how long my name is. It takes about three lifetimes, but I finally manage to scrawl out the letters

G E N E V I E V E G R A C E. At least I dropped one letter when I changed my last name from Larsen to Grace after my parents divorced.

Next, Dr. Derby asks me where I am, and what day it is. I take to the whiteboard again. When I apparently flub the date, he gives me a follow-up question of what year it is. Thankfully I get that one right.

The doctor turns to a computer and flicks through a few screens. Then he goes to the big ventilator machine parked next to my bed. The machine chirps in response as he presses a few keys. "I think we can extubate," he says. "Page Respiratory and put her on q fifteen-minute neuro checks for the first two hours. Call me for anything out of range. Oh, and put her on clear fluids until tomorrow night."

The redheaded nurse grabs a phone from the pocket of her scrubs and steps outside the room. The male nurse smiles at me. "Welcome back," he says. "The respiratory tech will be here soon. Just hang in there."

Like I have any other choice. I inhale deeply and the ventilator chirps again.

A couple of minutes later, an Indian girl who doesn't look much older than me pushes a cart into the room. "I'm Priya from the Respiratory department," she says. "It's lovely to see you awake, Miss Grace. I'm going to take that tube out of your throat." She starts to loosen the tape around my mouth.

And then I hear another voice, as sharp as a scalpel—my mother's.

"What's going on in here?" Her high heels rat-a-tat-tat across the tile floor like machine-gun fire. Everyone in the room looks like they want to take cover. "Why didn't you page me that she was awake?"

"I'm sorry, Dr. Grace. She literally just woke up," the male nurse says.

My mom pushes past him without replying. "Genevieve, honey. I was so worried about you."

I try to squeeze out a "Hi, Mom," which is probably inadequate, but it doesn't matter because I can't talk with the tube in my throat.

My mom glances around the room. "What are you waiting for? Extubate her."

Priya bends low with an empty syringe. She does something I can't see and then slowly pulls the tube out of my throat. For a second, I feel like someone is choking me, but then I gasp in relief. My mother hands me a tissue.

I wipe some crusty stuff from the corners of my mouth. "Hey," I manage. One word. Soft. Hoarse.

"Hey," my mom says. Her eyes start to water.

Wow, she must have been seriously frightened. My mom is one of those people who thinks crying is a sign of weakness and that signs of weakness are unacceptable. It's probably a good combination for a pediatric cardiac surgeon. Less so for a mom, or a wife. It's a miracle she and my dad stayed married as long as they did.

As if reading my mind, she says, "Your father is in the

waiting area." She gestures around the room. "A lot of your friends stopped by while you were . . . sleeping."

I wrap my arm around one of my bed rails and pull myself to a seated position. The room is full of colorful cards, balloons, and stuffed animals. Like *completely* full. What the hell? There must be stuff from fifty people here, which would be nice, except I only have two close friends. Maybe it's all from my mom's coworkers, or maybe Dallas's music industry friends sent a ton of crap.

I furrow my brow as I look past my mom, through the glass door of my room. A nurse in navy blue hurries by, the pocket of her scrubs bulging with syringes and other medical stuff. Behind her, doctors in white coats are clustered around a bank of computers.

"Where's Dallas?" I ask. He should be here right now.

Mom starts talking about the accident, but her words fade out, because suddenly I start to remember what happened.

CHAPTER 2

MAY 12

Dallas stood on the porch wearing ripped jeans and a designer T-shirt, his blond hair artfully arranged in soft spikes. He was clutching a bouquet of coral-colored roses and a plastic soda bottle of bright yellow fluid.

"Look at you," I said with a grin. "So smooth. Remember when we were both nerds?" I held open the door for him.

"You were never a nerd, Genna." He stepped into the foyer. "Lucky for me you just liked engaging in nerd pastimes."

I laughed. We met as freshmen in Premed Club, an after-school activity for kids who want to be doctors. We were still in that club, but finally we were seniors, which made us the automatic cool kids. Not that Dallas needed extra cool points. In the past three years he'd gone from "I started a YouTube channel to teach people how to play their favorite songs on the piano" to "I just released my first album." Dallas had close to a million Twitter followers. I had seventy-eight.

My mom materialized in the living room as if summoned

by the scent of roses. "How thoughtful of you, Dallas," she said. "But tonight is *your* special night. You didn't need to bring flowers for Genevieve."

"Oh, these are for you, Dr. Grace." He thrust the roses in my mom's direction. "I appreciate how supportive you've been, working around my music schedule and allowing me to pick up occasional shifts in your lab. I'm still planning on declaring premed, so that experience is really important to me."

My mom puffed up with pride as she accepted the bouquet, adding another inch to her already imposing five-foot-nine-inch frame. (I'm five foot three—not sure what happened there.) "If anyone can break records in the performing arts and medical fields both, I have no doubt that it's you," she said.

"Hey, what about me?" I said with pretend hurt. I actually have no interest in performing, unless acing my MCATs in a few years counts.

"Stick with medicine. We can't all be entertainers," Mom advised. "I'd better go see if I can find a vase. It's been a while since a man brought me flowers." She spun on her heel and headed toward the kitchen.

"I guess I could've brought her a vase too." Dallas fiddled with the rubber bracelet he always wore. It was black and white, like a set of piano keys wrapping around his wrist.

"No need. Not counting the one I broke when I was seven, I'm guessing she has about fifty." There was a point in my parents' marriage when my dad tried really, really hard.

"Cool." Dallas lowered his voice. "By the way, I find you plenty entertaining."

I gave him a playful punch in the arm. "Good to know."

He handed me the bottle of yellow fluid. "I know you don't like flowers, so this is for you."

I held the container up to eye level and sloshed the liquid back and forth. It resembled an unlabeled bottle of Mountain Dew, or maybe antifreeze. "You brought me a urine sample?" I joked.

"Yeah . . . no. Tyrell sent me a test batch of his energy drink to hand out to my friends. That's called Barely Legal, and apparently it's got enough caffeine and B-vitamins to keep you going for twelve hours straight. You're still getting up at five to go running every day, right? Wouldn't want you to fall asleep during your finals."

I had to swallow back a yawn at the mere mention of the word "sleep." "Barely Legal? Someone thought that was a good name? And you actually want me to drink this?" I unscrewed the cover and gave the fizzy liquid a sniff. "Are you sure it's not a urine sample?"

"Don't be a smartass," Dallas said. "Tyrell thinks that's going to compete with Red Bull. He and his brother are planning to go into production by midsummer to be able to market to kids by fall finals."

"Well. He's nothing if not confident," I replied. Tyrell James is featured in two songs on Dallas's album. I found it weird at first, the way a twenty-eight-year-old rapper from the north side of St. Louis wanted to collaborate with a teenage singer from what people who live in the city have been known to call "the sticks." But apparently they had the same producer or manager or something—I couldn't keep track of all the music industry jargon—and their sounds blended really well together. Plus, they both helped extend each other's fan base.

"He says ninety-five percent of success is confidence."

"What's the other five percent?" I asked. "Actual talent?"

"Energy drinks, I think," Dallas said with a grin. "You ready to go?"

"As ready as I'll ever be." I set the sample of Barely Legal on the coffee table and turned to follow Dallas out to his car. Like everything else about him, it was slick, shiny, and new. He swore he wasn't going to go crazy buying stuff, but it was probably impossible not to splurge a little when he signed his recording contract and suddenly felt rich.

We buckled up and Dallas backed slowly down the long driveway. He navigated the twisting back roads of my Lake St. Louis neighborhood like he'd been driving the car for years. We wound our way through an area of dense trees and then merged onto Highway 40 and headed for the city.

Dallas reached over and wrapped one of his hands around mine. "Thanks for coming with."

"You're welcome."

Dallas knew I felt uncomfortable going to parties with him. I liked his songs but I wasn't a huge music person in general, so a lot of the industry conversation was lost on me. Not to mention I'm kind of introverted, so I usually killed time in some quiet corner, texting my best friend, Shannon, or pretending to be responding to urgent emails while everyone else danced and mingled. When I was lucky enough that the parties were at private residences, I sometimes ended up on the floor somewhere playing with a dog or cat, or once a frisky pair of ferrets.

This particular party was at Tyrell James's house, which is in the ritzy Central West End neighborhood, between downtown St. Louis and Washington University. Dallas and I had both been accepted to Wash U for the fall. I had no idea how he thought he was going to manage our rigorous premed coursework with his new record label obligations, but my mom was right—if anyone could do it, he could.

The drive took us a little over an hour. Tyrell's assistant, Tricia, answered the door and ushered us into the great room, where most of the guests were hanging out. The room was a mix of old architecture and slick modern furnishings, the vaulted ceilings and crown molding blending surprisingly well with the black leather sofas and glass fireplace.

Tyrell sauntered over and greeted both of us. "What's up?" he asked.

Dallas gestured around at the crowd. "Pretty epic scene you've got going on here."

Tyrell laughed. "This is all you." He held out his fist.

As I watched Dallas execute an awkward fist bump, his pale freckled knuckles colliding with Tyrell's dark skin, I smiled at the idea that two musicians who were so different had created a song loved by so many people. Maybe there was hope for the world after all.

The two of them made the rounds along a string of strangers who pumped Dallas's hand and pressed business cards into his palm. Shaking my head at a couple of servers handing out hors d'oeuvres and glasses of champagne, I wandered toward the back of the house, where a set of stairs led down into the basement. I figured Tyrell had probably locked up his surprisingly lovable Rottweiler, Sable, in the laundry room as usual. I glanced back over my shoulder. My boyfriend was smiling his professional entertainer smile and nodding as a silver-haired guy showed him something on an iPhone. I opened the door to the basement with a creak and closed it behind me. Dallas would text me if he needed me.

Sable was smart enough not to bark when the door opened. Instead I heard the sound of her nails clicking across the cement floor as I flipped on the light. I'd only been there two other times, but either the dog remembered me or she was lonely enough to cuddle up to a stranger. She butted her head against my hand and then loped off into the darkness.

"Come here, girl." I sat on the floor and patted my legs to get her attention. "What are you doing?"

Sable found a ball behind the washing machine and trotted over to me, dropping it next to me with a hopeful look. I rolled the ball across the floor and Sable caught up to it in about two strides. She brought it back and deposited it into my lap.

"Gross. You drooled on it." I held it up like I was going to throw it and her mouth curled up into a smile. I smiled back—I've never been able to resist a smiling dog—and then flung the ball the length of the laundry room.

We played fetch until Sable was exhausted, and then she lay down on her side and looked up at me, her pink tongue dangling out of the corner of her mouth. I scratched her behind the ears.

"I'd much rather party with dogs," I told her. "I don't know why Tyrell locks you up. You are the cutest thing ever."

She chuffed in agreement, her dark eyes falling closed. I leaned my head back against the wall of the laundry room and stroked Sable's fur repeatedly. Above, a familiar beat started playing—Dallas's first single, "Younity," one of the tracks featuring Tyrell. The song is about kids and teens learning to support each other regardless of gender, race, wealth, etc. Fusion Records leaked the video in early spring and now it had more than seven million views.

When Dallas first transitioned from making instructional videos playing other people's songs to showcasing his original music online, he shot his own videos to upload to YouTube. I'm even featured in a couple of them. He wanted me to be in the video for "Younity" too, and I tried—I really did—but after one day on set, I quit and told him he'd be better off hiring a professional model.

Shannon said I was crazy, but she's a mega-extrovert. The idea of spending three days being dressed, made-up, and judged by strangers sounded *fun* to her. There is nothing fun about a group of people shaking their heads in exasperation because they hate the shape of your lips or the way your hair moves when you walk.

Dallas didn't seem to care about me bailing on him, especially when they replaced me with a willowy Swedish model named Annika Lux, and I was only too happy to escape to the sidelines, where I could snap pictures and share them with Shannon when no one was looking.

But a few weeks after the shoot, Dallas and I got into a fight and he told me that my dropping out of the video made him upset and embarrassed. Not only was it last-minute extra work for the producer, but he'd been tweeting about how excited he was that his beautiful blond girlfriend was going to be in his video, and suddenly everyone seemed to think he and Annika Lux were a couple.

Sable stirred in her sleep. I realized I should leave the dog alone and go find Dallas. I should *want* to go find Dallas, anyway.

I checked my phone to make sure I hadn't missed any messages and sighed when I saw that it wasn't even ten o'clock. Still, I'd been down there for almost an hour. I knew I should probably at least check in.

I headed back upstairs and cut through the kitchen area and back into the great room, where Dallas's album was still blaring and people were dancing, talking, or smashed onto the sofa playing video games. I didn't see Dallas anywhere. I pulled my phone out of my purse and started to tap out a text. Before I finished, a boy about my age wearing red leather pants and a black T-shirt so tight I could see the outline of his abs asked me to dance.

"Sorry. I don't dance." I tried not to stare at his overly defined muscles.

"That's cool," the boy said. "How about a drink?"

"I don't really drink either," I said. "Do you know where Dallas is?"

"Out there with some of his fan club." The boy gestured toward a set of French doors that led out onto the deck. "Too bad. You don't really look like a Kadet to me."

"Believe it or not, I'm the queen of the Kadets," I said.

I stepped out onto the deck, where a group of teens and twentysomethings were packed a little too tightly into Tyrell's hot tub. Behind them, a sprinkling of people stood clutching drinks. I scanned the crowd, but I still didn't find Dallas.

I approached a guy with a beer bottle in one hand and a cigarette in the other. "Have you seen Dallas by any chance?" I asked.

"Out there maybe?" The guy gestured toward the backyard with his beer.

I wandered to the edge of the deck and peered out into the night. The manicured lawn faded into blackness beyond the house lights.

"Dallas?" I called.

No one answered.

CHAPTER 3

"Genevieve?" My mom's voice slices the memory to pieces. "Are you listening to me?"

"Sorry. I was just trying to remember what happened." I shift slightly in bed and a sharp pain shoots through my left leg. I yank my blankets to the side and find my calf completely wrapped in gauze dressing. Gingerly, I reach out to touch the bandages.

"Nothing is broken, but a piece of metal cut into your muscle and the laceration required over twenty stitches," Mom says. "How's your head feeling?"

"Okay, I guess."

"I don't know how much the nurses told you before I arrived, but in addition to your leg, you suffered a skull fracture and an epidural hematoma requiring surgery. You also have a lot of scratches and bruises." Mom's voice wavers. She looks away for a second. "But it's nothing that won't heal."

"So where's Dallas?" I ask again. "Did he get hurt too?"

Mom's face tightens into her "concerned parent" look, the one that makes two little divots form in the space between her eyebrows. "Did you not hear *anything* I just said?"

I rub at my eyes. "I'm sorry. I zoned out. You were telling me about the accident, right?" I fish through my memory of the last couple of minutes, but the only things that surface are the words "head injury" and "unresponsive." She could have been talking about me.

My mom strides to the door of my room and snaps her fingers at my nurse as she passes by. "Get Derby back here."

I sink down in the bed. I hate it when she does the snapping thing. I thought she mostly reserved it for waiters, which still makes me cringe, but seeing her do it in the hospital makes me wonder if maybe everyone here hates her, if she's one of those mean surgeons the whole staff whispers about when she's not around.

"But we just did a neuro check and everything seems intact," the redheaded nurse says.

"I don't care. Get him on the phone for me."

The nurse looks ready to object again. Good for her for standing up to my mom, but I'm not sure she knows who she's dealing with. I cough feebly as a distraction. "Mom. You're not my doctor. You can't order people around."

My mom's lips tighten into a hard line. "And we might need Psych up here as well."

Of course, because if I'm standing up to her it's either a brain bleed or a mental disorder. "I don't need Psych," I say. "I just want to know what happened to Dallas. Is he hurt badly? Is that why he's not here?"

"Genevieve." My mom pulls a chair over to the side of the bed. She curls one hand around mine. "How much do you remember about the accident?"

My heart starts pounding. Images flicker through my brain: flashing lights, smoke, blood. But is any of it real? I'm not sure. For all I know, I'm still unconscious on a ventilator and this moment isn't even real. I bite down on my bottom lip until the pain makes my eyes water. "Just bits and pieces," I say.

"It was very serious—a head-on collision," my mom says softly. "I'm sorry, honey. Dallas didn't survive. He's dead."

"What?" I say, even though I heard her just fine. I must have known in some way, from the look on my mom's face, from the sound in her voice, that Dallas was gone, but hearing it stated so matter-of-factly is like a sledgehammer to the gut. "I don't—" My eyes start to water. My jaw trembles. I can't speak. I can't even breathe. I ball the fabric of my blanket in both fists. Through the blur of tears, I see my mom mouth "Psych" to the nurse. The nurse hurries from the room and Mom slides the glass door closed for privacy. She pulls a box of Kleenex from the counter and sets it on the bed next to me.

I grab a tissue and cover my face with it. "I don't under-stand," I choke out. "His first album just came out. How can he be *dead*?" I try to envision it in my mind—Dallas, lifeless—but I can't even picture the word "dead." I can't remember how to spell it. I might even be saying it wrong.

"They said he probably wasn't wearing his seat belt correctly, that airbags often don't work the way they're supposed to if you're not buckled in."

I barely hear the words my mom is saying. My brain keeps replaying, *Dallas didn't survive. He's dead.* The closest I've ever been to death is when Shannon had to go to Kansas City for her grandmother's funeral. Shannon didn't talk about it much and I didn't press her.

"I know how hard this is going to be," Mom says. "I just want you to know I'll be supporting you every step of the way. Nurses, psychologists, physical therapists. Whatever you need—I'll make sure you get it. I've overseen your care for the past week, I've—"

"Past *week?*" I peek over the edge of my tissue. "Wait. How long was I unconscious?"

"Five and a half days," my mom says. "They had to keep you sedated until the swelling in your brain went down."

"Oh my God." The tissue slips from my fingers and falls to the bed, getting lost in the white folds of my blanket. Five and a half days. Brain swelling. I almost died too. The word "dead" feels just as strange when I think about it to describe myself.

Tears stream silently down my cheeks. I stare straight ahead, at the thick glass door to my room. Beyond it, doctors and nurses stride past carrying clipboards and tablet computers. They're moving. Living. And I feel frozen in a single moment. *Dallas didn't survive. He's dead.*

Why Dallas instead of me?

"The police have been waiting to speak to you," my mom says. "But I'll tell them it can wait a little longer, until you're feeling a bit better."

I blink hard as I fight to regain control of my emotions, but now my mother has introduced fear into an already overwhelming mix of shock, grief, and pain. "Police? Why do the police want to talk to me?"

Mom's face twists up into a frown. "Because you were hit by some drunken miscreant, and they want to make sure he goes to jail."

"Is the other driver okay?"

My mom scoffs. "The people who cause the accidents always seem to come out on top. He was unresponsive at the scene but was resuscitated and woke up a couple of days ago with nothing but a concussion and a couple of scratches. He's claiming he doesn't remember anything. Too bad for him blood tests don't lie. I will never understand people who think it's okay to get wasted and then get behind the wheel of a car."

"I swear to you I didn't drink anything," I say softly.

"I know you didn't. The hospital did tox screens on both drivers, but I had no doubt what the results would be. You're a good girl, Genevieve. I'm sorry that bad things sometimes happen to good people."

The glass door to my room slides open and the redheaded nurse returns with a slender Asian man in tow. "It's time for another neuro check," she says brightly. "And I've brought Dr. Chao in case Genevieve feels like talking." She holds a portable phone out toward my mother. " I've also got Dr. Derby on the line for you."

Mom takes the phone. "Alex, one second," she says. She turns back to me. "Do you feel up to visiting with your father?"

I have spoken to my dad only a handful of times since he divorced my mom for another woman three years ago and moved fifteen hundred miles away. I've never really forgiven him for the way he broke up our family, but now doesn't seem like the time to hold a grudge. Plus, I guess it's nice that he flew in all the way from Utah to see me. "Yeah, he can come in." I glance around the room. "What time is it?"

"It's about four-thirty," Mom says. "I'll tell him to wait until Dr. Chao is finished." She turns her attention back to the phone as she clickety-clacks out of the room. I hear her ask something about cognitive processing speeds.

The nurse puts me through the same series of tests Dr. Derby did when I first woke up, asking me to hold out my arms, squeeze her hands, follow her flashlight with my eyes, etc. I ask her for pain medicine for my leg and she returns with a clear vial and a syringe.

Dr. Chao waits for her to administer the medicine and then closes the glass door behind her. He tells me he's from Psychiatric Services and gives me some general information about PTSD, anxiety, depression, and sleep disorders—all common side effects of serious accidents. I listen quietly, but my focus flickers in and out. I'm still replaying my mom's words in my head. *Dallas didn't survive. He's dead.*

"How are you really feeling?" Dr. Chao clears his throat. "Sorry, I know that's standard therapy talk, but the emotional and physical responses to traumatic events can vary widely, and finding the best course of treatment depends on knowing where the patient is at."

"I kind of lost it when my mom told me." I point at my red eyes. "But now I just . . . I don't know. It all seems sort of unreal. I think maybe I'm in shock. No one close to me has ever . . . you know." I can't bring myself to say "died."

"Well, you might be feeling numb from the pain medicine you received, but you'll be with us for a couple more days and then your mom asked me to recommend an outpatient therapist just in case. Between the two of us, we'll make sure you're covered for anything you need, okay?"

I nod. What I need is to rewind the past week and keep Dallas safe somehow, but I don't think Dr. Chao can prescribe me a time machine. I glance past him. My dad has appeared outside the closed glass door. He's pacing back and forth, his shirt rumpled, his hair sticking up. He looks like complete crap, and for some reason I find that comforting, like maybe he didn't get remarried and forget all about me.

Dr. Chao follows my gaze. "It appears someone is anxious to see you," he says. "I'll check back in tomorrow. In the meantime, read through these if you get a chance." He leaves a couple of pamphlets on dealing with grief on my nightstand and then heads back out into the ICU.

Dad strides into the room and comes immediately to my

bedside, where he slides into the chair Dr. Chao vacated. "Gene-vieve." He takes my left hand in both of his, expertly navigating multiple IV lines without pulling or pressing on anything. "I have never been so scared in my whole life."

I open my mouth to tell him I'm glad he's here, but what slips out is "You got old."

Dad laughs, and tears well in his eyes. "I never thought I'd be so happy to hear someone say that."

"Sorry. I think that might be the pain medicine talking."

"No, it's fine that my gorgeous teenage daughter thinks I'm old. But if you're referring to my gray hairs, I'm fairly certain all of them cropped up in the past few days."

"Too much time with Mom, huh?" Again, the words fall from my lips without much thought. Either the nurse gave me really good drugs, or my dad's presence is like one of those warm blankets she brought me earlier. I've been mad about the divorce for what feels like forever, but seeing him here reminds me of how things used to be. Suddenly I'm twelve years old again and my parents are still married. I never realized how good I had it back then.

Dad laughs again. "Pretty and funny. Some guy is going to be a lucky . . ." He trails off as he realizes what he's said. "My turn to apologize," he says. "I'm so sorry about Dallas. Such an incredibly talented young man. What a tragedy."

I nod. I don't want to talk about Dallas right now. I'll just end up crying again and I don't have the energy. Plus, there's something bothering me when I think about him—something more than just the fact that he's gone—but I'm not sure what it is. "I can't believe you're here," I say. "What about your cases?"

My dad is also a workaholic surgeon, but that's where the similarities end between him and my mom. Where Mom is high-strung and overdemanding, Dad is laid-back and was always kind of a slacker in the parent department. I think he viewed his role as more of a supporting one.

Dad rubs at his forehead. His blond hair is only beginning to recede, new threads of gray appearing at his temples since I last saw him. "I can't believe you can't believe I'm here." He shakes his head ruefully. "I messed things up between us so badly. Thank God I have another chance to be a decent father to you." He looks toward the ceiling for a second.

"Thank God?" As far as I know, my parents and I have all been atheists since I was old enough to decide for myself. "That's new."

"Yes, well. People change."

"Not easily," I say. "What happened? Did Rachael get you going to church?"

"Let's just say I'm trying to be more open-minded these days."

"I guess that's good." I pick at a loose thread on my blanket. "But it's hard to even imagine a God who would kill Dallas. Everyone loved him. He was destined for so many great things." My voice cracks and I look away. Neither one of my parents has ever been particularly skilled at handling my tears. I learned early on to do most of my crying in private.

Dad lifts one hand to my cheek. "Honey, I wish there was some way I could help. I know how close you and Dallas were."

I turn back to face my dad. "How do you know *that*?"

"Well, for one, your mother told me. But even before then, I've seen all the pictures of the two of you on your Instagram, the interviews where Dallas said some of the songs on his album were written for his girlfriend." Dad gives me a sad smile. "Just because we haven't talked much in the past couple of years doesn't mean I haven't been keeping up with how you're doing."

I'm not sure if I should be offended or flattered at the idea of my dad stalking me online. I really did think after he messed up royally with Mom and me that he just decided to cut his losses and start over with his new wife.

"We've been dating—I mean, we dated—for over two years, but we were kind of going through a rough spot," I say. "Dallas spent a lot of time working on his YouTube channel even before he got the offer to record the album, but it was never more than an obsessive hobby, you know? But once he started making real money, things changed."

"You felt left behind?" my dad asks.

"More like we just ended up on different paths," I say. "Maybe we would have broken up. I don't know."

"That doesn't make this any less traumatic for you." Dad squeezes my hand gently.

"Thanks." *Dallas didn't survive. He's dead.* It's like I have to keep replaying those words in order to believe them. I know the first stage of grief is denial, but I've always thought of that as an active thing, a violent refusal to accept reality. What I feel is just this passive shock, this numbness. Maybe it *is* just the medicine, like Dr. Chao said. At least my leg stopped aching.

"Right now it all feels fake," I say, more to myself than my dad. "Like I'm rehearsing for my role in the world's most terrible play."

I can't shake the idea that my real life, and Dallas, are out there somewhere waiting for me.

CHAPTER 4

Dad and I start watching a movie on his iPad. We're only about fifteen minutes in when my mom reappears, my backpack clutched in one of her fists. "Good news," she says to me, without so much as acknowledging my dad's presence. "Shannon dropped off your homework. I figured you'd want to start catching up as soon as possible."

"Is Shannon here?" I ask hopefully. Last year she had to spend the night in the hospital after she slipped on the diving board and hit her head. I stayed with her right up until she fell asleep, watching movies and working on homework together.

"I told her you weren't ready for visitors yet, but she'll be back tomorrow after school. Oh, and the police are going to come by and take a statement after dinner."

"Okay." There's a sick feeling in the pit of my stomach, and I'm not sure if it's from the idea of talking to the cops or the idea of trying to eat dinner for the first time in six days.

"How are your cases going?" Dad asks Mom, a safe attempt

to be polite. If there's one thing a surgeon is always willing to talk about, it's surgery.

"Good." Her eyes flick to his face for just a second and then back to mine. "Did two PFAs this week and a transplant in a two-year-old."

"Nice," my dad says. "You always did have a knack for the detail work. I prefer my hearts big enough that I can actually see the vessels I'm working on."

"Yes, well. We could talk all day about how you like easy, oversized things."

I wince. My stepmom, Rachael, is a park ranger who is five years older and about fifty pounds heavier than my mom. Mom had fun with that fact, telling all her friends that Dad had apparently developed a taste for overweight geriatric women.

"But at the moment I think it's best if we limit our interactions to what directly concerns our daughter," Mom continues. "How long will you be in town?"

Dad pauses the movie. "As long as Genevieve needs me."

My mother lifts her chin. "I'm quite sure I can take care of Genevieve. I've been doing it basically on my own for almost eighteen years."

Dad's face reddens. "That is not—"

I clear my throat. "Can you guys maybe not do this?"

My mom doesn't say anything for a moment. Then, "I'll let you and your father enjoy your movie and drop back by later after he's *left*."

"Good plan." Dad's jaw tightens.

Mom spins on her heel and leaves the room, the tails of her white coat flapping behind her.

"Sorry," he says, after she slides the door shut. "She still knows how to push my buttons."

"Yours and everyone else's," I say. "I thought she and my nurse were going to get into a fistfight."

Dad snickers. "It's good to know there are people who refuse to let her intimidate them."

"Good until those people start to mysteriously disappear, at least."

He pats me on the knee. "I'm glad to hear you making jokes. But hey, you don't have to put on a brave face for all this, okay? After everything that's happened, you're allowed to fall apart; your parents are both surgeons. We'll be here to put you back together if needed."

"Thanks, Dad. And thanks again for coming all this way." I tug at the loose thread on my blanket again.

"Stop thanking me for that." He leans forward so we're eye to eye. "You're always going to be the most important thing in my life."

"Says the guy who moved fifteen hundred miles away," I mumble.

"Says the guy who has been trying to get you to come visit him for three years."

That's the thing about surgeons for parents. They are always on their game. A weaker dad would have dissolved into apologies after my remark, but my dad counters with a legitimate point. I haven't gone to visit him once since he moved to Utah. I didn't even want to go to his wedding in the Bahamas, but he said I could bring a friend and Shannon had never gone anywhere outside the Midwest. Her eyes almost bugged out of her head when I told her. After that, I couldn't back out.

But the two of us hung out on the beach and kept to ourselves except for the actual ceremony and the bare minimum of time I felt obligated to stay at the reception. I expected my dad to act all wounded and lecture me, but instead he said he was glad I came, that it meant a lot to Rachael I was willing to be there.

"You're right," I admit. "I should've found the time to visit. I'm sorry if I hurt you, or Rachael." I glance around nervously. "I know you tried. I don't blame you for leaving anymore. I just wish you had done it differently."

"Me too," Dad says. "I hate that I hurt you."

I swallow hard. I'm in no condition to talk about the way my dad hurt me right now. It's weird that something he did years ago feels like a fresh wound, but thinking about Dallas being dead still feels hazy and unreal. Maybe it's my mind trying to protect me, holding back the emotional pain of the accident until my physical injuries start to heal.

I gesture at the iPad. "Let's get back to our movie."

For the next two hours, my dad and I hang out in comfortable silence, disturbed only by my nurse popping in occasionally to reprogram my IV pump and do neuro checks. As the credits start to roll across the screen of Dad's iPad, a man in black-and-white checked pants and a white coat knocks gently on the glass door.

My dad hops up and opens it.

"I have a clear fluids meal for Genevieve Grace," the man says, checking a paper list.

"Mmm-mmm good," Dad says. "Look, Genevieve. Dinner is served."

"Great," I say. "I've been clamoring for some chicken broth and Jell-O."

The man checks my hospital ID bracelet, makes a note on his list, and sets my tray on my bedside table. Dad pushes the chair he'd been sitting in back against the wall and helps raise the head of my bed all the way so I'm ready to eat.

The man heads for his next room and Dad lays out my silverware on a napkin.

"Are you going to hang out and watch me eat?" I ask. "I'll look the other way if you want to steal that Jell-O."

"Pass," Dad says. "You know I only like the green kind. I just want to be sure you can eat without aspirating."

I take a big slurp of soup—low salt, lukewarm, this is why people starve to death in hospitals—and when I don't suck it straight into my lungs, my dad smooths the wrinkles from his polo shirt and begins to gather his things.

A strange bout of preemptive loneliness hits me. I don't want to be in this room all by myself. "Do you know what happened to my phone?" I ask.

"I don't know if they ever recovered it from the accident, but I think there's a landline somewhere that works for local calls if you need to call someone." Dad scans the room.

Except I don't know Shannon's phone number. "I was just going to check my email and stuff." My eyes latch onto Dad's tablet.

"You want to borrow this?" He drops his iPad on the mattress next to me, bending over to kiss me on the forehead at the same time. "The latest Tess Gerritsen is on there if you need something to read. It's also full of my recent case study notes, if you need help getting to sleep later."

My lips curl upward. "Thanks, Dad."

The sliding glass door opens without warning and my mom reappears. I pull the blankets up to cover the iPad—I'm not sure why—and turn my attention to her. "You're just in time for the blandest dinner ever created. I think they brought me three bowls of colored water."

"See you tomorrow." Dad winks at me from the doorway.

Mom gives him a glare and then pulls up a chair next to my bedside table. "Are you doing all right swallowing?"

"Pretty good considering that everything tastes like nothing."

"I'll talk to Dr. Derby about getting you on a soft food diet by tomorrow night if you progress all right with the fluids."

"What's soft food? The one where everything tastes like mud?"

"If you're lucky." Mom smiles as she brushes my hair back

from my face. "The police will be here in about an hour. Do you want me to read you some of these cards while you eat?" She gestures around the room.

"Who is all that even from?" I ask.

She goes from gift to gift looking for cards as I struggle to make my way through my bowl of soup. There's a plush Dalmatian from Shannon, a silk flower arrangement from Dallas's parents, and then more stuffed animals from Tyrell and Dallas's record label. Some of Mom's colleagues chipped in for a bouquet of Mylar balloons. That accounts for about a quarter of the stuff. After that, some of it is from musicians I've never met, some from kids at school I barely talk to, and some of it doesn't even have cards.

"Do you think it's from Dallas's fans?" I ask.

"Possibly," Mom says. "The newspapers printed your name and that you were in critical condition."

I shake my head at the balloons and stuffed animals, at the brightly colored envelopes stacked on the counter. "Well, it's a nice gesture, I guess, but kind of unnecessary."

"You know how people are. Tragedies like this remind us how little control we have over our lives. Giving a gift makes people feel better." Mom points at my dinner tray. "Are you finished? I can help you brush your teeth before the detectives arrive."

"Good idea. My mouth tastes terrible."

Mom pushes my bedside table toward the wall. She finds my toothbrush and a travel-sized tube of toothpaste in an overnight bag she must have packed for me. She holds a pink plastic basin under my chin so that I have something to spit in after I brush my teeth.

"Gross," I say, as a bit of toothpaste drool runs down my chin and lands on the top of my blanket. "Is there any reason I can't get out of bed and walk to the sink?"

"Right now you're still hooked to too many tubes to be able to get out of bed safely. I'll make sure PT comes tomorrow. Dr. Derby will probably move you to the step-down too. A couple more nights and hopefully we can get you out of here. I'm sure you're dying to get back to school and see all your friends."

"Mostly just Shannon," I say.

After I brush my teeth, I ask my mom for a mirror. She hesitates just long enough for me to know there's something wrong with my face.

"What is it?" I ask. "Do I have a broken nose? A giant scar?"

Sighing, Mom hands me her phone so I can examine myself with her reverse camera. I'm a mess of cuts and bruises and there's a white bandage wrapped around my head, but I don't look as bad as I was expecting. I lift a hand to a long red gash along my cheekbone. My fingers trace the tiny black stitches.

"I had that stitched by one of the best guys from Plastics. It should fade completely in a year or two."

A year or two. I'll be a sophomore in college before this scar goes away. I finger the bandage wrapped around my head. "And this." I furrow my brow as I struggle to remember our earlier conversation. "You said . . . brain surgery?"

33

"A craniotomy, yes. They had to shave away part of your hair." Mom pulls a tissue from the box next to my bed, obviously expecting more waterworks. "They wanted to do half your head, but I convinced them they didn't need that much exposure, so it's not as bad as you think."

"Oh." I ignore the tissue my mom is holding out. Maybe there are stages of grief for hair loss too, or maybe I just can't bring myself to care about my appearance when Dallas is dead. I run one finger underneath the edge of the dressing and feel the smoothness of my skull.

"Don't mess with it. You don't want your incision to get infected." Mom blinks hard. She blots at her own eyes with the tissue.

"Mom . . ."

"I'm sorry. I've been a wreck all week. It took me a long time to get over losing your father, and I really thought I might lose you, too."

I'm not sure I've ever seen my mom cry. Even after the divorce, what I mostly saw was anger. If there were tears, she hid them from me. It feels weird comforting her when I'm the one who almost died, but I guess that's how it is in hospitals—the family members suffer just as much or more. I reach out for her hand and she lets me take it. For a little while, the two of us just sit there in silence. My eyelids fall shut and I start to doze off.

And then there's a knock at the door. I open my eyes to see two plainclothes policemen—well, one man and one woman—standing outside the room. The man is stocky and muscular, with dark brown skin and the beginnings of a beard. The woman is older, blond hair streaked with gray, dark circles under her eyes.

"Come on in." I gesture for them to enter, but my mom springs up from her seat.

As she slides open the door, she clears her throat. "I'm Genevieve's mother, Dr. Elena Grace, chief of Pediatric Cardiac Surgery." She keeps talking without giving the detectives a chance to introduce themselves. "My daughter suffered a traumatic injury to her brain, which is still healing. She hasn't regained her full memories of the accident yet."

"Dr. Grace. Thank you for letting us know Genevieve was awake," the blond woman says. She exchanges a look with her partner. "Do you think she might be more comfortable talking to us by herself?"

"Not a chance," my mom says. "She's a minor and I know her rights."

"What are *your* names?" I ask, a little embarrassed by the way my mom feels the need to introduce herself with her entire title and take over every conversation.

"I'm Detective Blake," the blond woman says. "And this is my partner, Detective Reed."

"Nice to meet you," I say.

My mom nods curtly to both of them and then returns to her seat.

The detectives pull chairs to the side of the bed opposite my mom and start by telling me they're going to record the interview. Detective Reed asks me to tell him what I do remember.

I close my eyes for a second and try to fish out more images from the blankness of the last few days, but I can't recall much beyond what I already told my mom. "Uh, I remember smoke and lights, the sound of people yelling. Firefighters, I think? And I remember blood. The windshield was missing, but there was blood on the dashboard . . . and on me. I had on a white top, and I remember all the red."

"And before that?" Reed probes gently.

"I remember us going to the release party. Dallas brought my mom flowers. He is . . . was always so kind, thinking of other people."

"Did anything special happen at the party?" Detective Blake asks.

"You'd have to ask . . ." I trail off. They can't ask Dallas. *Dallas didn't survive. He's dead.* I clear my throat and try again. "I'm not sure. Tyrell could tell you more about the party. I always felt kind of out of place at Dallas's events. I spent a lot of the night hanging out with Tyrell's Rottweiler."

Detective Blake gives me a small smile. She asks me why I was driving and it feels like a betrayal to admit that Dallas might have been drinking, but I guess now that he's gone it's no big deal if he was breaking the law. They want me to go back through everything I remember from that night, but the problem is I remember some of the party and then I have bits of memories of what happened after the crash, but the middle part is a total blank. "I'm sorry," I say. "I know you're looking for specifics about the accident, but I just don't remember."

"It's possible she'll regain full awareness of that night after she's had a chance to recuperate," my mom says crisply.

"We'll get out of your hair so you can rest." Detective Blake sets her business card on my bedside table. "Let us know if you remember anything else."

I nod. "Sorry I can't be more help."

"That's okay," Detective Reed says. "You've been through a lot. We're just glad you're doing better."

Detective Blake and her partner leave my room and Mom starts fussing with the equipment laid out on the counter. I think about the snide way she said the other driver was having trouble remembering. What if no one believes me, either?

The second the detectives are out of sight, I fake a huge yawn for Mom's benefit. "That was kind of tiring," I say. "I think I'm going to get some sleep."

"Okay," she says. "I should probably head home and take care of a few things there."

I can't imagine what Mom could possibly have to take care of at home. Pay the guy who trims the hedges? Make sure a second plastic-bagged newspaper doesn't pile up on the porch? But I don't care. Earlier I was terrified at the idea of being alone. Now I'm desperate for it. The not knowing is starting to weigh on me. I have to fill in some of the pieces from that night, and I know just the way to do it.

CHAPTER 5

The second Mom leaves, I fish Dad's iPad out from under the covers. Dallas was a big deal. There must be articles online about the accident by now. Maybe they'll help me fill in some of the gaps.

But first I want to email Shannon. I log into my account and am surprised to see I have over five hundred new messages. I click on my inbox. In addition to the usual spam, I've got several emails from Shannon and loads of messages from other kids at school. Some of them are Dallas's friends but a lot are kids whose names I only recognize in passing. Kids from different cliques, from different grades. I used to say that everyone loved Dallas, but I've never seen the visual evidence laid out the way it is here.

I click on the first one, from a girl named Ciara Clark. I know she runs a Dallas Kade fan site and we're in World History together, but we've never really talked.

Dear Genevieve,

I cannot even tell you how devastated I am about what's happened. The world has lost one of the greatest performers ever. And such a sweet guy too. I feel like one of my best friends has been stolen away.

I roll my eyes. Aside from one interview about the album, I'm pretty sure Dallas and Ciara Clark never exchanged two words.

I'm praying for a speedy recovery for you. Please email me back ASAP once you get this. I've reserved a feature spot on the blog for an interview with you about the accident. Dallas's adoring fans at sckadetkorps.com need you now more than ever!

Sincerely,

Ciara Clark

Founder and President of the St. Charles County Dallas Kade Fan Club

P.S. I shared your email address online because Dallas's fans wanted to send you their prayers and condolences. I hope you don't mind.

"Whatever," I mutter under my breath. That explains all the spam. I click on the second email. It's from one of Dallas's fans just wanting to say how sorry he is. Messages three and four are more of the same. A lump starts to form in my throat. I know these people mean well, but they're making me feel guilty for being the one who lived. After all, it's not like the whole world would miss me if I were gone.

The next email is from a girl who lives in Oklahoma wondering if it's okay if she sells Dallas Kade #NeverForget T-shirts online. "No idea, Tammy from Tulsa." I delete all five messages without responding.

Two more messages appear in my inbox, both from addresses I don't recognize. Ignoring them, I dash off a quick message to Shannon:

> Thanks for the homework, you big traitor ;) Have I told you lately that I miss you? Puh-lease come visit tomorrow if you have time. And if my mom gives you any crap about me needing to rest, ask my dad to sneak you in. I'm going crazy stuck in bed. I don't need rest. I need my best friend <3 I would call you but my phone got mashed in the accident and I'm on my dad's iPad.
> All the <333
> G

I send the message and close out my email. Now, to figure out what actually happened. I type the words "Dallas Kade" into the search box. Auto-complete gives me a list of choices:

Dallas Kade death
Dallas Kade accident
Dallas Kade Try This at Home

Dallas Kade Younity

Dallas Kade singer

Sucking in a deep breath, I highlight the top option and click search.

Hundreds of results come back—way more than I was expecting. Everyone has reported on the accident already and multiple major papers have written more than one article. I click on the most recent article written by the local newspaper.

THE ST. LOUIS TIMES

Man Who Hit and Killed Dallas Kade Charged with Driving While Intoxicated

BY R. J. CRUISE, 8 hours ago

The St. Charles County Sheriff's Department has released a report confirming that Bradley Freeman of Wentzville, Missouri, who was involved in the fatal car wreck that killed seventeen-year-old Dallas Kade, also of Wentzville, has been charged with driving while intoxicated. His BAC level was tested upon arrival at Lake St. Louis Medical Center, but the results have not been made public.

Kade was a passenger in a car belonging to him but being driven by his girlfriend, Genevieve Grace. Grace has been in a coma since the accident, but doctors are still hopeful she will recover. Kade was a senior at Ridgehaven Academy and had just released his first album. He is survived by his parents, Glen and Nora.

After three days of being unresponsive, Bradley Freeman awoke on Monday and issued a statement saying that his heart went out to the Kade and Grace families. Freeman incurred a head injury in the accident and is claiming to have no memory of the events leading up to it. This is Freeman's second DWI charge, but possible manslaughter charges in Kade's death are still pending. Freeman plans to plead not guilty to the DWI and says unequivocally that he was not driving drunk.

An investigation into the cause of the accident is ongoing. Anyone with information about this incident is requested to call the St. Charles County Sheriff's Department at 636-555-1919.

Comments 1–10 of 891

jenjenjenni: how can you plead not guilty to a dwi? i mean, even if he tests the blood somewhere else and gets a different result, isn't that still his word against the police department's? this is bull****

Mike Clinker: This whole thing stinks of some sort of cover-up. But Freeman used to work for the county and his dad was the sheriff out there for like 20 years, so of course they're trying not to charge him with anything serious.

Kadet4Ever: Poor Genevieve. Does anyone know if she's going to make it?

Slytherpuff: @Kadet4Ever: I heard things were looking grim for Kade's girlfriend, that even if she woke up she'd probably have brain damage.

pxs1228: Good to know Freeman's heart is going out to the family of the boy he killed and the girl he almost killed. They should've REALLY given his heart away before he woke up, donated his organs to more deserving people.

fullgrownkademaniac: #JusticeForDallas It's bad enough Freeman killed him, but now he's going to lie about it. Lock up this murderer already.

Billy Blitzen: My friend was out in Wentzville that night and he remembers seeing a red truck that looked just like Freeman's speeding and weaving erratically on Highway 70. He gave a statement to the cops.

Area51isReal: Wake up, sheeple! This was yet another event staged by our government to further its Big Brother agenda. A return to Prohibition is nearing. Mark my words.

Leftofleft: Maybe we should all chill out for a few days and let the cops do their jobs.

pxs1228: @Leftofleft: Is that you, Freeman? Let's see you chill out when it's your family member who gets killed and the murderer gets away with it.

I still can't believe Dallas and I got hit by a drunk driver. I click on an older article from the morning after the accident and scroll down until I get to the details.

At approximately 1:15 a.m., Kade and his girlfriend, Genevieve Grace, were returning home from an album release party when they were hit head-on by Bradley Freeman, age 38, on Highway Z. Kade was pronounced DOA at Lake St. Louis Medical Center. Freeman and Grace remain in critical condition. Authorities will not confirm whether either driver had been drinking. Freeman has a prior DWI conviction and blood tests are pending.

I close my eyes. One-fifteen in the morning. Highway Z. That old adage about how most accidents happen within a mile of home floats back to me. Why were we even on the road so late?

I click over to a third article and skim the text. This one is from a national news blog called *The Scoop*. It says basically the same thing, with the addition of mentioning that both a radar detector and a six-pack of beer were found in the wreckage of Freeman's truck.

I try to envision the truck that hit us. It doesn't come, but suddenly I can see the road. The twists and turns that felt less familiar to me in Dallas's car. I remember wanting to open my window, but it was raining. I remember the way Dallas's headlights glinted off the yellow lines in the middle of the road.

I click over to one more article, this one from *The National Wire*.

The same facts again, repeated in basically the same way. I study the pictures at the top of the post. Dallas's publicity photo. My senior picture—controlled smile, hair extra-shiny.

We're both blond and fresh-faced. We're so internet-friendly that we might as well be made of 1s and 0s. And then there's Freeman. He's not hideous or anything, but the picture they've used of him appears to be a mug shot. His eyes are red and the fluorescent lighting emphasizes the deep lines etched into his wide forehead. His dark beard is flecked with gray and his lips are turned down in a scowl, like he's angry. Like he's a bad man.

I stare at the picture, waiting for it to make me feel something. I should hate this guy, this stranger who drove drunk and killed Dallas, nearly killing me too. But as with the idea of Dallas being dead, all I feel is a numbness when I look at Brad Freeman. Like he's not a real person. Like he's just another actor in the world's worst play. I wonder if he's somewhere right now, looking at my picture and feeling numb too.

My eyes are drawn back to Dallas's photo. Unlike me, he's showing a lot of teeth. I remember when he got his braces off, the summer after tenth grade. He was so excited. He kept rubbing his tongue over his teeth, reaching up to feel them with his fingertips. I caught him checking out his reflection in every shiny surface we passed.

"Yeah. You're hot now. Get over yourself," I teased.

"You don't get it," he tried to explain. "Imagine wearing glasses or a bra or something for two straight years, never ever taking it off. And then finally you're free forever."

Back then I never thought about how short forever could be, and I'm pretty sure Dallas didn't either. Neither one of us had ever gone to a funeral. I bet his parents have already buried him. My chest grows tight at the thought. A tear leaks out of my eye. The last time I saw Dallas, he was beginning this amazing new chapter in his life. How do you go from that to a box underground? I swallow back a sob.

The door to my room slides open, startling me so badly I almost drop Dad's iPad on the floor. My redheaded nurse is standing in the doorway. "Hey. I brought your night nurse for our shift change report."

An older woman with short brown hair smiles at me. "I'm Debbie," she says.

"Hi." I wipe at the tear, hoping neither nurse noticed it.

The nurses pass by me to get to the IV pump, where my day nurse explains something about my IVs to Debbie.

"How's your pain?" Debbie asks. "On a scale of zero to ten."

"Not too bad. Maybe a three or four?" I'm still thinking about Dallas in a coffin. Would he look like himself, his injuries cleverly disguised by some mortician with makeup and hair products? Or would he look like I do, bruised and broken?

My lower lip starts to tremble and I clamp down hard on it with my teeth. The nurses seem nice, and so does Dr. Chao, but I don't want to talk to anyone here about the accident. They're strangers—crying on them would feel weird.

"What are you looking at?" Debbie asks, gesturing at the iPad. Three faces still stare up at me from the screen. Me. Dallas. Brad Freeman.

"Just news stuff." With shaking fingers, I hurriedly close the tab, another jolt of pain arcing through me as the images wink out of sight. *Dallas didn't survive. He's dead.* It hits me that the one person I want to talk to about everything is the person who is gone forever.

CHAPTER 6

Two days later, I'm discharged from the hospital. My mom informs me that the goal is to get me back to school as soon as possible. I'd rather finish out the rest of the semester at home while I continue to heal, but once Mom has made a decision about something, arguing is pointless.

After a weekend of watching me like a hawk, she hires a nurse named Connie to look after me while she's at work. Connie is an older lady who changes the dressing on my leg and forces me to get out of bed every few hours. My leg still aches and every time I pass something remotely shiny I see my scarred and bruised reflection staring back at me, my hair hanging unevenly where some of it was cut away.

But honestly, that stuff doesn't even bother me. I don't care that I'm ugly. I don't care that I've run three miles a day, five times a week, for the past five years and now I can barely walk. I just want them to let me stay in bed. I never knew how exhausting grief could be. I haven't even cried that much since

I left the hospital. The numbness has worn off and the pain has definitely found me, but it's like my body can't find the energy to produce actual tears.

So I just lie in bed, hour after hour, day after day, trying to make sense of what happened. I keep coming back to how unfair it is that Dallas died and the other driver and I both got to live. Brad Freeman must feel horrible. I can't imagine what it would be like to kill someone drinking and driving. My mom sat me down before I even got a learner's permit and told me that she realized kids drink sometimes, and that if I was ever anywhere and needed a ride home she would come get me, no questions asked. I know that must have been hard for her—she's not a no-questions-asked kind of person. If only Freeman had called someone.

I still haven't been able to bring myself to hate him, though. Part of me wishes I could—that I could just blame him for everything and stop caring about filling in the blanks from that night. But a bigger part of me needs answers.

And that means more pain. Just thinking about things leaves my muscles weak, my head throbbing with the endless ache that comes from concentrating too hard. I pull my covers up over my head, blocking out the light, blocking out the world. Pressing my fingertips to my temples, I once again replay each individual second of that night that I remember. I was looking for Dallas outside on Tyrell's deck. And later, flashing lights, firefighters, and blood. But in the middle? Still nothing.

• • •

Dallas's parents come to visit me the Thursday after I arrive home. It's eleven a.m. and I'm tucked safely beneath the patchwork quilt my grandmother made me for my thirteenth birthday. It's a mix of tan and turquoise squares, with images of different breeds of horses sewn between them.

Connie knocks sharply on my door. "Genevieve. You need to get up."

I pull the quilt up over my head and hide between an Appaloosa and a quarter horse. I pretend like I'm still sleeping, even though I've been awake for hours. She opens the door and claps her hands so loudly that I flinch.

"Get up," she says again. "The Kades are here." Connie steps inside my room and closes the door behind her. "Come on. I'll help you look presentable."

Mom said the Kades stopped by my ICU room a couple of times before I woke up, but this will be the first time I've spoken to them since the accident. "I don't need to look presentable," I mutter. "Just stall them for a few minutes so I can brush my teeth."

"Will do. Tyrell James called earlier too, by the way. He said to let you know he's thinking of you."

"Thanks." Tyrell came to see me the day before I left the hospital. We took turns exchanging awkward condolences and then he showed me some video clips he had of Dallas from their recording sessions. I should call him back because I know he's hurting too, but it's hard. I'm barely keeping it together myself. I'm not sure I have much to give to another person right now.

"Call me if you need help," Connie adds. She heads for the hallway. After she's gone I pull a hooded sweatshirt over my pajama top and trade my bottoms for a pair of track pants. I brush my teeth and splash a little water on my face, pausing for a second to consider whether my appearance will upset Dallas's mom. I'm still wrapping my craniotomy incision in gauze even though I don't need to, because I don't want to look at that big bald spot. I decide I can't look any worse now than I did in the ICU.

I try my hardest not to limp as I make my way into the living room, where Glen and Nora Kade are sitting on our white leather sofa. I can't remember the last time anyone sat on that. Mom and I do our limited lounging in our family room at the other end of the house.

"Oh, Genevieve." Dallas's mom starts to cry the second she sees me, which makes me start to cry. Connie produces a box of tissues from somewhere and Nora and I each take one. Nora slouches over as she enfolds me in a gentle hug, patting me awkwardly on the back. "I'm so sorry," we whisper at the same time. I sob into the collar of her shirt, thinking about how different she feels—smells, even—than my mom. My mom is not a sloucher. She's also not a hugger, but if she were I'd end up with my face against the sharpness of her collarbone. I'd smell the clean scent of her fabric softener and maybe a hint of the surgical hand scrub that she uses at the hospital. Dallas's mom smells like a mix of lavender and vanilla.

I cling to her for a few seconds as she pets the ends of my hair.

Connie sets the tissues onto our pristine glass coffee table. "I'll be in the kitchen if you need me," she says softly.

Pulling away from Nora, I take a seat on the chaise lounge across from the sofa, another piece of furniture that's always been more for show than actual use. The living room curtains are pulled completely closed, but I can see the occasional shadow of someone moving on the other side of them.

"Did the vultures harass you?" I ask.

When I came home from the hospital, Mom shielded me from the reporters the best she could, but I wasn't prepared for the microphones thrust under my nose, for the barrage of questions. I shudder just thinking about it.

Dallas's dad looks toward the closed curtains for a moment. "We've gotten pretty good at saying 'No comment,' so they weren't too bad." He looks back to me and clears his throat. "Look. Genevieve. We wanted to apologize for going ahead with the services for Dallas without you."

It turns out that Dallas's parents held his funeral the day before I woke up from my coma. Mom didn't mention it at the hospital because she thought I'd be upset, but after I got home, Shannon sent me a YouTube link where someone recorded the whole thing. The church was packed and hundreds of people waited outside to be part of the graveside ceremony.

"It's okay," I say. "You didn't know if I was even going to live." I look down at my hands, my trembling fingers making tiny tears in the Kleenex I'm clutching. "Plus, I kind of want to remember Dallas the way he was, you know?"

Nora nods rapidly, her eyes filling with tears again. She grabs for a second tissue.

"Dallas didn't have a will, of course," Glen says. "Not for his earnings or his personal effects, but we know how close the two of you were."

My eyes widen. "Oh. I don't need or expect stuff from him. We weren't, like, getting engaged or anything."

Nora smiles through her tears. "I could tell that he loved you, even though he didn't talk about that kind of stuff with me. But wow, when I listen to the album, I realize just how deep things ran between the two of you."

I've heard the whole album, of course. Dallas tried to tell me that all the songs about romance were inspired by me, but I could tell which of them actually were and which were just cool ideas that he and his producer dreamed up together.

Nora swallows back a lump in her throat. "Is there anything you would like . . . his laptop, his clothing, perhaps photographs of you two?"

I blink hard and then look down at my lap. The Kleenex I've been holding is a mess of torn fragments. I hadn't thought about everything Dallas left behind. Not just people and an album sure to go platinum—or whatever successful albums go—but little things like his collection of pop culture T-shirts, his notebook of partially written songs, and our junior prom picture wedged in his dresser mirror.

"Pictures would be good," I whisper. "I'm not sure if I can—"

"We don't need to do this now," Glen says. "We just wanted

to come see you and wish you well, and make sure there wasn't anything specific that you wanted."

I want Dallas to be alive, I think. But I don't say it, because his mom has finally stopped crying, and I don't want to be the reason she starts again.

After Dallas's parents leave, I head back to my room, but Connie follows me. "Good news," she says, just as I'm about to crawl back into bed. "Most of the reporters followed the Kades when they left, which means that for the time being your paparazzi have dwindled down to just two. How about a walk around the block? I'm sure you could use some fresh air."

"I'm not really feeling up to it," I mumble.

"You know, not exercising is going to delay your recovery. Aren't you anxious to get back into your running shoes?"

Yes. So I can run away from all this.

My new phone chirps with a text, a sadistic reminder of how I'll never be able to escape completely. I swipe at the screen. It's Shannon.

> Her: When are you coming back to school? I am dying without you.
>
> Me: I am just plain dying :P
>
> Her: Oh, G. I wish I were there to give you a hug :(
>
> Me: It's okay. I'm fine. Just a little overwhelmed.
>
> Her: It's okay if you're not fine, you know?

Why does everyone keep saying that? It's like they missed the actual accident, so they want me to crash and burn a second time so they can witness the wreckage.

Me: I gotta run. Evil Nurse is forcing me to exercise.

Her: Yay! If you can exercise, you can sit through all your boring classes.

Me: Ha. Maybe.

Her: All the hugs.

Me: All the <333

I turn back to Connie. I could refuse her, but if I do, my mom will end up making me go for a walk later. At least now there're no kids from school outside. I think of the unread emails in my inbox. I don't want to hear about how sorry they are. It won't change anything. It won't *fix* anything. "Get rid of the remaining vultures, and I'm all yours."

"I'll do my best." Connie disappears and returns about ten minutes later. "I told them their presence was hindering your recovery and suggested they take a lunch break."

"And they agreed to that?"

"No, but I called your mother and she said to let them choose between a small payout to leave you alone or dealing with her lawyer."

"How small is small?"

"Two hundred bucks each."

"Good to know I'm such a cash cow," I mutter. "All right, let's do this."

"Are you sure you don't want to . . . freshen up a bit first?"

I glance in the mirror and debate trying to fix myself up, but there's no point in putting lipstick on a pig, like my dad used to say. I look like crap, and no amount of foundation or mascara is going to hide it. "Nah, let's just get it over with."

The two of us head for the front door. Connie helps me down the porch steps and I blink rapidly in the bright sun. It makes me think of a line from a movie I saw with Dallas: *Why do my eyes hurt? You've never used them before.* I feel sort of like that, as if I'm seeing everything differently now.

Connie walks next to me on the side with my injured leg. I step with my good leg and pull the other one behind me. I'm lucky that it's just pain I'm wrestling with, that there wasn't any nerve damage. Eventually my leg will return to its pre-accident state, even if the rest of me won't.

The smell of fresh-cut grass wafts over from the neighbor's lawn. A flag mounted above the mailbox snaps in the breeze. A face peers out from living room window. Mrs. Ernst. I used to see her power-walking in the early mornings while I was running. We exchanged waves and smiles, but that's all, because I always had my headphones in. Dallas used to make me playlists. At first he named them for the days of the week, but later he got more creative. Now my iPod is full of lists like "Feelin' Good Mix," "Running Sucks So Why Do I Keep Going?" and "Songs for Genna." That last one was a mix of stuff he wrote for me and other songs he said made him think of me.

Mrs. Ernst lifts her hand in recognition. I force a smile. My cheek muscles feel stiff, like it's the first time I've used them too.

Connie and I make our way slowly around the block. Very slowly, like "lapped by an old lady with tennis balls on the bottom of her walker" speed. Okay, not really—we only have to pass one person on our walk—Mrs. Henderson, whose daughter ran cross-country with me back when I was in middle school. But if an old lady with a walker had been out with us, I guarantee she would've kicked my ass.

"It's good to see you, Genevieve." Mrs. Henderson beams like I'm one of those internet videos of a baby sloth getting a bath or something.

"You too." I manage a second smile in return.

"Looks like you'll be back running in no time!" she chirps.

"Hope so," I say, limping off at a speed that might just rival that of a baby sloth.

When my mom gets home, I stand outside her study and eavesdrop on Connie giving her a progress report.

"She's moving around just fine. A bit slow, but her endurance is good. Didn't want help getting dressed. Even made lunch for the two of us."

"Excellent. Thank you so much for taking such good care of her." Mom sounds pleased.

I have a feeling I know what's coming next, and I want no part of it. Before either Mom or Connie can catch me eavesdropping, I head back to my room. I hide away until it's time for dinner.

Later, when I'm setting the table, Mom sneaks up behind me. She rests a hand on my shoulder and I flinch, dropping a fork onto the clean kitchen floor.

Mom reaches down and snatches up the fork in her nimble surgeon hands before I can even say I'm sorry. She goes to the dishwasher and deposits the dirty utensil into one of the plastic baskets. Then she turns back to me. "Connie says you're moving around without needing help, doing basic things for yourself. That's great. I think you should try going back to school on Monday."

"But Mom." I retrieve a new fork from the top drawer of our kitchen island. "There are only two weeks left in the semester. Do I *have* to?"

"Dr. Chao told me the best thing for you would be to get back to a normal routine as soon as possible."

"Get back to normal?" I grip the fork tightly. The world might have flipped some terrible switch and stolen away my boyfriend, but I don't have a switch I can flick to be okay with it. "Dallas is dead. That is never going to feel *normal.*"

"I know, honey. But wallowing in your grief isn't going to help. If you want, I can bring you by the grave site. The stone won't be up for a couple of months, but all the things his fans have left are lovely. Maybe it would help you find closure."

"I don't need *closure,*" I tell her. "It's not like we broke up."

She plucks a piece of lint from the front of her blouse. "Is this about how you look?"

"What? No!" Okay, the giant creepy scars and big bald stripe across my head don't exactly increase my desire to spend all day in public, but it's not like I have anyone I need to look good for. And it's not like everyone at school won't be staring at me already.

"What then?"

"I just don't want to deal with any of it—the sympathy, the staring, the inappropriate questions."

"Maybe you should give your friends more credit," Mom says. "I don't think they're going to pump you for gory details."

"It's not my friends I'm worried about," I mutter, thinking back to the random emails from people who didn't even know Dallas.

"Genevieve, you have to try." Mom glances at the black marble wall clock and then back to me. "Can you do that for me? At least try?"

A surge of guilt moves through me. I talk a lot of crap about my mom being a dictator, but the reality is that she works her ass off to take care of both of us. Yeah, I wish she cut me more slack, but maybe maintaining a household without much support from anyone requires ruling with an iron fist. I *should* try, for her. Maybe school won't be as bad as I think. Maybe I can just zone out—pretend I'm hiding in my bed all day and then come home and do my assignments in the quiet safety of my room.

"Okay," I say. "I'll try."

"Thank you." Mom checks the time again. "The food was supposed to be here five minutes ago. I'm going to give them a call." She swipes at her phone and turns away to look at something in the backyard, tapping one foot while she waits for the call to connect.

I head back to my room and start mentally preparing for going back to school. I grab my phone to text Shannon but then decide it might be fun to surprise her. Peering at my reflection in the mirror, I try to cover the scar on my cheekbone with some concealer, but it just makes it look more obvious. At least I got the stitches out the other day.

There is, however, still an extremely creepy line of staples in my skull. I don't want to show up with my head bandaged, but I'm not allowed to wear hats in the classroom, so covering it up will require a bit of creativity. I scan my room for ideas. My eyes fall on a rack of patterned scarves I wear mostly in the fall and winter. I pull a pink one from the rack and fold it into thirds and tie it around my head.

Not terrible. I look like I should be reading someone's fortune at a carnival, but at least I don't look like a Halloween monster. I shrug at my reflection. It's all just pretend anyway. Making myself look normal on the outside isn't going to change the way I feel inside. Hollow. Empty. About as far away from normal as I can get.

CHAPTER 7

School is every bit the nightmare I expected it to be. Pre-accident, my day usually went like this: Up at 5:00 a.m. to jog. Shower. Eat breakfast. School by 7:00 a.m. Look over home-work, aka help Shannon with her homework, before first hour. Three lecture classes where no one paid me much attention. Lunch with Shannon and Dallas and some of his friends. Poetry class, technology lab, and last period gym. On a normal day, I probably spoke to fifteen people max.

Today I speak to almost fifteen people before I even make it to first period. The first two are Krissi and Mandy Sanchez, identical twins who play on our soccer team. My mom drops me off at school and Krissi nearly bumps into me as I'm limping my way up the front steps. Her eyes widen when she recognizes me.

"Oh my God, Genevieve. It's so good to see you," she says.

"You look great," Mandy adds. "I like your shirt."

I force a smile. I've gotten surprisingly good at that in the past few days. "Thanks." My shirt is just a striped T-shirt from a local department store, but I'm sure Mandy just wanted to say something nice and couldn't find anything else to compliment.

"I'm sorry about Dal—" she continues, cutting off when her sister elbows her in the ribs.

"We're just happy to see you back at school so soon." Krissi smiles brightly.

"Thanks," I say again. The girls are both wearing their soccer jerseys. I gesture at their outfits. "Do you have a game tonight?"

"District playoffs," they say in unison. They giggle.

"Awesome. I hope you win." I fidget with one end of the scarf tied around my head, wondering if it looks weird.

We all turn and head into the school lobby together. Halfway to the main hallway, Krissi and Mandy get waylaid by a couple of senior boys and I continue toward my locker by myself.

Three girls I've never seen before suddenly appear in my peripheral vision. They have their heads together whispering as I slowly make my way down the corridor.

The tallest of the three flounces up to me. She's almost as tall as my mom, but thin and coltish, with knobby knees and long limbs. A freshman, probably. "Genevieve. I just wanted to say I am so sorry. We all are." Her minions quickly nod like a couple of bobblehead dolls. Tall Girl lowers her voice. "We hope the guy who killed Dallas goes to jail forever."

The guy who killed Dallas. He doesn't even have a name to these girls. He's probably not even human. I wish I didn't know his name either. I wish he wasn't human to me. I think back to the three pictures from the online article, Dallas and I looking so fresh-faced and full of hope, Brad Freeman looking like a criminal. I wonder if that picture is who he really is. I wonder if his numbness has worn off too, if he's hurting even worse than I am, if he'll ever be able to forgive himself.

The second-tallest girl shoos curious onlookers out of the way while the leftover member of the trio timidly offers to carry my backpack.

"I'm okay," I say, my fake smile materializing out of nowhere. "But I've got to get to my locker. See you later." Or not.

I head down the corridor as fast as I can manage, leaving the freshmen behind, but accepting two more messages of sympathy—one from a teacher I had in tenth grade and another from our senior class president, a girl who I've shared at least six classes with during the past four years but only spoken to once or twice.

When I turn the corner and head down the main hallway, I'm relieved to see the one person I actually want to talk to rooting through our locker. Shannon. She's wearing the cutest skinny jeans and tunic outfit and has her hair done up into three buns down the back of her head, what she likes to call her superhero hairdo.

"Oh my God, ohmygod, yay!" Shannon literally jumps up and down when she sees me approaching. "Why didn't you tell me you were coming back today?"

"Surprise." I grin.

Shannon wraps me in a tight hug. "I can't believe you're here! I'm so sorry I haven't been by the house the past couple days, but my parents dragged me to Carlyle Lake this weekend and we didn't get home until nine last night. I hate coming over late because I always feel like I'm pissing off your mom."

"You and me both," I say, wincing a little in her embrace. "Easy, I've still got a lot of cuts and bruises."

"You poor thing." Shannon steps back and the fluorescent lights reflect off her lip gloss, nearly blinding me. "I can't believe you came back so soon."

"Well, you know my mom. Pretty sure I'd be back here by now even if I broke every bone in my body."

"Truth. Can you imagine sitting through school in, like, a full body cast? A janitor would have to roll you from class to class on one of those dollies."

"That sounds almost as much fun as a coma."

Shannon laughs, and for a few brief seconds life feels like it did before the accident, just me and my best friend getting ready to do her homework and then head off to first hour.

And then someone taps me on the shoulder. I spin around. It's another girl I don't know. Her face is stained with tears and she's wearing a "Students Against Drunk Driving" T-shirt. A tiny bouquet of daisies is clutched in one hand.

She thrusts the flowers at me. "I am so sorry," she says. "My boyfriend also died in a drunk driving accident."

"Thank you." I accept the flowers. "I'm sorry for your loss."

"You're welcome." Tears start to leak from her eyes, but before I can say anything else, she turns and skitters down the hallway.

Shannon takes the flowers out of my hands and reads the

card. "From one of Dallas's biggest fans and someone who knows what you're going through. May our hearts heal together. #NeverForget Sincerely, Cassandra 636-555-8989."

I shake my head. "I can't handle all these people."

"They mean well." Shannon hands the bouquet of daisies to me and I set them at the bottom of my locker.

"She did, maybe," I say. "But my hospital room was full of gifts from strangers, and random people have been emailing me and asking me sketchy Dallas-related stuff."

"Forget email. Have you seen your Twitter lately?" Shannon's eyes widen beneath her expertly applied cat-eye eyeliner.

"No. I haven't even downloaded the app onto my new phone. Why?"

"You have like eight thousand followers."

"What?" I dig my phone out of my purse and open up Twitter in a browser window. Sure enough, I have 8,231 followers and more than two thousand new interactions. "This is insane." I skim the most recent tweets that have tagged me:

Shelly Webster @ericdismylove • 6m

@GenevieveLGrace OMG. I heard that our #PrayForGenevieve campaign worked and you're back at school! Is it true??

Justine @Kadet4Ever • 11m

@GenevieveLGrace I can't wait until you get your memory back so you can testify against #BradFreeman. He's a #drunkdriver and a #murderer.

Patrick S @pxs1228 • 14m

So @GenevieveLGrace is doing okay, but #BradFreeman is

still a #liar and a #murderer who should pay for his crimes.
#HumanWaste

Meera Malik @vivalameera • 15m

@GenevieveLGrace @RealTyrellJames I heard there was an
eyewitness to the actual accident. Is that true?

Izzy Rocks @izrockin • 17m

@GenevieveLGrace Been listening to Younity all day. Might go
get some #JusticeForDallas myself. #BradTheMurderer

The last tweet has an animated GIF of an automatic weapon
spraying bullets into the air. Shannon pulls out her phone and
responds to it. Another tweet appears in my feed:

Shannon Tate @shanrocks900 • 6s

@izrockin @GenevieveLGrace Ha! I like the way you think!
#JusticeForDallas #BradTheMurderer

I close the browser window and stuff my phone back into my
purse. "Don't do that, okay?"

"Do what?" Shannon flips to the camera function on her
phone and checks her makeup. She rubs at a smudge of eyeliner
with the tip of her pinky.

"Feed the trolls."

The smile fades from Shannon's face. "I was just showing my
support for you and Dallas."

"I know," I say. "But there's nothing funny about death
threats. And killing someone in a car accident doesn't make you
a murderer."

"You're right," Shannon says. "But that Freeman guy is old.
He probably doesn't even have a Twitter."

"He can still read it, you know." I give her a pointed look.

"I'm sorry, Gen. I'll delete it. Twitter will probably delete the original tweet too." Shannon drops her voice. "But why are you defending Brad Freeman?"

"I don't know," I say honestly. "Some of the stuff people are saying, especially online, is really uncalled for. I guess I know what it's like to feel guilty that Dallas died and I didn't."

"But Freeman *deserves* to feel guilty," Shannon says.

"Yeah, but still. No one's asinine tweets are going to bring back Dallas." My voice gets louder with each sentence. "I just wish everyone would stop talking about it."

Shannon glances around. The girls at the next locker are staring at me. One of them is wearing a "Try This at Home" T-shirt.

"Sorry," I mutter. I lower my voice as I turn back to Shannon. "I know everyone misses him. I know they feel bad. But what am I supposed to say to all these people? Thank you? Me too? I'm sorry I didn't die instead of him?"

"Genevieve." Shannon's face goes pale. She reaches for my hand. "No one thinks you should've died instead of Dallas."

"Forget it." I lower myself to the tile floor of the hallway, wincing as I extend my injured leg out in front of me. "So you need my Calc homework or what?"

"You're caught up on your homework?" Shannon asks incredulously.

"It gave me something to do when I wasn't reliving every moment of that night over and over trying to remember what happened."

"You seriously don't remember?"

"Nope. The doctors say I probably will eventually, but right now it's mostly a blank." I pull my Calculus textbook out of my backpack. "Fortunately for you, I still remember Pappus's Theorem."

"Well, in that case, let's compare answers." Shannon grabs her own book from the locker and sits next to me, stretching her long legs out in front of her.

"Wait wait wait. *You* did your Calc homework?"

"You've been out of class for two weeks, Gen. I only had two options—learn to do my own work or find a replacement for you. Do you know how hard it is to find someone both smart enough to get A's in Calc and cool enough that I actually want to spend time with them?"

"Yeah," I say. "That's probably why I do my own work too." Well, that and the fact that my mom would probably disown me if she caught me cheating.

We quickly go through our assignment, stopping to recheck and correct a couple of problems where we ended up with different answers. "I can't believe we're going to be out of here in two weeks," Shannon says. "Are you still going to work in your mom's lab?"

"I think so. Mom is a big fan of faking it till you make it. She won't want me to change my plans because of . . . everything."

"You know I'm here if you ever need to talk, right?"

I nod. "Right now I just can't." Back in the hospital I might have opened up to Shannon, but I've spent so many days thinking about the accident that for me there's nothing left to say. All I really want is to know what happened, and why. Shannon can't help me with either of those things.

"Okay. God, I'm so glad you're back. The last couple weeks have been hell." Shannon adjusts the lowest of her three buns, shaking out the hair and reworking it back into a tight circle. "Oh, random, but why are you wearing a scarf on your head?"

"Good question. It covers the ginormous bald stripe and scary staples I am currently rocking. I thought maybe I could bring back the nineties."

Shannon makes a face. "More like the seventies. And probably not." She cocks her head to the side and studies me. "Would a headband cover it? A thicker one, like Alison in *Orphan Black*?"

Shannon is a self-taught hairstyle expert who vlogs about style and hair design. She also manages to stay current on a wide variety of TV shows. "Is Alison the soccer mom?" I ask. "Maybe. But will that make me look thirty-five?"

"Possibly, but you won't look like a time traveler. Let me think on it." Shannon hops to her feet and then bends down to help me back up. She slams her locker and gives me another quick hug. "See you at lunch."

Her buns remain firmly in place, like the spikes down the back of a stegosaurus, as she heads for her first class. A dull ache blooms in the pit of my stomach. I wish I could follow her. Sighing, I grab my own books and head for AP Physics.

And then the rest of the day goes downhill like an out-of-control skier.

Exhibit A: In first period, my teacher pauses for a moment right in the middle of taking attendance to welcome me back. "My deepest condolences, Miss Grace," she says. "Please know that if you need to cry or otherwise express yourself, that is completely acceptable and my classroom is a safe space free from judgment."

"Thank you. I'll try my hardest to refrain from . . . emotional outbursts." Everyone turns to look at me, and I'm half expecting the class to rise into a standing ovation or burst into spontaneous applause. Instead, the girl in the front row who sometimes gets misty-eyed during "The Star-Spangled Banner" sniffles into a Kleenex and most of the boys slouch awkwardly or stare right through me.

Exhibit B: On the way to second-period Calculus, I pass at least three different kids playing "Younity" on their phones. One of them is crying, I mean all-out bawling, as if Dallas were her brother or best friend or something. When I see all those tears, I can't help but think about what Dallas would say if he were here. "I didn't realize she and I were so close," Ghost-Dallas murmurs in my ear. "What's her name again?"

"No idea," I say.

The janitor happens to be passing by with a mop and bucket and gives me a strange look.

Nothing to see here, I think. *Just a crazy girl talking to a dead boy.*

Exhibit C: Ciara Clark, the girl who emailed me about a feature post on her KadetKorps fan site, corners me the second I walk into third hour. "Genevieve," she squeals, her dark curls bouncing as she practically skips over to my desk. She wraps an arm around my shoulder like we're suddenly best friends. "OMG. I am so sorry for your loss. Well, the whole world's loss, really." Before I can even answer, she's got her phone out, snapping a picture of the two of us.

"What are you doing?" I back away from her.

"My readers know that I go to school with you. I have to give them something. You wouldn't be willing to share Dallas's last words, would you? It'd be a great exclusive for SCCKadet-Korps-dot-com."

"No," I say. "I still don't remember that night and I don't want to be on your website, Ciara."

"Oh, come on," she wheedles. "You look great. You know, considering. You can even make up some last words if you want. I'd go with something super-romantic, like—"

Luckily, the bell rings and Ciara is forced to shuffle off to her seat on the other side of the room before she can finish her thought. But as my World History teacher starts taking attendance, I keep thinking about how messed up it is that I *don't* know Dallas's last words. Did I even get a chance to say goodbye? The pressure of not knowing wraps itself around me, crushing down on my chest. I spend the entire lecture going through that night again. Why can't I remember?

Just when I thought the day couldn't possibly get any worse, my teacher runs out of slides about the Vikings and tells us to spend the last fifteen minutes of class reading the next chapter in the textbook. I stare at the print, but the words are just a blur of ink.

The kid sitting next to me, a dark-haired guy named Jake who gets a lot of in-school suspensions, passes me a note. I don't want to read it but he's staring at me like I'm stupid, so I unfold the page with a sigh.

> Sorry about Dallas. You got any notes or T-shirts or stuff of his you want to get rid of? There's a huge demand for his stuff on eBay. I can do the posting and selling and split the profits 50/50. Oh, and if you have any pictures of the accident or the smashed-up cars, that would also be an epic moneymaker.

My throat starts to close up. Is this guy seriously asking me to help him profit from Dallas's death? I crumple up the note and shove it in my pocket. Without looking at Jake, I slide out of my chair and limp up to the teacher's desk. "Can I get a bathroom pass?" I ask. "I meant to go between classes, but it takes me forever to go up and down the stairs and I ran out of time."

"Of course, Genevieve," my teacher says soothingly. He starts to write my name on a slip of paper. "Did you want one of the other girls in the class to go with you?"

"Um, no. I think I can pee by myself, but I'm going to bring my books so I can go straight to lunch if that's all right." I snatch the pass from his hand without waiting for an answer.

Out in the hallway, I take in a deep breath of air. The crushing feeling dissipates slightly. I pass right by the bathroom and back to my locker. Someone has decorated the outside of it with sympathy cards and pictures of Dallas they printed out online. Seriously? In what world do people think calling attention to the fact my boyfriend is dead every five seconds could possibly be helpful? Tears well in my eyes as I pull down the pictures. "Everyone loved you," I whisper. "It should've been me."

I shove my books into my bag and slam my locker. "I tried, Mom," I mutter under my breath. Then I head for home.

CHAPTER 8

My mom calls at what should be the end of sixth period but instead is me back in bed with the covers pulled over my head.

I have never cut class before. I've never even thought about cutting class. I have no idea if she's going to tear into me or have Dr. Chao make a house call. I cross my fingers that it won't be the first one. The half-mile walk home took me twice as long as usual, and I don't have the energy to get into an argument with her. I take in a deep breath, blow it out, and then answer the phone.

"Genevieve. Where are you? The school called and said you never showed up to your afternoon classes."

"I went home early."

"Why? What's wrong?"

"I tried, Mom. But school is . . ." I pause for a second to come up with the right word. "Unbearable."

She exhales in a way that indicates a forthcoming lecture. "Why is it *unbearable*?"

"People won't stop talking about Dallas." I hear someone in the background ask for more 5.0 Prolene and it occurs to me that my mom is talking to me in the middle of some kid's heart surgery. "We can talk about this tonight if you're busy," I say.

"Stitch," she says sharply, and then to me, "I can multitask. Dallas was their friend and your boyfriend. Your grief is their grief too."

It's similar to what Shannon said, and I'm sure for some kids that it's true. But I feel like half the school are misery-mongers, people who just want to get in on a big event so they can post about it on their blog or Facebook later.

"Genevieve?" my mom prompts.

"I know," I say. "But some people really suck. This girl in third hour took my picture to post on her KadetKorps blog and then this boy asked me if I had any Dallas memorabilia he could sell on eBay. I don't want to go back. I'm not ready to deal with all that."

"Stitch." A pause and then another sigh. "I forgot how thoughtless kids could be. We'll talk about it later, all right?"

"All right. Thanks, Mom."

"I love you," she says.

I wait for the "but" that usually follows those three words, as in "You know I love you, but you're being overdramatic or too sensitive. . . ."

This time my mom doesn't feel the need to tack on a qualifier. A warm feeling spreads in my chest. "I love you too," I say.

Just as I hang up, my phone buzzes again. I realize I have

four texts from Shannon.

> Shannon: Where are you? Someone said you went to the bathroom in World History and never came back.
>
> Shannon: Did you fall in? Seriously, G. Are you skipping lunch today or what?
>
> Shannon: Did you go to the nurse? Are you skipping class?? Please respond. I'm worried about you.
>
> Shannon: You have five minutes to answer this or I'm calling the hospital and having them page your mom.
>
> Me: Sorry. I didn't mean to ignore you. I was resting.
>
> Shannon: Resting?
>
> Me: I went home.
>
> Shannon: Why?
>
> Me: Because our classmates are idiots. This kid in 3rd hour wanted to know if I had any of Dallas's stuff to sell and Ciara Clark asked me if I'd tell her Dallas's last words for a blog exclusive.
>
> Shannon: WTF? I hate that girl. Were you and Dallas still fighting when it happened?
>
> Me: What?
>
> Shannon: You know. You texted me that night and said you thought it was over.

My phone starts to shake in my hands.

> Me: What did I say exactly? Can you screen shot it for me?
>
> Shannon: Sure. You don't remember that either? I figured you just didn't want to talk about it.

I wait for the image of my text to appear. I skim the words.

> Me: Thanks. I gotta go.

Shannon: Are you all right? Do you want me to come by? I can bail on swim practice if you need me.

The last thing I want is for this whole thing to mess up Shannon's life too.

Me: I'm fine. Don't skip practice for me. I'll text you later.

Shannon: Okay, if you're sure. All the hugs.

Me: All the <333

I read and reread the texts I sent her that night, and another memory begins to piece itself together in my brain.

CHAPTER 9

MAY 12

I was just about to head back inside when a silhouette at the far side of the yard, almost all the way to Tyrell's six-foot privacy fence, caught my eye. I squeezed past the partygoers and took the narrow wooden steps down to the grass. I froze up as I got close. It was Dallas, but he wasn't alone. He was talking to a girl I didn't recognize. She rested one hand on his shoulder in a way that looked more than familiar. "Dallas?" I said, trying to hold my voice steady.

The girl spun around, her hand falling from his shoulder back to her side. "We'll talk more later," she said. She gave Dallas a beauty pageant wave and then headed across the lawn.

He had a look on his face that I couldn't quite interpret—a mix of surprise and amusement, with a twist of something else thrown in. Something like . . . pleasure.

"Was that her?" I kicked one foot at the damp grass.

"Huh?" Dallas ran a hand through his hair. "Who?"

"You know who," I snapped.

Dallas looked from me to the girl's disappearing form and back to me, as if maybe he missed something. "What are you talking about, Genna?"

"The girl you hooked up with," I said through gritted teeth. "Was that her?"

Dallas sighed deeply. "This again?"

I lifted up my hands in mock surrender. "Oh, sorry. Am I making too big of a deal out of you cheating on me?"

Dallas swore under his breath. "That was Tyrell's half sister, Raelyn."

"Pretty," I said. And then, "That doesn't answer the question."

"No, Genevieve. That's not the girl I hooked up with," Dallas said.

Just hearing him say the words was like being given a series of injections, the type that burn going in and then make you feel achy and sore later.

"She was all over you," I said calmly.

He shrugged. "She's kind of touchy-feely. She's also dating a football player from Mizzou."

"So why were you guys out here all alone?" I glanced around the yard, making sure there was no one lingering nearby who might've been eavesdropping. After Dallas became famous, I realized that our words were no longer our own unless we protected them. As beloved as he was in the media, I was sure there were plenty of bloggers and reporters who would've loved to break a juicy story about clean-cut, boy-next-door

Dallas Kade being a cheater.

"We were talking about Tyrell. He's been working his ass off promoting our songs and my album, so I wanted to buy him something as a surprise. I was DMing Raelyn on Twitter the other day and she promised she'd try to come up with some ideas." He paused. "That's what we were doing *out here all alone*."

I saw in his expression that he was telling the truth. I also saw that he was pissed. "I'm sorry," I said. "But can you blame me? You know what they say. Once a cheater, always a cheater."

"Who's *they*?" Dallas asked. "Your mom?"

I winced. "Leave her out of this. It's not like I told her what you did."

"Why not? *They* also say that honesty is the best policy, right? But clearly that isn't always true. Sometimes I wish I'd never told you. It's only screwed everything up between us."

"Don't say that. Lying to me wouldn't make things better."

"Wouldn't it? I get wasted at a party—one you could've been at, I might add—and end up doing something stupid." Dallas lowered his voice. "I feel terrible and I confess everything, because I think you deserve to know the truth and that we'll be able to get past it. But ever since that night, I feel like you don't trust me at all."

I hugged my arms across my middle. "It's hard, Dallas, seeing all these girls practically drooling on you."

"Well, I can't exactly be rude to them." He rested his head in his hands. "Maybe it was better when you didn't come with me to these things."

"So now you don't want me around?"

Above our heads, thunder rumbled. Storm clouds painted the black sky gray.

"Oh, come on. You don't want to be here. Before, you were fine just to send me off and then meet up later to do something we both wanted to do. But now you're here because you feel like you have to watch me, right? This isn't my girlfriend supporting me. This is my girlfriend keeping tabs on me."

He was mostly right. If people at the party saw Dallas and me arriving together, if I was in some of the pictures that ended up on the KadetKorps Tumblr and Instagram accounts, it would amplify my presence in his life. It would make girls less likely to throw themselves at him, at least in theory.

"That's what I thought," he finished.

"It's just that every time I see you with a girl, a little voice in my head reminds me that one girl persuaded you to cheat on me. And if one can do it, why not more than one?"

Dallas shook his head. "You told me you forgave me."

"I did." I blinked hard. "But forgetting is harder than forgiving."

"Well, if you're going to hold it over my head forever, then you should just break up with me," Dallas said. "I screwed up and I hurt you. I will always regret that. But I won't spend the rest of my life being punished for one mistake, no matter how big it was." He waited for me to respond, and when I didn't he threw up his hands, spun around, and stalked back toward the house.

"Dallas, wait." I ran after him. My fingers closed around his forearm. I led him over to the custom playground equipment Tyrell had installed for his kids. We sat on a pair of tire swings, gently rocking back and forth. "It's not just . . . what you did. It's everything. A couple of years ago we both wanted all the same things, you know? College. Med school. Making the world a better place. The YouTube thing was just a hobby, something you did because you liked messing around on the piano."

"Yeah," he said. "And now everything is different. No one could've predicted this. I know you think it's shallow, writing music, performing for people. But I think it's *also* a platform for making the world a better place. I mean, look at what Tyrell has done for the city."

Dallas had a point, not about me thinking his newfound fame was superficial, but about Tyrell making real changes to the city. Tyrell James had been instrumental in creating safe spaces for inner-city youth across St. Louis. He funded a number of after-school programs where local high school and college kids volunteer to teach sports, writing, art, filmmaking, etc., in areas where the more common after-school activities revolve around gangs and drugs.

"I don't think it's shallow," I said. "But you're right. I don't have fun at these parties. I haven't been coming just to keep an eye on you, though. I've been trying to be the girlfriend I thought you wanted me to be. I figured maybe if I compromised and tried to be more involved in your world, it might help fix things between us."

"Genna, nothing between us is broken."

"Not to you, maybe," I said, my voice growing hoarse.

"I just want for you to trust me again. I want for things to go back to the way that they were."

Another clap of thunder startled me out of the swing. A bolt of lightning split the night into pieces. There was a squeal from the hot tub as people started heading back to the house.

I peered up at the sky. "Are you trying to hang on to us because you want to hang on to us? Or is it because you're worried about how a breakup right when your album releases might look? Are you worried I'll tell people you cheated on me?"

Dallas's face blanched ghost pale against the dark backdrop of Tyrell's yard. "You did not just ask me that."

"I'm sorry, but—"

"No. You know what? I can't even believe you're pulling this shit tonight." He rose up from his swing and headed back toward the house.

"Dallas," I called after him. "Where are you going?"

"I need to be away from you right now," he called back over his shoulder.

I let him go. For a few minutes, I swung idly back and forth on the tire swing, waiting to be swept up in a storm that never arrived.

Then I returned to the safety of the laundry room, and Sable, but this time her doggie smile couldn't lift my spirits. I grabbed my phone and sent Shannon a text.

Me: Dallas and I got into a fight :(

Her: That's been happening a lot lately, hasn't it?

Shannon didn't know Dallas had cheated on me. It wasn't that I didn't trust her—I knew she'd keep it a secret. But Shannon used to live next door to me before her parents divorced, and the two of us were almost inseparable from first grade until sophomore year. Then I started dating Dallas and she admitted she was a little jealous of the time I spent with him. Things had improved between the two of them over the past year, but he still wasn't her favorite person. If she found out he cheated on me, she would have told me to break up with him, and I didn't feel like explaining to her why I wasn't going to, how what he did was different from what my dad did. Dallas had gotten drunk and caved to temptation—a one-time thing. My dad had given up on his marriage and fallen in love with another woman behind my mom's back. And where Dad had lied about it for months, Dallas came clean right away.

But Shannon wouldn't have seen it that way. She would've told me I needed to have more self-respect. And maybe that was true. Maybe by staying with Dallas, all I did was prove to him that he could treat me like crap if he wanted to.

Me: I think it might be over.

Her: Is it because he's taking a year off before he goes to college?

I started to shake. As far as I knew, Dallas and I were supposed to be starting at Wash U together in the fall. After that, we both planned to attend med school together and then try to match for a residency in the same city. If Dallas was taking a year off, our whole lives would be off track.

Me: Where did you hear that?

Her: IDK. I probably read it online somewhere.

Me: Well this is the first I've heard of it.

Her: Well then it's probably not true.

Me: I bet it is and he just didn't tell me because he knew I'd be upset. I don't know if we can survive this.

Her: You're just saying that because you're upset now.

I looked away from my phone and sucked in a deep breath. I let it out, slowly, calmly. My shaking dissipated.

Me: What if I'm not upset? What if I feel like I'm seeing things clearly for the first time in months?

Her: What kind of things?

Me: I don't want to talk about this via text. If I come over in like an hour and a half, will you still be awake?

Her: Sure. Or if not, just go around back and knock on my window.

Me: Thanks, Shan.

Her: Anything for you, G.

I headed back to the great room, where Dallas was sitting on the sofa smashed between two girls I'd never seen before. One of them had her hand on his leg, playing with a fraying thread on his jeans. He looked up at me with an expression just daring me to say something, but I bit my tongue. I wasn't interested in seeing myself on YouTube as "Dallas Kade's psycho girlfriend."

"Hey," I said sweetly. "Can I talk to you for a couple of minutes?"

The girls glared at me as Dallas slid out from between them

and followed me through the dining room and into a back hall-way.

"Are you really taking a year off before you go to college?" I asked.

Dallas didn't say anything for a couple of seconds, but the look on his face—surprise, discomfort, guilt—was all the answer I needed. He cleared his throat to speak. "Uh, well, the thing is—"

"How could you?" I asked. "How could you make this deci-sion and share it with other people and not me? You promised you would never lie to me, Dallas."

We'd made a pact to always tell the truth back before we ever started dating. We were fifteen at the time and Dallas was walking me home after Premed Club. He was so proud because we'd been doing microbiology and he'd figured out the unknown organism before I did, but when I didn't respond to his gloating, he knew something was wrong.

"What is it?" he asked. "You've been acting weird all day."

"My parents are getting a divorce," I said. "My dad's leav-ing."

"Like *leaving* leaving?"

"He's moving to Montana or something. I don't know. I quit listening after the part about how he'd fallen in love with another woman." I choked back a sob. I had refused to cry for my father, my father who I caught humming under his breath while he was packing.

"I'm so sorry, Genna." Dallas took my hand.

I looked away. "Whatever, you know. If he wants to leave,

then he should leave. I just wish he hadn't lied about it."

"Everybody lies sometimes," Dallas said.

"I don't," I snapped.

"Yes you do. What about all day at school when I asked you what was wrong and you said nothing?"

He had a point. "Well, at least my lies aren't to cover up anything bad that I'm doing."

"Let's make a pact," Dallas said. "Right here. Right now."

I remember we were coming up on the train tracks we had to cross to get to my house. We had stood and watched as the brick-red boxcars of a freight train rolled past.

"I promise I will never lie to you," Dallas said.

"I promise I will never lie to you." I held my hand out, pinkie extended.

"Pinkie swear, huh?" he said with a grin. "Serious business."

"Serious business," I agreed.

"Pinkie swear," I now reminded him, as he slouched back against the wall of Tyrell's house.

Dallas rubbed at his temples. "I didn't *lie*. I just didn't want to tell you anything until it was definite, because I knew you'd be . . . disappointed. My parents and I talked it over and we all think me taking a year off before I start college is a good idea. That way I can do a good job promoting the album and staying engaged with fans without potentially sacrificing my grades."

"But don't you think there will be a second album?"

"Maybe." He shrugged. "I don't know, Genna. So far, I only signed for one. I love making music, but not enough to skip going to college and exploring other opportunities when I'm ready."

"But we were going to go to med school together," I said. "And what about matching for a residency?"

"That's a million years away," Dallas said. "Who knows what could change by then? We might not even still want to be doctors after a couple years of college."

"Well, I know I will," I said hotly.

"Even if we do, maybe you can take a year off after college and we can still apply for med school together."

"I'm supposed to take a year off because you suddenly aren't sure if you want to be a doctor?"

"A lot of people take gap years. It's no big deal. Why are you being like this tonight?" Dallas asked. "This album release is really important to me. Can you just *try* to be supportive for the next couple of hours?"

"I don't know." I gnawed on my lower lip. "I can't stop looking around at all these girls and imagining each of them as the girl you hooked up with. Is she here?"

"No," Dallas said flatly. "If you really want to know—"

Someone coughed gently from the doorway to the dining room. Tricia, Tyrell's assistant. "Everything okay?" she asked.

"Sorry, Tricia," Dallas replied. "Everything is fine. I'll be back in a couple minutes."

I held my breath as I waited to see if he was going to finish his sentence and tell me about the girl.

He turned to me. "We should probably talk about this later."

"I'm sorry," I said. "You're right. Now is not the time or place. Can we maybe just get out of here?"

Dallas looked at his phone. "It's eleven-thirty. Even if we leave right now, it'll be after twelve-thirty by the time we get home. Plus, it looks like it's going to rain and I'm not sure I'm in any condition to drive. I was thinking we could just crash here and head home in the morning."

I fidgeted, thinking about how I told Shannon I was coming over. "I really want to get home."

Dallas sighed. "You can have your own room if that's what you're worried about."

"It's not that. I just shouldn't have come here with you. I hate that this is your special night and I'm wrecking it. Maybe I can just call a cab."

"A cab from here to your house would be like two hundred dollars," Dallas said. "We can go if you really want to." He yawned. "But I should probably slam a quick cup of coffee first."

"I can drive," I said quickly. "I haven't drunk anything at all."

"It's a bigger car than you're used to."

"I have a MINI Cooper. Every car is a bigger car than I'm used to. It'll be fine—I've driven my mom's car plenty of times," I said. "I'll drop you off at home, take the car to my house, and then I can get it back to you tomorrow."

"Fine." Dallas tossed me his car keys. "I just have to say good-bye to a few people first."

"I'll wait for you outside." I headed for the front door.

CHAPTER 10

Someone knocks on my own front door, interrupting the memory that's been coalescing in my brain. Maybe Shannon decided to skip swim practice and come by anyway. It wouldn't be the first time she's blown off her responsibilities for me.

But when I open the door, it isn't Shannon. It's a girl wearing khakis and a polo shirt with a number five emblazoned just below the collar. She tosses her stick-straight blond hair back from her face in a way that makes it cascade across her shoulders. Definitely a move she's practiced before. A cameraman hovers behind her, looking as if he's trying to maintain a safe distance from me.

"What are you doing?" I ask. "Don't you have to stay down there?" I point at the curb. I managed to avoid all the reporters on the way home from school by circling around and cutting through the backyard, entering the house through the garage. It never occurred to me they might just come knock on the door.

"Hi, Genevieve!" The girl's voice is unnaturally cheery, like she's here to interview me about my National Merit Scholarship instead of my dead boyfriend. "I'm Ashley Losito from Channel Five News. I just thought now that you're feeling better and back to school that you might want to share your thoughts about what happened?"

"No comment," I say. In the back of my mind, the memory of that night is still filling itself in, a piece at a time, and I just want this girl to go away so I can focus. I see Dallas leave Tyrell's house. He gets into the car. I pull away from the curb and head for the highway.

I start to close the door on Ashley and her perfect blond hair.

She sticks her foot in the crack. "Is there anything you want to say to Brad Freeman, the man who almost killed you?"

"No comment," I repeat.

"What about Dallas's fans, the Kadet Korps? Surely you have something to say to them." She's still got one foot inside my house, but she quickly repositions her body so her cameraman can get us both in the frame. It makes me think of Ciara trying to take a selfie with me.

"Don't touch me," I snap, as her arm brushes against mine. "All of you need to get a life. Get off my porch."

In my head, Dallas and I are driving. The road is dark. Rain starts to fall.

"Genevieve. Why are you getting angry?" Ashley asks. "We're on your side. We just want to tell your story."

"I said no comment!" The memory is fading now. I lift a hand to my forehead as if I can manually grab hold of it. With my other hand, I reach toward Ashley Losito, intending to push her backward so I can shut the door.

"What are you doing?" She steps back quickly.

From the depths of my brain I hear Dallas ask the same thing. *Genna, what are you doing?* I analyze the sound of his voice, the volume, the sharpness, the velocity of his speech. He sounds . . . terrified. But why? There's a flash of an image. Lightning illuminates the car's interior. Dallas is wide-eyed and reaching toward me. Beyond him, I see dark pavement and a ravine running along the side of the road.

Ashley decides to press her luck. "Are you remembering something? What's the last thing you remember before the accident?"

"Just leave me alone!" I push Ashley backward with both hands.

Startled, she bumps into her cameraman and they both almost end up on their butts in my mom's rosebushes. I slam the door, lock it, and slide the dead bolt into place. Then I head for the safety of my bedroom.

The memory of the night Dallas died is gone, leaving me with a mess of words and images that I can't fit together in any way that makes sense. What happened between the time I pulled away from the curb in front of Tyrell's house and later when the firefighters had to cut me out of the wreckage? I picture myself in Dallas's car. I picture myself on Highway Z. *Genna, what are you doing?* Why was Dallas so scared? What *was* I doing? I see the flash of lightning, the dark road, and the ravine through the passenger window. But how could I see the road beyond Dallas? We were on a two-lane highway. That would mean I was driving on the left side, wouldn't it?

For the first time, I wonder if somehow the accident might have been my fault.

CHAPTER 11

My laptop sits open on my desk. My wallpaper is a picture of Dallas and me from when we first started dating. Even though I kind of hate how frizzy my hair is and it's before Dallas got his braces off, this has always been my favorite picture of the two of us. Things seemed so simple back then. It was before Dallas was approached by a manager for his YouTube channel, before I was spending every free moment worrying about getting high enough SAT scores to get into Wash U. Neither one of us even had a job. We'd go to school, come home and study together, and then watch TV or read books.

"I think I might have screwed up big-time, Dallas," I say.

You got your memory back, huh?

It's weird how easily I can form Dallas's responses even though he's not here. I can practically hear his voice in my head. "Only part of it. I think it means something bad, but what if I'm wrong?"

You're never wrong.

"Everybody's wrong sometimes." I really, really want to be wrong this time.

I close the laptop and Dallas disappears. I need to talk to someone about this—someone who's alive.

I check the time. It's almost four p.m. Shannon will be at swim practice until five. This doesn't feel like it can wait. If I don't tell someone what I'm thinking right now, I'm going to convince myself that I made the whole thing up in my head— that Ashley Losito upset me by being so aggressive and my memories got mixed up with what was happening in the real world.

I drum my fingertips on my leg. My mom is usually out of surgery by now. She'll know what to do. If anyone is always right, it's her. I call her cell phone and she picks up on the first ring.

"Hey, hon. Are you okay?" she asks.

"I don't know," I admit. "I'm sorry for bothering you at work, but I needed to talk to someone and Shannon is at practice."

"It's fine. I'm in my office just entering some surgical notes. What's going on?"

"What if the accident was my fault?" I blurt out.

"Genevieve!" My mom can make one word cut like a Ginsu knife. "Why would you even say that?"

"I don't know. Dallas had just gotten that car, so I had never driven it and it was dark and rainy and—" My voice breaks apart as I start crying. I can't believe Dallas is gone. I can't believe he's gone and I don't remember what happened.

"Honey," my mom starts. "You were driving and that makes you think you should have somehow prevented this. But that's wrong. Even if you might have responded differently in your own car, that is not a crime. The man who hit you was drinking and driving. He broke the law, he killed Dallas, and he almost killed you too. He's the criminal here, okay? Not you."

I wipe my eyes with the back of my hand. "I remembered part of that night. Dallas and I were fighting at Tyrell's house. I found out he was going to take a year off—that he wasn't going to start at Wash U in the fall. I made him leave. He wanted to stay there overnight but I wanted to go home."

"Oh, Genevieve," my mom says. "You couldn't have known what was going to happen."

I keep going without responding. "Then today this reporter knocked on the door and she was bothering me and she said something and it triggered another memory—Dallas saying, 'What are you doing?' He sounded scared, Mom." I pause. "And I saw the road through the passenger window, but Highway Z is only two lanes, so that would mean I was on the wrong side of the road, only I don't know why that would be the case. I know it sounds crazy, but I just have this weird feeling that I did something horrible."

My mom sighs. "It doesn't sound crazy. It sounds like you want to blame yourself because you were driving and you're the reason the two of you left the party. But honey, who knows if that memory is even real? Or if it is, it could be from another time when you were passing someone. Bradley Freeman was drinking and driving. You can't go around telling people you think you might be responsible for the accident, okay? You'll end up muddying the case against him. Plus, you could get yourself in trouble."

I think about the nasty comments I've read online—the people calling for Freeman to be thrown in jail, or worse. The hashtags dance in my head. #DrunkDriver, #WhiteTrash, #HumanWaste, #Murderer. What would they say about me if it turned out the accident was my fault? Would they call me a #Murderer too?

"But what if he's not to blame?" I ask.

"He *is* to blame. I know it's hard because you don't remember everything and you want to give people the benefit of the doubt, but there are multiple witnesses who saw him driving recklessly that night. You don't want to put a drunk driver back out on the streets, do you?"

"I guess not," I say. My mom is probably right. My brain is making stuff up because I feel guilty about forcing Dallas to leave the party. If only I hadn't been so insecure that night, thinking every girl he talked to was trying to steal him away from me. *#JealousBitch #ControlFreak*. Great. My conscience has started speaking in hashtags.

"Are you sure you don't want to talk to a therapist about this?"

Dr. Chao tried to refer me to one of the outpatient doctors who worked for the hospital, but it felt like he'd be just one more person showering me with sympathy and making me feel guilty about surviving the accident.

"I don't need a shrink," I say, my voice wavering. "I just needed my mom. Thanks for listening."

"Anytime." Mom clears her throat. "Look. I know I haven't always been there for you since your father left, and I know I'm gone a lot now, but I'm trying to be better, okay?"

"I know you are," I say.

"Good. We'll talk more tonight."

"Okay. Bye." I hang up the phone, but the uneasy feeling I had before I called my mom is still lingering.

My mom shows up a little after six p.m., still dressed in her powder blue surgical scrubs. Normally she finishes up her cases, showers, changes into business clothes, and then goes to each of the units to see her currently admitted patients. Mom in scrubs means she's had a rough day.

"You okay?" I ask tentatively. "I could try to make some dinner?"

"Let's order out," she says. "Do you mind calling for something while I shower and change?"

I shake my head. "What do you want?"

"Anything is fine."

I nod. Anything-is-fine days are the worst days of all. I feel bad for adding to her stress.

I dial a local pizza joint and order a gluten-free pizza, hoping to appease both of Mom's major dietary preferences after a hard day—healthy food and comfort food. By the time she's out of the shower, I'm arranging the pizza and a couple of different drinks—sparkling water for me, a choice of heart-healthy red wines for her—on our dining room table.

Mom opens a bottle of merlot with the corkscrew I've laid out. She pours herself a glass of wine, takes a seat across from me, and reaches for a slice of pizza. I slide a piece onto my own plate and sip hesitantly at my water.

"So," Mom starts, her brown eyes studying me carefully. "Are you feeling better about before?"

I nod. "I know you're right. And I know you just want to protect me."

"Good. So then do you want to discuss what else happened today?"

"Meaning?" I fidget in my chair, preparing for a lecture on skipping school.

"What's this about you assaulting Ashley Losito from Channel Five News?"

"Oh, that." I exhale slightly. "She was being pushy and she was half in the house where I couldn't shut the door. I just nudged her. Why? Is she mad or something?" I bite into the tip of my slice of pizza.

"I don't know," Mom says. "I ran into Mrs. Ernst outside and she mentioned it to me."

Nosy old Mrs. Ernst, always peeking out those curtains. I swallow hard. "Are the reporters still out there?"

"Yes." Mom swirls her wine around in her glass, more interested in staring at it than drinking it. She nibbles at her pizza.

"Are they ever going to go away?"

"Eventually, yes. But I don't know when. In the meantime, you're going to have to control your temper. Ashley Losito could file charges against you."

"She touched me first," I say.

"Yes, but she didn't *push* you, did she?"

My eyes fill with tears. I rise from my seat and go to the front window. I peek through a tiny crack in the curtains. The number of reporters has doubled since I got home from school. When Connie was here to shield me from them, they were just an annoyance, but if they're willing to knock on the door, who's to say they're not going to hunt me down on my way home from school? Or even harass Shannon if she comes over to visit? "Why is it okay for them to bother us?" I ask, shuffling back to my seat at the table.

"Because it's their job," my mom says softly. "And if Freeman is officially charged with manslaughter, there will be even more of them out there."

"I don't want to deal with them, Mom," I say. "Can I go away somewhere? Stay with Grandma and Grandpa for a while, maybe?" My grandparents are retired doctors who live in a house on Lake Michigan. It would suck to be away from Shannon, but we could text and talk and I could come back once things calmed down.

"What about school?" Mom asks.

"I can finish it as independent study," I say. "I have all A's.

My teachers won't care if I turn in my last few assignments from home."

Mom runs one finger around the base of her wineglass. "Your grandparents are actually going to be spending most of the summer in Kenya doing volunteer work with children afflicted by hydrocephalus."

"Oh." Kenya sounds perfect—I'd like to see Ashley Losito and her cameraman follow me there—but I know there's no way my mom is going to let me jet off to Africa. Still, it makes me think of something I learned in psychology class last semester called "door-in-the-face technique." Ask for something crazy and then, after being refused, ask for something reasonable in comparison and you're more likely to get it. "Can I go with them?" I ask brightly. "It'd be a great experience."

"Out of the question," my mom says. "You're still healing, Genevieve. Physically and mentally. You can't be someplace without reliable medical care."

"Well, what about Grandma and Grandpa Larsen?"

Mom frowns. "I'm not sure a working farm would be—"

I take in a deep breath. "Or maybe I just could go visit Dad?"

"In Utah?" Mom says shrilly, like it's farther away than Kenya, like maybe I just asked her to strap me into a spaceship and send me to the moon.

"I know it seems crazy, but didn't you say most of his neighbors are retirees from Arizona and California? Old people have probably never even heard of Dallas Kade. I could go there and get my mind off everything."

"I suppose." Mom picks at her pizza. "Of course there's always a chance reporters might find you there, but like you said, the accident wouldn't necessarily be newsworthy to the people of Springdale."

I push forward while she seems to be seriously considering it. "And didn't you say Zion National Park is really pretty? Maybe being in nature would be therapeutic." Rachael works at the park, but I'm careful not to mention her name in front of my mother.

"It is lovely," Mom says grudgingly. "Let me think about it and then talk it over with your father."

"Okay," I say, praying that she decides it's a good idea. "Maybe a change of scenery would help me heal. It'd be a whole new environment—a fresh start."

It'd be running away, a voice in my head says.

Maybe, but after everything that's happened, I think I deserve a chance to escape, at least for a little while.

CHAPTER 12

Mom and I hem and haw about the possibility of Utah for a couple of days, but then a witness to the actual accident comes forward and Brad Freeman is officially charged with vehicular manslaughter. The number of reporters outside our house grows from ten to twenty overnight and Mom decides she doesn't want me to have to deal with it. Springdale, Utah, here I come.

It turns out a spaceship to the moon might have been quicker, because I have to take three different planes just to get close to where Dad lives. First I fly from St. Louis to Phoenix, then to Salt Lake City, and then into the town of St. George, which is about forty miles from Springdale. By the time I get off the third flight, I've logged an impressive eleven hours of traveling.

My dad is sitting on a bench, tapping away at his iPad when I enter the baggage claim area. I figure he's probably doing something work-related, so I walk right past him and head for the black conveyor belt to grab my own bags.

"Uh, excuse me," he says. "Father here, waiting for some sort of acknowledgment."

I stop and turn back to face him. He's made quite a recovery since I last saw him—freshly shaven, hair artfully arranged in a style that hides his gray. No more rumpled shirt or dark circles under his eyes. I wonder if he's thinking the same thing about me. My injuries are healing nicely and I've "regained full mobility," physical therapist talk for saying I don't walk like a one-legged turtle anymore. "I saw you. I just didn't want to disturb you. I can grab my own bags."

"You could never disturb me." My dad rises up from the bench, leaving his computer completely unattended while he pulls me into a hug.

I squeeze him somewhat awkwardly. He left St. Louis the day before I got out of the hospital, so this is our first real hug in quite a while. Right after I had almost died and it was just him—no stepmom—it was easy to forget that I had spent the last couple of years mad at him, not just for breaking up our family, but for the way he did it, cheating on my mom for months and lying about it. But now I'm going to be face-to-face with that woman in less than an hour and my body is tight with tension.

"Someone's going to steal your iPad," I mumble into his armpit.

Dad pulls back and gathers his things. "Sorry, I didn't mean to smother you. I'm just so glad you're here."

We turn toward the baggage carousel together. There's only

one, because this entire airport has only one gate.

"And like most men, I live to tote around heavy luggage for beautiful women," my dad adds.

"Be careful what you wish for," I say, as I pull the first of two shiny purple hardtop Samsonite suitcases onto the carpeted floor of the airport.

Dad tests it with one hand and fakes like he can't even lift it. I point out my second bag—an even bigger one—as it nears us. He heaves that bag from the conveyor belt and arches an eyebrow at me. "Could there possibly be more?"

"Nah, that's it."

We each take one of my bags and head for the exit. "Thank you for coming to get me," I say. "I figured you'd have patients to see, so you'd have to . . ."

"Send Rachael?" Dad arches a blond eyebrow.

"Yeah, I guess." I fiddle with the handle of my suitcase, suddenly focused on peeling off the black-and-white airline tag.

"I had a valve replacement and a pacemaker insertion, but I finished surgery by four so I could do my rounds and come get you." He pauses. "But I hope you're going to cut Rachael a little slack while you're here. She and I both made mistakes, but I'm the one who hurt you and your mom, okay?"

I nod. I'm pretty sure Mom blames Rachael as much as she blames Dad, but I don't really know the details and I don't want to. Rachael tried hard to get to know me when she and Dad got engaged, but after I made it clear I had no interest in that, she left me alone. So basically, as far as stepmoms go, I could do a lot worse. "I will," I say.

"Good. She's really looking forward to seeing you again," Dad says. "Now please tell me you're hungry, because I haven't eaten since this morning."

"Oh my God. All I got on the plane was a small bag of low-fat pretzels. I'm hungry enough to eat an entire cow."

"I think there might be restaurants here where that's possible," he teases. "How do you feel about pizza? Real pizza, with meat and cheese. Not that gluten-free, vegetarian, flavorless crap your mom likes."

"Sounds good."

"Perfect. There's a great pizza place in Springdale, so if you can last another forty-five minutes or so, we'll wait until we get home and then walk over."

"You live walking distance from a pizza place?"

"Almost everything is walking distance in Springdale," Dad says. "Or if not, the national park runs a free shuttle through the town that anyone can hop on and off."

"Cool," I say. But then on the way out to the car, I notice a couple of girls with hot pink and white zebra-print luggage staring at me. It's not their luggage that grabs my attention. It's the black-and-white piano key bracelets they're both wearing. Just like the bracelet Dallas used to wear.

I drop my sunglasses back over my eyes and lift a hand to my hair to make sure my headband is still covering the craniotomy scar. Mom took me shopping yesterday and bought me a pack of five headbands so I could wear them every day. She also let

Shannon dye my hair brown so I would be less recognizable in Utah, though according to Mom I was being "a little paranoid."

"So what's with the new look?" Dad asks. "Testing that theory about whether blondes have more fun?"

Brown hair plus my new "soccer mom hairstyle," as Shannon called it, mean I look nothing like the senior picture still being splashed all over the internet. I shrug. "I just needed a change."

"Well, it's very pretty," Dad says.

"Thanks."

Dad stops in front of a modest-looking midsize car and clicks his key fob to unlock the doors. He pops the trunk and lifts my suitcases into it one at a time.

"A Prius, huh? Who *are* you?" I open the car door and slip into the passenger seat.

"I'm a guy who screwed up when he was younger and made it all about the things instead of the experiences. But it's never too late to change, right?" Dad slides into the driver's seat and looks over at me. "Not that this isn't a nice car."

I fall silent as we pull away from the airport. It's miles outside town, so all I can see are reddish-brown hills stretching off into forever. It reminds me of the way Mars usually looks when they show it in movies.

"So," I say. "Is this what Utah looks like? Just piles of dirt everywhere?"

Dad snorts. "I don't know. Is Missouri just one big cornfield?"

"Okay. Good point," I say. "I guess I was just expecting

something different. The internet made it sound like the whole state is full of breathtaking monuments."

"There are quite a few monuments," Dad says. "Just not right next to the airport." Gradually the desolate landscape transforms into suburbs as we exit onto Interstate 15 and pass through St. George. Dad chats about some of his recent surgical cases. I try to focus but my eyes keep scanning everywhere. Aside from the mountains off in the distance, this city doesn't look much different from Wentzville, the town where Dallas lived.

A few miles later, we leave the outskirts of St. George and the landscape grows barren again. We start to climb in elevation. Off in the distance, soft sweeping mountains give way to higher, sharper rock formations. The sky is so blue and bright, like it's being lit up by a turbocharged sun in some other galaxy.

Dad exits the interstate and turns onto Highway 9. We hit the edge of a town called Hurricane and pass a couple of small subdivisions and a paintball place.

He drums his fingertips on the steering wheel. "I'm so glad you're getting a chance to see all this."

I'm about to ask what he means by "all this" when the sprawling parking lot of a Walmart Supercenter comes into view. "Hey, there's a monument," I say.

"Ha." Dad glances over at me. "When you see how tiny Springdale is, you'll be begging to borrow my car so you can drive back here."

"Doubtful," I mutter. "I'm not big on driving these days." My

MINI Cooper has sat in the garage since the accident. Mom tried to get me to take it out and drive it around the block a couple of times to keep everything running smoothly, but just the thought of crawling behind a steering wheel made me almost throw up.

We pass through two more small towns called La Verkin and Virgin. Just as I start thinking how awkward it would be to live in a town called Virgin, Dad points out the river running alongside the road. "That's the Virgin River," he says. "It runs all the way through Zion National Park."

"It's cute," I say. The rivers back in St. Louis are wide and full of barges and floating casinos. This looks more like a stream.

"Well, when you see Springdale and Zion Canyon, keep in mind the whole thing was formed by that *cute* river."

When we finally hit Springdale, it looks more like a small town in a movie than a place where people actually live. The buildings are made mostly of wood or stucco, with hand-painted signs in front advertising businesses like the Zion Prospector and Springdale Candy Company. People walk along the side of the road, some dressed in shorts and T-shirts and some in more rugged-looking hiking gear.

"They like rocks here, huh?" I ask, after we pass a second store with big bins of quartz and other stones for sale out front.

A smile plays at Dad's lips. "They do like their rocks." He gestures out into the distance.

Set back from the road, walls of red rock, banded with stripes of pink and white, rise up on either side of us, bright green vegetation sprouting improbably from the lower areas.

"It's like driving into a painting," I say. "What do you even call all this? They're not mountains, exactly."

"Cliffs?" Dad offers. "Plateaus? I'm not sure, but Rachael can tell you all about the geology of this area if you're interested."

"I was just curious. I can Google it."

Dad turns off the main street and pulls the car into the driveway of a modest-looking ranch house. "We'll just drop off your stuff and then head to the pizza place."

As I slide out of the car, I see another girl about my age walking along the edge of the road. She's not paying us any attention, but I can't stop thinking about the girls at the airport. I figured Dallas wouldn't be well-known here since most of the locals are older people. But I completely forgot about all the tourists who come through Springdale to go to Zion National Park. We've passed at least six motels on this road alone. Suddenly brown hair and sunglasses don't seem like enough of a disguise.

"On second thought, I'm kind of tired," I say. "And I should probably take a shower after all those plane rides. Any chance we can get that pizza for delivery?"

"Sure. Or better yet, I can pick it up while you settle in." Dad lifts both of my suitcases out of the trunk of his car and we each wheel one up to the porch. He unlocks the front door and we step into an airy living room with a mildly vaulted ceiling, two overstuffed sofas, and a big-screen TV with surround sound. The décor is mostly earth tones, with one wall taken up by a stone fireplace.

"This is nice," I say.

"Thanks. I assure you I had nothing to do with any of the decorating, unless you count picking out the television."

I give him a sideways glance. "It's smaller than the one at Mom's."

"Yes it is. As I said, I'm trying to exercise a bit of restraint in my old age." Dad turns down a hallway before I can reply. "Rachael and I set you up a bedroom, but there's a second spare room at the back of the house, so you're welcome to whichever one you prefer."

"I'm sure whatever you guys set up will be fine."

Dad pushes the door open and immediately I can see how much effort he put into decorating it. He must have gotten Grandma Larsen to make another horse-themed patchwork quilt at some point, because the one on this bed is almost exactly the same as the one I have at home. There's also a desk and chair that look like they were hurriedly assembled from IKEA, and a wooden shelf protruding from the wall that's stocked with paperback novels.

Dad and I used to trade books back when I was in middle school. He'd give me the latest medical thriller by Tess Gerritsen or Robin Cook and I'd give him something by Dean Koontz or James Patterson, and then we'd compare notes at our weekly Sunday brunch, occasionally held on Monday night if Mom or Dad were on call that weekend. My mom thinks reading fiction is a brain-melting pursuit, so after Dad and I finished discussing a book she'd give us the highlights of the latest scholarly paper she'd read, twisting the clinical findings so that they sounded like a thriller novel.

I miss those days.

"This is great, Dad. Thanks."

He exhales deeply, his body visibly relaxing. "Oh, good. I was worried you might hate it. The bathroom is right across the hall. You should be able to find towels and washcloths and all manner of girlie shower products you might need in the linen closet."

"Sounds good," I say.

"I'll order the pizza and probably just walk down the street to pick it up." He shifts his weight from one foot to the other. "Call me if you need anything."

"Okay." I close the door to my room and lie back on the bed. It's surprisingly comfortable and I peel back the lavender sheets to find a memory foam mattress. Wow. Dad really went all out for me.

I curl onto my side and notice a series of pictures hung along a recessed area of the wall. Three photos of my dad and me from when I was young. In the first one we're both riding horses out by Six Flags. I'm about eight years old but I look tiny sitting up on the giant horse the stable gave me. Dad has his horse pulled up right next to mine, so close our legs are touching. The second one is the two of us at a water park for my fourteenth birthday. I remember my mom taking this photo. Both of my parents seemed so happy that day—I felt like we were the perfect family. Now I'm wondering how much of that was an illusion, if my parents' marriage was already starting to fracture, but I was just too blind to see it.

The third picture is of my dad standing behind me while I'm on a rocking horse, a Christmas present he built for me when I was three. I blink back tears. I loved that horse.

I turn away from the pictures and pull my smaller suitcase up on the bed. I start grabbing what I'll need for a shower, trying to ignore the rumbling in my stomach.

My phone buzzes with a text. Shannon. I debate ignoring it for a second. I just got here and I want to enjoy the feeling of having completely escaped St. Louis. But it's Shannon, and if she ignored me, I'd be hurt. I swipe at the screen.

Her: Are we there yet or what?

Me: Just got to Dad's house. Preparing to wash off the airplane cooties and eat a crapload of pizza.

Her: I can't believe it took you all day to go three states.

Me: They're big states :P

Her: I know you're going to be happier getting away from everything for a bit, but I miss the hell out of you already.

Me: Miss you too.

Even though I'm relieved to have escaped the reporters and the nosy kids at school, I really do miss Shannon. My dad said I could bring her with me if I wanted, but she'd already committed to a summer job in St. Louis and her mom wouldn't let her back out.

Her: Don't go replacing me with some cowgirl who says "Yee-haw" or anything.

Me: You know you're irreplaceable <3

Her: You too, G. Call me later if you want.

Me: Okay. All the <333

Her: All the hugs.

Before I can even set the phone down it starts to ring. Mom.

"Hi," I say. "I made it. I'm here."

"You're all the way to Springdale?" my mom asks.

"Yeah. Sorry, I should've called you from the airport. I was distracted by hunger, I think. Dad's actually picking up a pizza right now."

Mom clucks her tongue in disapproval. "That man is going to end up just like his patients."

I should have known better than to mention my father. "Yeah, okay. I'll keep in touch while I'm here," I promise.

"Yes, do," my mom says. "Oh, but I called for another reason. Detective Blake needs you to call her."

So much for completely escaping. "What for?"

"She just wants to check and see if you've remembered anything else that might be helpful with the case the DA is building against Brad Freeman. I told her you'd call tonight."

"Ugh, Mom. Couldn't you have just told her no for me?"

"I tried, but she said she needs to hear it from you for it to be official." Mom sniffs. "I get the feeling she thinks I'm a bit overbearing."

Normally that would make me smile. Mom? Overbearing? Where would anyone get that idea? But there's a weird gnawing feeling in the pit of my stomach when I think about talking to the detectives again.

Mom rattles off the number I'm supposed to call and I scribble it down on a piece of scrap paper from my purse. "If you don't call her, she's going to call you."

"Okay. I can do it right now." It's almost eight p.m. in St. Louis. Hopefully, Detective Blake will be gone for the day and I can just leave a message.

"I'm assuming you haven't remembered anything else?"

"Not yet," I say.

"Then keep in mind what we talked about, all right?"

"I will. I'm not going to say anything stupid." I think about the onslaught of words and images that hit me while Ashley Losito was trying to push herself into the house. The rain. The dark pavement. *Genna, what are you doing?* What if I really was on the left side of the road?

But I can't tell the police about a bunch of memory fragments and some vague hunch that I might have been responsible for the accident with nothing else to go on. It'll just mess up their case, like my mom said.

I hang up and call Detective Blake. The phone rings once . . . twice . . . three times. I breathe a sigh of relief and start to compose a voicemail message in my head.

But then a voice says, "This is Blake."

Pain knifes through me as my heart skips a beat. I can't believe she's answering her work phone so late.

"Hello?" she says.

I debate hanging up, but then I realize she's almost definitely got caller ID and it will take her two seconds to find out who I am and call me back. "Hi, this is Genevieve Grace," I say rapidly. I continue talking without giving her a chance to reply. "My mom said you wanted to know if I remembered anything else about the crash."

"Genevieve. Thanks for getting back to me," Detective Blake says. "As you know, Brad Freeman has been charged with manslaughter. The DA just wanted me to check in with you to see if you remembered anything more from that night that might help."

My heart skips another beat. I take in a deep breath. "Unfortunately, I don't have anything that can help with your case. I'm sorry."

"So you haven't regained your memory of the accident then?"

"I haven't," I say. "I'm sorry. I mean, I wish I had." I need to stop apologizing. It probably sounds fishy.

"Well, you have my number, so let us know if you remember anything, all right, even if you're not sure it's useful."

"Will do," I force out, my voice high and unnatural. My heart makes up for those skipped beats by pounding double-time as I disconnect the call. It's not like anything I said was a lie, but it still feels like I've done something wrong. Almost criminal.

Like I've crossed a line that I can't come back from.

CHAPTER 13

I try to put the phone call to Detective Blake out of my mind. I'm fine. Everything is fine. There's a blood test and eyewitnesses that prove Freeman is at fault. I'm just freaking out because I can't remember. I take a quick shower and then return to my room, where I put on clean clothes and start combing the tangles from my hair.

Someone knocks gently on the door.

"Come in," I say.

Rachael peeks in from the hallway, and then when I don't object she slides all the way into the room. She looks the same as I remember her from the wedding—tanned, reddish-brown hair, a kind, welcoming face and slightly overweight body that hasn't been starved and exercised to perfection like my mom's. She's wearing olive green pants and a gray button-up shirt, a National Park Service patch on her shoulder.

"Hi, Genevieve. Your dad wanted me to let you know that the pizza is here."

"Thanks," I say. "Good to see you again," I add, like she's some kid I knew in kindergarten who I bumped into at the grocery store.

"You too. Better come quickly before he eats it all." The skin around her eyes crinkles a little as she smiles.

"I'll be right there." I manage to squeeze out half a smile in return.

I know firsthand how difficult it can be to please, or even satisfy, my mother, so I can totally understand how my dad would have gravitated to someone like Rachael—appreciative, laid-back, nice. But still, up until the day Dad sat me down at the dining room table and told me he and my mom were getting a divorce, I had kind of the perfect life. Successful but doting parents, only child. It was a sweet gig.

After that, Mom took on more and more work under the pretense that we suddenly needed the money, but I knew enough about how divorces worked to know that Dad would be paying her heaps of cash until I graduated from college.

The truth is, I reminded her of things she didn't want to think about, so she alternated between avoiding me and berating me. I think of how I debated dodging Shannon's text earlier and I wonder if I'm following in my mom's footsteps, hiding from things I don't want to deal with by hurting the people who care about me.

"I'm sorry I was a bitch to you, Rachael," I blurt out, before I can change my mind. "You tried really hard to get to know me and I shouldn't have avoided you."

Rachael's cheeks redden slightly. "I know I was pushy. I wanted you to accept me so badly. Part of me worried that if you weren't okay with me then your dad might change his mind."

"Part of you worried for nothing," I say wryly.

"Perhaps," Rachael says. "But your opinion means a lot to him. And I don't want you to think that because I quit reaching out means I quit thinking about you. Your dad said to give you time, so that's what I did."

I nod. "I appreciate it. And thank you for letting me stay here."

"Genevieve," she says softly. "You're family now, whether you like it or not. And family will always be welcome here."

I bite my lip. "I'm sorry I've never treated you like family."

"Given the circumstances, I think you've been remarkably understanding," Rachael says. "And I want you to know, I'm not expecting anything from you while you're here. I'd love to get to know you better, but this visit is about you having a safe place to recover. If that means steering clear of me, I can respect that."

"That's cool of you," I say. "I've got a bunch of stuff to do for school that will take most of the next week, but after that I'm sure the two of us can . . . hang out or whatever. Maybe you can show me around the park?"

"I'd love to." Rachael pats me on the shoulder. "Now let's go eat before your dad picks off all the pepperoni." She turns toward the door.

"Eew. He still does that?" I make a face as I follow Rachael out of my bedroom and down the hall to the kitchen. I don't want my dad's hands all over my pizza, but it's good to know that not everything has changed.

I spend the next few days holed up in my room working on last-minute school stuff, not venturing farther away from the house than going outside to grab the mail from the curb. On the weekend, Dad and Rachael invite me to go with them to a barbecue that one of Dad's colleagues is throwing in St. George, but I tell them I have to study for finals.

Then on Tuesday I wake up at five a.m. when my phone starts to blow up with text alerts. It's Shannon.

> Her: I know you're probably sleeping, but call me when you get this.
>
> Her: It's not true what people are saying, is it? I'm your best friend. You would tell me, right?
>
> Her: It makes a weird sort of sense, though. It would explain why you were so upset at school, and why you were in such a hurry to get out of town.

Panic rattles my insides. I don't know what Shannon is going on about, but whatever it is, it can't be good.

> Me: I WAS sleeping. What are you talking about?
>
> Her: This.

There's a link attached to the message. I exhale a deep breath before I open it.

THE SCOOP
Was Dallas Kade About to Be a Father?
QUINN KING, 2 hours ago

New information has come to light regarding the death of YouTube sensation Dallas Kade, a Fusion recording artist whose first single "Younity (featuring Tyrell James)" debuted at number eleven on the Billboard Top 40 charts and has been at number one for the past two weeks.

Kade's girlfriend, Genevieve Grace, who was driving Kade's car the night he died, has vanished, leaving the people of her affluent Lake St. Louis community to wonder where she went . . . and why.

Sources close to Genevieve have informed us that she was pregnant the night of the car accident, and that her abrupt departure is because she has gone into seclusion after the loss of her unborn baby. Neither Genevieve nor her mother, Elena Grace, MD, were available to comment on this story.

Criminal defense attorney Max Collier from Collier and Dunst Legal, who is not personally involved in this case, informed us that if Grace was in fact pregnant the night of the accident, and the accident was determined to have ended her pregnancy, Brad Freeman might find himself charged with not one, but two counts of vehicular manslaughter.

Recent Comments:

dallasismybae: awww. this is so sad :(i hope it's wrong and that genevieve has just gone into hiding so she can have the baby without people bothering her. she seems so nice.

SoccerStar5151: Two of my friends go to school with Genevieve and apparently one of the teachers said she's still pregnant and her doctor might have put her on bedrest until the baby is born.

pxs1228: If she really had a miscarriage because of the accident, I hope they decide to charge Freeman with murder, or at least two counts of manslaughter.

 CeliaRN0612: it might depend on how far along she was, whether the fetus was viable outside the womb at the time of the accident.

Kadet4Ever: I read on a message board that the source for this article was actually a member of Dallas's family.

 Lila Ferrier: link?

"This is ridiculous," I mutter. It's no one's business where I am or whether I'm pregnant, and there's no way my teachers or anyone in Dallas's family would be gossiping about it. I can't help but feel a slight sense of relief, though. If people believe this is true, they'll probably be less likely to try to hunt me down.

I log on to Twitter and sure enough, almost all the tweets mentioning me are talking about this story and how everyone should #PrayForGenevieve and #RememberDallas and demand #JusticeForDallas. I scroll through the first few tweets in my notifications feed:

Karla French @klf1222 • 6m

@GenevieveLGrace omg gurl. i lost a baby in a car accident too. I know just how ur feeling. hang tight. and remember god is luv.

Aksel @VictoryIzzMine • 11m

@GenevieveLGrace I hope that SOB #BradFreeman gets charged with 2 murders. Don't let him scare you away from testifying!! #JusticeForDallas

The Mad Marvel @psylockeshock • 17m

Hey @GenevieveLGrace, the #KadetKorps has got your back. Wherever you are, we're all thinking of you and wishing you well #PrayForGenevieve

I notice that my followers have increased from eight thousand to twelve thousand. I log off Twitter and call Shannon. "I am not, nor have I ever been, pregnant," I tell her. "I don't know who these 'sources' are, but they need to stop making shit up."

"I'm so relieved," she says. "I mean, of course I would support you if it were true. But just the thought that you felt like you had to go to Utah and avoid all your friends was horrible. You know you can always confide in me, right?"

"I know," I say softly. And I wish it were true. But I feel like there's a statute of limitations on secrets. If I tell her I'm worried I might have caused the accident, she'll want to know everything that happened at Tyrell's house, and that probably means telling her about Dallas cheating on me. And if I tell her that, she's going to be hurt that I kept it a secret for so long. "Hey," I say, as my feed updates with additional notifications. "I'm going to delete my social media accounts so random strangers will quit bothering me."

"Seriously?" Shannon asks. "But . . . what will you do? I mean, how will you talk to people?"

"Shan, you're one of the only people I want to talk to, and you'll still be my friend if I don't like all your Instagrams and YouTube vids, right?"

"Of course. I just . . . I can't imagine giving up social media. Aren't you going to be bored?"

"I don't know. Rachael says I should go outside or something. But I don't want you to think I'm avoiding you, okay? You'd better still text me."

"I will," Shannon says. "Outside, huh? Like, for fun? Very retro-chic. I trust you will email me some pictures of small-town Southwestern style so I can poach anything good and pretend I invented it?"

I snicker. "You know it."

"I just wish I was closer so I could give you a hug."

"All the hugs for you," I say.

"And all the hearts for you," Shannon says.

It's the way we usually sign off on our texts, only reversed.

Shannon swallows back a yawn. "I should go find some coffee so I don't fall asleep during one of my finals."

"Just think. A few more days and you'll be able to sleep in."

"Hardly. I have to be at the pool by seven a.m."

"Oh, right, I almost forgot." Shannon works as a lifeguard during the summer. My only summer job has been working for my mom in her lab. I suddenly dread the idea of an entire summer without any specific place to be. Maybe I can find a coffee shop or something around here that needs someone for part-time work.

But as soon as I think of that, I think of handing over my driver's license to some college-aged hiring manager. She'll see the name Genevieve Grace and ask where she's seen it before. Or she'll just Google me.

Maybe I can register for an online college course or two instead.

"I should go call my mom so she doesn't freak out if she saw this article," I say. "We'll talk soon, okay?"

"Okay. Take care," Shannon says. "And remember, send me some pictures!"

"Will do." I end the call and find my mom's number in my contacts menu. It's going on six-thirty a.m. there, so she's probably already at work. For a minute I debate letting it go—after all, she's probably not stalking the Dallas Kade newsfeeds. Then again, it would be bad if she heard about my fake pregnancy from one of the scrub nurses. With a sinking feeling, I tap the screen.

The phone rings twice and then my mom comes on the line. "Are you calling about the newest articles?" she asks. No "Hello, how are you?" No "I miss you." Straight to business—that's my mom for you.

"Yeah. Sorry to call so early. I just wanted to assure you I'm not, nor have I ever been, pregnant."

"Oh, I know that, honey. The hospital does a pregnancy test on everyone of childbearing age before they're given any kind of scan. Of course your initial CT was emergent and done before the results came back, but if you were pregnant, your father and I would've been informed." She pauses. "I'm more worried about the other rumor."

"What other rumor?"

"The one that says the real reason you left town was because Brad Freeman threatened you. Did that man make any kind of contact with you?"

"What? Someone is saying *that* now? No, Mom. I have had no contact with Brad Freeman. How can people write articles that aren't true? Do you think I should respond and tell them they're wrong?"

"I wouldn't," my mom says. "It'll just fan the flames. Plus, it'll make it easier for tech-savvy types to find out where you are."

"Good point. I didn't even think of that. Has anyone asked you where I am?"

"The police know, but they won't tell anyone. Some reporter called me on the phone and I told him you were spending the summer with your grandparents. Let him hunt for you in South Dakota or Michigan, or Africa for that matter."

"Do you think they'll eventually find me?"

"I don't know. It depends on how deep they dig. Hopefully something else will come along to distract them," my mom says. "But enough about all that. What else is going on? Why are you awake so early?"

"Shannon texted me. That's how I found out about the article."

"Ah. Are you still working on stuff for Ridgehaven?"

"I'm almost finished," I say. "I already emailed in three final projects. I just need Dad to watch me take a couple of online exams and sign off on them. But I should finish everything by the deadline, so I'll get my grades on time."

"Good, good," my mom says. "And you're sure you won't regret not walking in your graduation ceremony?"

I heard before I left that graduation was going to be dedicated to Dallas's memory, with a slide show of him before the ceremony and music from his album playing on the way in and out of the auditorium. I'm surprised no one asked me to give a speech.

"Positive," I say. "It's high school. It doesn't mean that much."

"I see," Mom says. "So what else are you doing there? I assume your stepmother has taken you to see the national park?"

"I haven't done much of anything yet," I admit. "I'll get out and see some stuff once I finish my finals."

"Are you unhappy? You can always come home if you want." My mom says it lightly, but I can sense the loneliness beneath her words.

"I'm okay," I say. "I guess I'm just afraid someone will recognize me and start asking me questions."

"Oh, honey. You are completely entitled to tell anyone who bothers you that what happened is none of their business. Please don't let that fear keep you cooped up in the house all summer. Your father and I might not see eye to eye on most things, but I completely agree with him that where he lives has breathtaking scenery and loads of outdoor activities, and you should take advantage of that stuff while you're there."

"You're right," I say. "I will. Thanks, Mom."

"I love you," she says.

"Love you too." I disconnect the call and set my cell phone back onto my nightstand. Maybe I do need to get over my obsessive fear of being recognized. But that doesn't mean I have to listen to people spreading lies about me online.

I go from Twitter to Tumblr to Instagram to YouTube to Facebook, deleting all my social media profiles. Each time I zap another electronic version of Genevieve Grace out of existence, I feel a little bit lighter. I might not be able to escape my own thoughts about the accident, but I can escape everyone else's.

Running away, that voice in my head reminds me.

I shush it. There's nothing wrong with tuning out a bunch of hurtful gossip and speculation from random strangers. If anyone has anything important to say, I'm sure I'll hear about it one way or another.

CHAPTER 14

My fingertips are trembling as I close my laptop. I take in a deep breath and shake out my muscles. I go to my bedroom window and slide open the glass. The early morning sky looks in at me, all purple-black and hazy, wide swatches of clouds blotting out the moon. The desert breeze snaps the silky cloth of an American flag hanging in front of the house across the street.

Yawning, I open up the dresser and pull out a pair of running shorts and a top. Quietly, I change into my clothes and tie my hair back into a ponytail, covering my scar with a purple headband. I slip on my shoes and open my door a crack.

There's a light on under the bathroom door, which means either Dad or Rachael is already awake. Not surprising, since they both start work early. I tiptoe quickly down the hallway and let myself out the front door.

Outside, the desert wraps around me—walls of red sandstone, the rounded silhouettes of prickly pear cacti, grains of sand swirling like miniature storms at my ankles. Stars peek through breaks in the clouds. I had no idea anywhere could be so beautiful in the dark.

I turn in the direction of the national park and start running. My feet pound the asphalt. I breathe in deeply. This is the first time I've run since the accident, and my body aches from the impact of each stride, but it's a good kind of pain, like my muscles are waking up after a long nap. My heart keeps pace with my feet.

My mind stays blissfully blank as I run, my eyes taking in the scenery that's waking up around me. The shop windows are all still dark, but as the sky lightens, the massive rock formations off in the distance become clearer. I remember what my dad said in the car about how the Virgin River carved out this whole area between the cliffs. Not such a weak river after all.

It takes me about fifteen minutes of running to reach the entrance to Zion. There's a separate entrance for pedestrians across a parking lot of restaurants and camping shops. The sun is just starting to peek over the horizon and there's no one in the ticket booth yet, so I can just wander right in. I pause inside the gate to consider a map of the park so I don't get lost.

Even though it's still early, the air is already beginning to grow warm. I wish I'd brought something to drink with me. I glance around, looking for a place to get water. The Zion Canyon Visitor Center complex is huge—a sprawling network of concrete filled with educational displays. The actual building is centrally located and not open yet, but there's a second building across the way.

I squint and can just barely make out a sign that says

"Restrooms" and a water fountain between the men's and ladies' rooms. Perfect. I cross the parking lot, cutting in front of a white pickup truck.

A guy in a gray uniform shirt that looks like Rachael's is sitting in the driver's seat. He's staring down at his phone, his thumbs rapidly tapping out a message to someone.

The guy doesn't even look up as I head for the drinking fountain. Bending over, I gulp some cool water. As I'm heading back out to the road, the guy gets out of the truck and I realize he's about the same age as me.

He puts down the truck bed and starts to unload a long beam of lumber. His arm muscles go tense beneath skin that is tanned from outdoor work, but I can tell he's not plain white like me. Part Hawaiian maybe, or Native American.

The wood is probably ten feet long, and even though this boy's biceps are pretty massive, he's struggling a bit due to the awkward proportions.

"Do you need some help?" I ask. This is the first sentence I've spoken to anyone in Utah who isn't Dad or Rachael.

The boy turns toward the sound of my voice and nearly hits me with the beam he's carrying. "Jesus," he mutters. And then, "Sorry. You scared the shit out of me." His dark eyes take in my outfit. "Early morning run?"

"Yeah." I scoot out of the way so he has more room to maneuver the beam.

"Do you have a park pass?"

"Uh . . ." I start. "There was no one in the booth. I was just curious to look around. I didn't mean to sneak in." I back away from him slightly.

His lips twitch. "So you're just out trespassing and sneaking up on park staff?"

"I didn't mean to sneak up on you either. I'll leave if you want. That just looks awkward, like maybe you could use a second set of hands."

"I'm supposed to have some help, but I don't think he's going to show." The boy shakes his head in disgust. "The problem with volunteers is that they mean well, but there's no sense of commitment."

"I can commit to helping carry all four of those," I offer, pointing at the wood. "You know, in exchange for my breaking and entering."

The boy chuckles. "If there's been any breaking, I don't want to know about it." He looks me up and down again, as if he's not convinced I can even carry half of a beam. "This would be faster with a second person. You don't mind?"

"I don't mind."

"Okay, then." The boy sets the beam on the ground and grabs a pair of gloves out of the cab of the truck. He tosses them to me. They're about three sizes too big, but they'll protect my hands from getting splinters.

"I'm Elliott," he says. "We're just taking these over there to where that railing is damaged." He points at an area that overlooks the Virgin River. "I'm going to cut them down with a power saw later."

"Okay." I take the back half of the beam and we set off across the clearing together. We're almost there when a rustling down by my feet makes me stop sharply.

Elliott glances back over his shoulder. "Rock squirrel. They're everywhere."

The little rodent dashes across the clearing and disappears behind a sagebrush plant. Elliott and I set the beam down in a grassy area. As he bends over, a carved pendant on a black cord slips out from beneath his collar. He tucks it under his shirt as we both turn back to the truck.

We're on the fourth and final beam when the walkie-talkie on Elliott's waistband crackles to life.

He grabs it without even missing a step. "What's up?" he asks.

The voice on the other side is male, but I can't make out what he says.

"Okay," Elliott says. "I'll check it out in a few minutes. Oh and FYI, Eric didn't show up again. Tell Rachael we need another aide for the summer, or at least a reliable volunteer."

Rachael! Elliott must work for my stepmom. Small world.

We set the last beam on the pile. Elliott still has the walkie to his ear, so I smile a good-bye at him and head for the street.

"Hey, wait." He hooks the walkie-talkie back on his belt. "Aren't you even going to tell me your name?"

I pause. This is an issue I should have realized would come up eventually and already dealt with in my mind. If I tell people my name is Genevieve and they've seen any of the coverage of the accident, they're going to put it together. "It's, uh—"

"You don't have to, if you don't want to," Elliott says. "I can just think of you as my mysterious beam-carrying benefactor."

I smile, this time for real. "My name is Gen," I say, hoping he'll assume it's J-E-N as in Jennifer. That's got to be one of the most common names ever.

"Thanks for the help," Elliott says. "And be careful if you're exploring the park by yourself. I just got a call about a mountain lion sighting out on one of the trails. They don't usually mess with people, but you're kind of small, so if you see one, don't run from it, but don't approach it, either."

"So . . . just stand there?"

"Um, no. If a mountain lion comes near you, make a lot of noise and try to make yourself look big. It's probably a nonissue now that the sun's up. Usually the sightings happen at dawn and dusk."

Holy crap. The sun rose completely while we were unloading the beams and all of a sudden I'm outside the house in broad daylight without sunglasses, where anyone might see me. And recognize me. "Got it. Thanks for the tip. Bye!" I wave and then head back toward town.

That night at dinner, I tell Dad and Rachael how I ran down to the park.

"I'm glad you're back running," Dad says. "Sounds like your body has almost completely recovered."

"Yeah, maybe."

"Are you finished with your stuff for school?" he asks.

"Almost. I have two finals left I was hoping one of you guys might proctor tomorrow night. Once those are graded, my guidance counselor said they'll mail my diploma to Mom."

"So what do you want to do this summer now that you've basically graduated?" Rachael asks. "I could use a reliable volunteer if you're interested. We just had another one quit."

I remember Elliott's frustration about the missing volunteer. I wonder if he told her about his mysterious beam-carrying benefactor. "Why?" I ask. "Are you a mean boss?"

"I don't think so, but maybe I am," Rachael says, her dark eyes twinkling.

Dad snorts. "Trust me, you're not. On a completely unrelated note, Genevieve, have you talked to your mother lately?"

"This morning, actually. I decided to touch base after someone posted an article speculating about why I left St. Louis."

Dad makes a face. "Those people need to get a life. Is your mom doing okay? Letting you come here for the whole summer must have been tough."

Dad's concern surprises me. I figured he hated my mom as much as she seems to hate him, that how she was coping without me would be the furthest thing from his mind, except possibly to gloat. "She seemed a little lonely, but you know Mom. She's a survivor." I pause. "But back to the volunteering thing. If you're serious, I think I'd like to give it a try."

The old Genevieve Grace was not much for hiking or camping, or even spending time outside. Except for the running I did most mornings, I really only went outside to transfer from the house to the car and then back inside on the other end. It was all about studying for me. That was what my mom wanted and what I wanted for myself. But I can't deny that being outside today made me feel better.

"That's great, Genevieve." Rachael beams. "I just know you're going to love it there."

"I'm assuming I'll have to wear a name badge. Would it be okay if I went by Jen with a *J*? That way people will be less likely to figure out who I am."

"Hon, you can spell your name any way you want," Rachael says.

"And you'll call me Jen?"

"If it keeps that smile on your face? Sure thing."

Rachael took my dad's last name, Larsen, but all the news articles are calling me Genevieve Grace since I changed my name to my mom's last name after my parents got divorced. It should work. Even when people find out I'm her stepdaughter, they won't automatically put the pieces together.

"We had our seasonal volunteer training sessions a couple weeks ago, so I'll have to pair you up with some of my more experienced staff. They can get you caught up on how we run things at the park. How does Friday sound for a first day?"

"Sure," I say.

Rachael pulls out her phone and swipes at the screen a couple of times. "What's your email address?"

I give it to her and a message pops up, "Subject: NPS Training

Materials." I open it and download a twenty-page PDF.

"That's a lot of training materials for a volunteer," I say.

"Well, the park is a government-run facility," Rachael says, smiling. "I wouldn't be doing my job if I didn't bury you in tedious and difficult-to-understand paperwork."

I give Rachael a quick hug. "Thank you for this," I say. "I think being outside in this beautiful environment will be exactly what I need."

For the first time since the accident, I actually feel excited about something. I wonder if I'll see that Elliott guy again. I liked the way he didn't pressure me to talk about myself. He seems like the kind of guy who keeps his head down and focuses on the work. That's exactly the kind of person I need around me right now.

CHAPTER 15

On Friday, my alarm goes off at six a.m. I brush my teeth, wash my face, and then look for something to wear. Rachael said because I'm not an official government employee that I can wear what I want as long as it's clean and not too revealing.

I opt for a pair of jeans and a T-shirt with the molecular structure of caffeine on it. Dallas had a shirt just like this. A ripple of sadness moves through me as I realize I've managed to go almost two days without thinking much about the accident. I've been focusing on finishing my finals and reading up on my Zion volunteer training materials, but still. It feels wrong.

I open my laptop to the wallpaper with the picture of us. "I'm wearing my caffeine shirt," I tell him. "Remember when we got matching shirts together at the mall?"

You look good, Genna.

"Do I really?" I ask.

Well, I liked you better as a blonde, but brown hair is pretty too.

"Glad you approve," I say with a wry grin.

Rachael knocks gently on the door to my room. "Gen? You on the phone?"

I shut the laptop. "Uh, yeah," I call through the door. "Sorry. I'll be ready in a couple of minutes."

I pull my hair back in the same ponytail-and-thick-headband combo I had on when I was running. It covers up my bald spot, but unfortunately leaves the scar on my cheekbone visible. I try my best to camouflage it with a bit of concealer, but all I can manage is lightening the red line into a pink one. Frowning in the mirror, I reach for an eyeliner pencil. Maybe if I emphasize my blue eyes it'll make people less likely to notice all my facial imperfections.

Rachael parks her National Park Service Jeep in the lot behind the Zion Canyon Visitor Center. We head inside, where she introduces me to a girl about the same age as me. She has the kind of skin that looks naturally flushed, and long, sandy blond hair that hangs over her shoulders in two thick braids. She's dressed just like Rachael except for the tan cowboy boots peeking out from beneath the hem of her olive green workpants.

"This is Halley. She's a student park guide, and this is her third summer as a Zion staff member," Rachael says. "Today you can shadow her and help out at the pedestrian entrance station. You'll also be with Clint—he's a ranger. The two of them will get you acclimated so you know where everything is, both in the booth and in the layout of the park."

"Sounds good," I say, but I can't bring myself to meet Halley's eyes. I've just noticed what she's wearing on her wrist—a black-and-white rubber piano key bracelet. "My name is Jen," I add, before Rachael can mess up and introduce me as Genevieve.

"Nice to meet you, Jen," Halley says. "Let's get going."

Halley and I leave the Visitor Center and follow the path to the entrance station, which vaguely resembles a tollbooth. The sun is already bright and hot. It's going to be a scorcher of a day.

"Working the entrance station is a very important job," Halley lectures as we pass several educational displays outside the Visitor Center. The Virgin River runs along the edge of the parking lot. The water is a greenish-gray color, and so shallow that rocks are poking through the surface. I read in my training material that the park's most popular hike is called the Narrows, and this river is a trail that people can follow for miles. Halley clears her throat and I realize she caught me zoning out.

"Sorry. You were saying?" I swallow back a yawn and direct my full attention back to her. Well, three-fourths of my attention. Part of my brain is wondering where I can get a cup of coffee.

"One of the reasons rangers always work this booth is that we're the first people visitors will interact with and we set the tone for their entire stay. If we come across as rude, disinterested, or unknowledgeable, it could affect their view of the entire National Park System."

"Makes sense." I want to do a good job for Rachael, so I listen closely as Halley runs down a list of issues that non-ranger employees should never try to answer on their own.

"Often, people will ask you if it's safe for their grandma or their child to hike on such-and-such trail. It can be tempting to say yes. After all, it's a national park, right? Of course it's safe." She pauses for a second and gestures up at the majestic cliffs. "But nature is unpredictable. A trail that's safe one day might be treacherous the next. People die here sometimes. They fall, or they drown, and then their family members want to sue. So if anyone asks you if it's safe to hike a trail, you'll want to refer them to our trails specialists at the Visitor Center."

"Got it," I say.

Halley unlocks the booth that we'll be spending the next several hours in together and shows me where I can set my purse. "I recommend bringing a water bottle," she says. "Sometimes we do lots of talking."

I gesture at my caffeine T-shirt. "Actually, what I need is coffee."

"You can get a cup from the staff lounge at the Visitor Center," Halley says. "You might want to run back over there now, before we get busy."

"Okay. I can bring you a cup too if you want."

"I don't drink coffee," Halley says.

"Really?" This time I can't swallow back the yawn. I cover my mouth with my hand. "Sorry. I pretty much live on it."

"I'm a Mormon. We're not supposed to drink coffee."

"Holy crap," I say. "Er, sorry. I mean, wow. I knew Mormons weren't supposed to drink or smoke, but I didn't know they couldn't have coffee. That's harsh."

"It's not that big of a deal," she says, shrugging. "Go ahead and get yourself a cup so you don't fall asleep. I'll get set up in here and then we'll go over everything once you're back."

I run over to the Visitor Center and get myself a cup of coffee from the staff lounge. Rachael is standing behind the Park Information desk, flipping through some kind of report.

"Did Halley drive you off already?" Rachael asks, smiling. "She can be kind of intense."

"Oh, no, she seems nice. She recommended a water bottle and I realized I needed some coffee."

"Ah, okay. Well. Have fun. And just so you know, I plan on putting you outside tomorrow, if you're game. Halley was supposed to start helping me with a special project, but we had someone call in sick for the entrance station today, so it seemed like a good way to cover the post and help you get acclimated to where everything is."

"Definitely," I say. "I guess I'll see you later."

Rachael's phone rings and she smiles a good-bye as she answers the call.

I return to the booth, where Halley has everything organized and ready to go. She gestures at a wall of maps and brochures, pointing out which ones are for Zion and which are for some of the other parks in the area. My eyes are drawn to one for a place called Bryce Canyon. The rock formations are even more breathtaking than what's around me now.

Halley catches me looking. "Bryce is one of my favorite places. Have you been there?"

"I haven't been anywhere in Utah except for here," I say. "I'm spending most of the summer with my dad."

"Oh, nice." Halley logs on to the computer and checks the time. "Are you in high school or college or what?"

"I just graduated from high school. I'm going to be a college freshman in the fall."

"Sweet. Me too." She pulls a roll of white credit card tape from a low shelf and starts feeding it through the machine.

I watch her fingers work, my eyes once again being drawn to her black-and-white bracelet. I make a mental note to Google the bracelets later and see why they're popping up everywhere. It has to be related to Dallas.

"Where are you going?" she adds.

Crap. This is another question I should have anticipated. Even though my craniotomy scar is hidden by my headband, I still have the scar on my cheekbone. If I tell her Wash U, will that be enough for her to put the pieces together?

"Northwestern," I say. It's a school that's the same tier as Wash U and only one state away, so it's not really a lie. I mean, it is, but I could have gotten accepted to Northwestern if I'd wanted, so it's not like I'm lying to make myself look better.

I don't know when I became a person who classifies lies as "lying" and "not really." I always hated people who lied to me growing up. My parents did it for a little while about the divorce and it made me so angry. I guess they thought I couldn't cope with the truth, so they tried to pretend everything was fine for as long as they could. And now here I am, lying to hide my identity. I'm not sure that's any better.

Luckily I'm saved from this train of thought by Ranger Clint arriving. He's a broad-shouldered guy about my dad's age wearing a sheriff-style hat.

"Hey, Clint." Halley waves.

"Hi," I say.

"Morning, ladies," he says. "Halley, who's your friend?"

"This is Jen. She's a new volunteer."

"Is that so?" Clint extends his hand. "Nice to meet you, Jen."

"Nice to meet you too." I wrap my fingers around his and he pumps my arm up and down.

"Well, since there's two of you in here, I'll hang out outside for a bit and greet people as they arrive. Flag me down if you have any questions."

"Will do," Halley says brightly.

Clint heads outside and a couple of minutes later our first family arrives—a mom with two sons. Halley greets them and runs through the schedule of fees, pointing out that if they're going to visit any of the other national parks nearby, it might be cheaper for them to buy an annual pass. The mom springs for the pass and Halley swipes their credit card and hands them a receipt.

Business stays steady for the next couple of hours. I'm impressed by the way Halley chats with the tourists—she manages to sound enthusiastic and young, yet completely professional.

When it's time for our lunch break a few hours later, Clint

steps inside the booth, followed by a second ranger, an Asian woman who introduces herself as Min. Halley and I grab our purses and slip out of the booth.

"You are really good with people," I say, as we head back toward the Visitor Center. "Were you in student government or something?"

She shakes her head at me. "I've been homeschooled since seventh grade."

"Seriously?" My voice rises in pitch. "People who say homeschooled kids struggle socially need to hang out with you for a while."

Halley laughs. "My parents own the Springdale Family Kitchen. I guess you could say I've been unofficially in the customer service field since I was ten. But I'm also required to participate in one extracurricular activity at Hurricane High, where the other kids from Springdale go to school. Last year I joined the debate club."

"Hurricane High." I try to remember if Dad and I passed it on the drive from the airport. "Is that where Elliott goes?" I step inside the air-conditioned building and hold the door for her.

"How do you know Elliott?" Halley's voice takes on a playful tone.

"I ran into him earlier in the week when I was running."

"Ah. Yes, that's where Elliott graduated from. He just finished his first year of college at Dixie State down in St. George. You'll probably see him tomorrow if you're working with me again. The two of us are supposed to break ground on a new trail project."

"That's sounds cool," I say. It definitely sounds like something I've never done before.

Halley scoffs. "If you enjoy hard labor." Then she smiles. "Just kidding. It'll be fun. We're actually working on creating a touch trail for kids. Rachael has been trying to get a budget for it for years and she finally got approval for the materials."

"What's a touch trail?"

"Kind of like the educational stuff around the Visitor Center, but with more stuff little kids can interact with. A lot of people bring small children here, but there's not much geared for that age group."

"Cool," I say again. "Elliott is the only other person our age I've met besides you. Are there other teens working here?"

"Not so many who are park guides, but there are some high schoolers in the Junior Ranger Program and lots of college kids who work for Zion Lodge. Oh, and if you want to meet more people, you're welcome to come to church with me some Sunday."

"I'll think about it," I say, wondering what Halley's friends would think if she brought an atheist to Sunday services.

Rachael is still at the Park Information desk, along with another ranger who doesn't look much older than Elliott. A couple my grandparents' age are leaning against the counter, poring over a map that Rachael is pointing at.

"I'm not sure what you want to do for food," Halley says. "I've got a packed lunch in the staff refrigerator, but if you want to buy food, the Zion Canyon Brew Pub is pretty good and right over there." She points across the parking lot. "There's also a market over there with sandwiches and stuff."

"I think I'll see what Rachael is doing. She's actually my stepmom," I say.

"Oh. I didn't realize that." Halley looks back and forth from Rachael to me. "Having divorced parents must be hard. But I guess if you have to have a stepmom, you hit the jackpot with Rachael. Everyone loves her around here."

"This is my first time really getting to know her," I say. "But I can see why she's so well liked."

The couple at the Park Information desk take the folded map Rachael offers them and head for the parking lot. Halley disappears into the staff lounge, leaving me to stare awkwardly at Rachael from across the counter.

"I was wondering what you were doing for lunch," I say.

"I was going to invite you to lunch at the brew pub," she says. "It's got standard bar food—burgers, fries, soups, salads—but also some fancier choices if you're feeling like pasta or steak. Sound good?"

I glance at my phone. "Is there time?"

"You're a volunteer. You can take a few extra minutes if you need. And I have a radio, so if anything major comes up, Josh will let me know, right?" She glances at the ranger next to her.

"You know it." Josh smiles at me before turning his attention to a pair of college girls who are clutching a copy of the

Zion-Springdale Guide.

Rachael strolls around from behind the counter. Then the two of us head off to lunch.

It feels almost normal, which feels really strange.

CHAPTER 16

The rest of my first day as a Zion volunteer goes really well. At lunch, Rachael tells me about the trail project I'll be working on tomorrow.

"It's called the Zion Canyon Touch Trail and the idea is for it to be a quarter-mile loop, and every hundred and fifty feet or so we're going to have an educational display that kids can touch or interact with. This trail will be flat and paved, with a handrail, so it'll be fully handicapped-accessible. And for the surface we'll be using local dirt and mixing it with a natural polymer that's resistant to wear and better for the environment than asphalt."

"So what will I get to do?" I bite into my applewood-bacon cheeseburger, which is cooked perfectly. I blot at a strand of cheese that sticks to my lips.

"I'm going to leave that up to Elliott." Rachael spears a forkful of her salad. "He's one of my seasonal employees. Very hardworking and nice. I'll be out on patrol tomorrow, so he'll be supervising. I would definitely be prepared to get dirty and sweaty, though."

"I actually met him the other day when I was running," I say. "He was parked by the Visitor Center when I stopped to get a drink."

"Dark hair, dark eyes, big biceps?" Rachael asks.

"Yeah, that sounds like him. I mean, I'm not really checking out guys' biceps these days, or anything."

Rachael swallows her bite of salad. "Sorry. Of course you're not," she says quietly. She takes a sip of her water. "Look, I know the two of us aren't that close, but if you ever need to talk, I'm here. Sometimes it's easier to talk to someone who's a little more distant from the situation."

I concentrate on my burger. "Sure. Okay." I know Rachael is trying, but I can't imagine opening up to her. There's not even really anything to talk about. Dallas is gone. I miss him. I feel like what happened was partially my fault. I don't understand why he died and I didn't. All those things hurt, and no amount of talking is going to change any of them.

We finish our meals and I head back to the booth, where Halley and I spend the rest of the afternoon with Clint, taking payments and handing out maps of the park. She lets me work the window the last hour of our shift, just so I can test myself on how well I know the parking procedure and how to get to the various campgrounds, picnic shelters, and trailheads.

When the clock hits five, Halley grabs her purse. "And we're done for the day."

"You ladies have a nice evening," Clint says.

"He stays until seven," Halley explains as we exit the booth and Clint waves.

I turn back to Halley. "Well, thanks for showing me around today. I'll see you tomorrow."

"You're welcome," she says. "Oh, and tomorrow? You're definitely going to want a water bottle and sunscreen."

"Right. Trail building. Good looking out."

I meet Rachael back inside the Visitor Center and she drives me home. We stop at Zion Pizza and Noodle Company on the way and pick my dad up his favorite meat-lovers pizza, hilariously called the Cholesterol Hiker. I look over the choices and smile when I see there's one called the "Good For You" pizza. That'd be my mom's choice for sure.

"Will this be okay for you?" Rachael asks. "Or would you like me to order you something different? The salads here are pretty good."

I skim over the Cholesterol Hiker's ingredients—a lot of cheese and a lot of meat. "This is fine," I say. "It's a little high fat for me, but Halley told me I'll be getting a major workout tomorrow."

Rachael grins. "You have no idea how excited I am to have you helping me out on this trail. It means so much to me." She pauses. "And *you* mean so much to me. I'm sorry about the circumstances that brought you here, but I'm really glad we're getting another chance to get to know each other."

"Me too," I say, and I mean it. Rachael invited me into her

home when I needed a place to escape to, she offered me a job and saved me from a long hot summer of hiding in my bedroom, and she's been nothing but nice to me since I got here. I used to think that liking her would be a betrayal of my mom, but now I think that even my mom would like her under different circumstances.

While we wait for the pizza to cook, I look up the piano key bracelets on my phone and see that I was right—there are about ten different websites selling them as a Dallas Kade memorabilia item. It's a nice gesture, I guess, but seeing them everywhere is just one more thing that's going to remind me of the accident, of the fact that if I hadn't been so petty and jealous, Dallas would still be alive.

It doesn't take me long to figure out what Halley meant about hard labor. Rachael drops me off at the Zion Lodge the next day, a little ways up the road from the Visitor Center. By the time I swill my very necessary cup of morning coffee, Elliott has gone somewhere and returned, his pickup truck brimming with tools and supplies. It looks more like we're going mining than building a trail.

He pulls what looks like a couple of axes out of the bed of the truck and hands one to me. It weighs twice as much as I'm expecting and I almost drop it on my foot.

"Do you know what that is?" Elliott asks.

I'm guessing it's something I'm not qualified to hold, let alone use. "An ax?"

"It's a Pulaski. Forget the ax side. You're going to use the adze side."

"The what?" I consider the other side of the tool. It's got a sturdy metal head on it with a blunt edge that resembles a garden hoe.

"Adze," Elliott repeats. He gives Halley and me each a pair of work gloves and then tosses her a cloth tape measure and a bundle of bright orange flags. "Halley, your job is to mark the lines so Jen and I know where to break up the ground. You've got the diagram Rachael sent, right?"

Halley pulls a folded piece of paper from the back pocket of her jeans. "On it." Her blond braids swing back and forth as she jogs across a big grassy clearing in front of the lodge to an area closer to the river that's a mix of sagebrush and sandy soil.

I start to follow her, the deceptively heavy ax, no, adze, hanging at my side.

"Hold up," Elliott says. "I'm going to show you how to use that, but not here where all the old men are staring at you."

I glance around quickly, fidgeting with my headband to make sure my scar is covered. Sure enough, a couple of men about my dad's age are leaning against a minivan in the parking lot and checking me out. Almost without thinking, I check their wrists for black-and-white bracelets. If these guys are wearing them, I can't see them. Middle-aged men aren't exactly the demographic Dallas and his producer were shooting for, but back when he was teaching piano online he had fans of all ages.

"Creepy," I mutter.

"Yep. The local people here are awesome, but you never know what you're going to get with the tourists." Elliott takes me out into the sandy area a few yards away from where Halley is marking. "Have you ever swung one of these?" he asks. "Or an ax?"

"Uh, no. I've never even swung a hammer."

"Seriously? Well, you're about to get an education, rookie. And a workout."

Elliott takes his Pulaski in both hands and has me mimic the way he's holding it. I feel a strange combination of ridiculous and badass, like when I dressed up as Black Widow for Halloween and wore my costume all day at school. Dallas went as Captain America, which I joked was barely even a costume given his all-American good looks and boy-next-door demeanor. I think that was a lot of what shocked me about his cheating—he was always so nice, so proper. I never thought he would hurt me like that.

I try to push the thought out of my mind. I shouldn't be thinking about the bad things, not now that Dallas is gone. But part of me wonders if someday that girl will come forward, sell her story to some tabloid website for a few bucks.

Elliott lifts the tool about waist high and slams it down into the sunbaked dirt.

I jump. "Sorry," I say. "I'm paying attention. I swear."

"Good." He does it a few more times and I can see the chunks of earth breaking apart.

I'm not convinced I'm going to be able to mimic his form with the heavy tool. "Wouldn't a shovel be easier?"

"Nope," he says. "But there's one in the back of the pickup if you're afraid to give this a try."

"I'm not afraid." I do my best to replicate Elliott's form with the Pulaski, surprised when the ground cracks under the force of my stroke.

"Nice job, Crusher," he says. "Only about two million more to go."

I consider the twisting path of flags that Halley is meticulously placing. Two million might be a conservative estimate. "Are we the only people working on this?"

"We are today. This is Rachael's baby, so it's primarily her team handling it. That's Halley and me and two other park guides . . . and you, I guess."

I snicker. I'm on Rachael's team. God, my mom would die.

"What's so funny?"

"Nothing," I say.

Elliott and I join Halley and start to break up the ground between the red flags that she's carefully inserting in the ground every five feet.

"How deep do we need to go?" I ask.

"At least six inches," he says.

Crap. I'm only getting about half that deep. I try to put more force behind my strokes, letting the blade of the tool fall with gravity instead of trying to keep control over it.

"Now you know what working on a chain gang would be like," Halley teases. "I guess this explains why all our volunteers have quit."

"Don't listen to her," Elliott says. "She's hoping to do this full-time after college. She likes the pain."

I shrug. "At least it's a good workout." It's also helping to clear my mind. I focus on the way my body moves with the tool, on the way my muscles relax and contract during each strike. The repetitive motion reminds me of running.

Elliott and I are mostly quiet except for the repeated thunking of our Pulaskis hitting the dirt. Halley chatters to both of us as she measures out the trail and marks it with flags.

"So what's your deal, Jen? What kind of stuff do you like to do?"

"Um . . . running?" I offer. "Reading? Studying. My school was really intense, so I didn't have a lot of time for outside stuff."

"Okay, so what kind of stuff would you do if you *had* free time?" Halley presses.

The truth is, I spent most of my free time with Dallas. When we didn't have Premed Club, we hung out at my house a lot since we could walk there after school. We usually ended up studying, messing around online, or hooking up if there was no chance of being caught. Sometimes all three if my mom was working late.

I try to come up with answers that are true but that won't give away my identity. "I like horses," I say. "And running . . . which I already said. And I took a poetry class that I ended up liking more than I thought, so maybe that too."

"Awesome," Halley says. "You know, there's a horse corral right over there." She points at a spot across a far parking lot, just on the other side of the Virgin River.

"Really? Maybe we can ride sometime when I'm here."

"Sure. They do two different options, a one-hour or a three-hour ride."

I make a mental note to ask Rachael about it later. "What do you like?" I ask Halley. I've become pretty good at deflecting questions back on other people.

"Well. Like you, my school curriculum was very rigorous, and I sometimes help my parents out at their restaurant in the evenings. But when there's time, horses, hiking, camping, hanging out with my friends." Halley pauses. "Do you have a boyfriend?"

I feel my skin blanch. I swallow hard before answering. "I used to," I say. "But it . . . didn't work out."

Elliott's eyes meet mine for a moment. His expression softens. "So everyone is single and everyone likes horses. Glad we got that settled."

I flash him a grateful smile. He must have picked up on my discomfort.

"I thought you were afraid of horses," Halley says.

He scoffs. "I'm not *afraid*. I simply respect the fact that they're big and strong and that they could kill me." He turns back to me. "I work at a veterinary clinic in St. George during the school year. I've helped restrain horses so my boss can do exams."

Halley turns her attention to Elliott. "I can't wait for college. I hope it won't be too hard to make new friends."

"I'm sure you'll do just fine." He tugs on one of her braids. "You're rooming with a friend of yours, right? So you'll have a head start."

"Yeah. Tazmyn and I are rooming together at BYU," Halley says. "Tazmyn is my best friend," she explains to me. "We went to the same elementary school, and we're in the same ward at church."

"Nice," I say. I'm curious to ask Elliott more about his college experiences so far, but I know that every question I ask will invite a question in response. Right now there are a lot of questions I don't want to answer.

Elliott drops his Pulaski for a second to look over Halley's progress, adjusting a few of her flags so the marked trail goes around a small cluster of sagebrush and not right through it. "Remember, Rachael said whenever possible not to disturb the natural flora."

"Right. Sorry." Halley studies the diagram from Rachael again and goes back to her marking. She's quiet for a few minutes, but then she says, "Hey, Elliott? I heard that the lodge staff are having their secret Fourth of July party again this year. Are you going?"

"Would you like me to go?"

"Heck yes!" Halley exclaims.

"Halley likes to party with the cool kids who work at Zion Lodge in the summer, but she needs a man to show up with in order to feel legit," Elliott explains.

Halley rolls her eyes. "More like I need a ride, since the

shuttle won't be running that late."

"I'll think about it," Elliott says.

I smile, but focus on my digging, surprised and strangely proud at the line of dirt I've broken up. I blot the sweat from my forehead, noticing that my headband is drenched. I'm sure all the makeup I tried to use to cover my scar has also melted off. I stop and take a long swig from my water bottle.

"How are your hands?" Halley asks. "Sometimes even with gloves you end up getting a blister from working with tools like that."

I tug off one of my gloves. The area between my thumb and first finger is pink, but there are no blisters forming as far as I can tell. "They're okay."

"Your face is red. Did you remember sunscreen?"

I nod. "I put it on at home and I can reapply at lunchtime."

"Okay," Halley says. "But you're a volunteer. Just remember you can take a break whenever you need."

I shake my head. "I'm fine."

"You're so quiet," she says. "I feel like you could totally be miserable and we wouldn't even know it."

"You talk enough for all three of us," Elliott tells Halley.

She grins. "That's because I have a lot to say."

"You'd better hurry up with those flags or Crusher here is going to lap you." The two of them go back and forth teasing each other for a couple of minutes. I start breaking up a new area of ground and Halley returns to her measuring and marking.

Rachael shows up at lunchtime with sandwiches and cold

drinks. I'm reaching for a can of Coca-Cola when Elliott grabs my wrist. I'm so surprised by the touch that I drop the Coke right back into the cooler.

"Try this." Elliott holds out a different can of soda in my direction. It's bright orange.

"Cactus Cooler?" I say dubiously. "It's not prickly pear flavored or anything, is it?"

"You'll like it. Trust me."

Shrugging, I pop the top. "Looks like orange soda to me." I take a long drink, surprised by the twist of something tangy running through the sweetness. "Wow, that's tasty."

"It's orange-pineapple," Elliott explains.

"Yeah, it's okay," Halley says. "But FYI, prickly pear is delicious." She gestures toward the lodge behind us. "The gift shop sells prickly pear everything—chocolate, caramels, jelly, you name it."

"Prickly pear jelly?" I wrinkle up my nose.

"Don't knock it till you try it," Rachael says. She drops down to the ground next to the rest of us and starts distributing the sandwiches. The three of us eat mostly in silence. I watch some of the lodge guests toss a Frisbee around. A Zion Park shuttle pulls up and a bunch of people pour out—mostly retirees and families with little kids. I smile to myself when I think about how soon they'll have a special trail just for them.

After we finish eating, I return to digging the trench. Rachael hangs out with us and helps for a while. She verifies Halley's placement of the flags and moves a couple to adjust the path of the trail just slightly. Then she picks up a Pulaski and goes to town on the dirt. She doesn't necessarily look like she's in good shape, but she has incredible strength and endurance.

"I'm amazed by how much progress we've made in a single day," she says.

"Me too," Elliott says. "You didn't tell us your stepdaughter was Superwoman."

I grin. My hands and arms and back are aching from using the Pulaski for hours, but there's no denying that the three of us did a ton of work today.

"See you tomorrow," Elliott says as I hop into Rachael's Jeep.

"Bye." I give him a half wave.

My phone buzzes with a text. Before I can even fumble it out of my pocket, another text comes in. My fingers close around my warm plastic case and I tap at the screen. Two messages from Shannon. The first one says: Genevieve? Are you there? The second one is marked 911 but it's just two words: Call me.

CHAPTER 17

The second I'm home and inside the safety of my room, I call Shannon back.

"What's up?" I ask when she answers the phone.

"Freeman is trying to pin the accident on you," she says.

"What? What do you mean?"

"Everyone figures that this is a ploy cooked up by his attorney. Since you never remembered exactly what happened that night and the crash site evidence was deemed inconclusive, if Freeman can convince jurors you caused the wreck, it might be enough to create reasonable doubt."

"Oh." I lie back on my bed, my brain spinning. With everything going on at Zion, I had almost managed to forget about Brad Freeman.

"Oh?" Shannon repeats, her voice incredulous. "I figured you would be, like, screaming mad. This asshole gets drunk, gets behind the wheel, hits you, kills your boyfriend, causes you to need dangerous brain surgery, causes so much interference in your life that you move across the country to escape it, and now he's trying to say it was all your fault. And your response is 'Oh'?"

"Sorry," I say, my voice wavering. "I'm just in shock, I guess. What about the eyewitnesses? And the DWI?"

"Freeman is insisting that the blood test is inaccurate. He admits to having a couple of drinks after work that night, but not enough to impair his driving or put him over the legal limit. The bartender and two of his coworkers are vouching for him not being drunk, and apparently he and his lawyer are contesting the BAC results because the hospital did the test different than police officers do it or some bullshit."

"Wow."

"Wow, indeed. And according to his lawyer, none of the eyewitnesses are credible. The one who saw the actual accident is supposedly a huge Dallas Kade fan who couldn't have clearly seen the road that night from her bedroom window as claimed." Shannon huffs. "And there are some lovely quotes online from Freeman's lawyer about the rate of accidents among teenage drivers, and how isn't it possible that you were reaching down to change a CD or texting or something?"

"No, because Dallas's car didn't even have a CD player, and who would I be texting at one-fifteen in the morning?"

"Right? And they could pull your phone records to verify that. Don't panic. I'm so sorry to bring this up. I just wanted you to hear it from me."

"It's okay. I appreciate it." Blood pounds in my ears. *Genna, what are you doing?* The fear in Dallas's voice was almost palpable. But was it real? I close my eyes and try to return to that moment. I see the road. I see the rain. And then I see the flashing lights and firefighters.

I swear under my breath.

"What?" Shannon says.

"Sorry. I was just thinking about something. Anything *good* to report?"

"Let's see. There's a totally hot lifeguard who started working at the pool with me. His name is Niko. He says he's Greek, but I'm pretty sure he's just a regular American with a decent fake accent. I mean, who moves from Greece to Wentzville, Missouri?"

"Good point. What's he like aside from being a possible fraud?"

"Well, I can't say I know him that well yet. It's only been a few days." She pauses to take a breath and then launches into the story of how they met.

I let Shannon tell me all about Niko while I log on to my laptop and do a search for Brad Freeman. A slew of articles pop up. I click on the first one from today.

REALE NEWS NOW
Bradley Freeman Claims Innocence in Dallas Kade Death
CHRIS REALE, 4 hours ago

In his first press interview since waking up in the hospital after being part of a car crash on May 13 that left Fusion

Records performer and YouTube sensation Dallas Kade dead, Bradley Freeman insists it was Genevieve Grace, not him, who caused the accident.

Freeman said he recently regained all memories from that night, and he can clearly recall being in his proper lane on Highway Z as he returned home from work, seeing the glow of headlights from around a bend in the road, and then making the curve only to find the other car in his path with barely any time to brake and no time to figure out how to get out of the way.

Normally in fatal crashes, an accident reconstruction team can analyze the position of the cars after impact, the skid marks on the road, and other technical elements of the event to determine what really happened. However, heavy rain the night of the accident washed away skid marks as well as bits of glass and debris that could have been helpful.

Freeman was charged with DWI and one count of vehicular manslaughter after his BAC came back at .083. One eyewitness who lives on Highway Z claims to have seen the accident, and two others came forward to say they had seen him driving erratically that night. Freeman's lawyer, Roderick De Laurentis, said he plans to challenge the BAC results and that the eyewitness testimony would prove unreliable in this case.

Genevieve Grace was not available for comment, but a spokesperson for the Grace family was quick to point out that Grace has a spotless driving record. Grace suffered a life-threatening brain injury in the crash and has still not recovered her memories.

Recent Comments:

DadsagainstDD: WHAT A BUNCH OF BULL****. WHAT KIND OF GROWN MAN USES A TEEN GIRL'S MEMORY LOSS AND TRIES TO BLAME HER FOR AN ACCIDENT AFTER HE ADMITS TO DRINKING AND DRIVING?

> **Jayden Pierce:** A delusional one. Or one with a really savvy lawyer. This dude needs to be locked up.

pxs1228: How do you suppose he is affording Roderick De Laurentis anyway?

> **Izrockin:** [Comment has been removed by an administrator.]

Chris Reale: I heard De Laurentis is doing this case pro bono. I respect your passion, commenters, but please remember to abide by the terms and conditions of posting on Reale News Now. Death threats or verbal abuse will not be tolerated.

Allison_in_Hell: What's funny is that if you drive drunk and hit a homeless veteran, no one cares, but hit a YouTube star and you're Public Enemy #1. Sometimes I hate the world we live in.

A spokesperson for the Grace family. I wonder if that was my mother or if she opted to get her lawyer involved to handle the inquiries.

Shannon is now telling me each thing Niko has said to her since they met, overanalyzing his words to find some hidden meaning. "Do you think he likes me?"

"Uh . . . it sounds promising," I say. I hit the back button on my browser and scan the next article about Freeman.

THE SCOOP
Brad Freeman Blames Dallas Kade's Girlfriend for Accident
QUINN KING, 3 hours ago

Cyberspace is buzzing today after Brad Freeman, the former paramedic charged with vehicular manslaughter in the death of Fusion recording artist Dallas Kade, made a public statement blaming Genevieve Grace for the accident that left Kade dead and Freeman and Grace in critical condition early last month.

According to Freeman, he didn't drink enough for his driving to be impaired and it was Grace, not he, who caused the accident by veering onto his side of Highway Z in Wentzville, Missouri. Several eyewitnesses to Freeman's erratic driving have come forward, including one who witnessed the accident through her bedroom window, but Freeman and his lawyer say those people are all mistaken.

What do you think, Scoopers? Sound off in the comments like I know you love to.

Recent Comments:

The Black Death: Freeman better watch his back. I am Justice and I am coming for him, and ain't gonna be pretty.

boxxofmonkees: Hey guys. I started a Fire Brad Freeman Facebook page if you're interested. Every person who posts on it has been tagging Eight Ball Bar & Grill in New Melle, MO, Freeman's place of employment. Be sure to share it and tell your friends to boycott Eight Ball until they fire this lying sack of ****

Brad_Freeman27: My lawyer told me not to comment on any of these articles but I'm sick of hiding. Please take down that Facebook page and stop calling my work. I understand why people are angry, but I've been charged and there's going to be a trial. Please don't get me fired. I need my job.

> **pxs1228:** Well look who it is. You should have thought about how you needed your job before you got wasted after work, got in your truck, and killed a rising celebrity.

> **Brad_Freeman27:** I didn't get wasted and I didn't kill anyone. You'll see.

> **pxs1228:** Says you. I feel sorry for your mother, having to watch her son take advantage of a teen girl's brain injury to try to prove his "innocence."

> **shanthewoman:** Hey Freeman, why don't you just go die, you degenerate piece of redneck scum?

> **Never Forget DK:** If there was any justice in this world, you never would have woken up.

I shut my laptop with shaking fingers. There's a crushing pain around my chest, and for a second I imagine my ribs folding and breaking, jagged shrapnel stabbing me in all my organs.

"Genevieve? Are you still there?" Shannon asks.

"Yeah." My voice cracks. "You're not responding to any of the articles, are you?"

"No," Shannon says. "I might have retweeted a couple of things because they were so well worded, but nothing bad."

"Look. Sorry, Shan. I have to run," I say. "Literally. I'll talk to you later." I disconnect the call before she can protest and go immediately to the small chest of drawers. I trade my jeans and boots for shorts and running shoes and head for the front door, a sheen of sweat already coating my face. I need air. I need space. I need to get out of here before I lose it in front of Dad and Rachael.

They're both in the kitchen. He's standing at the counter chopping lettuce for a salad while she stirs a pot of spaghetti sauce.

"There you are," she says. "I told your dad you were working that phone like a madwoman in the car and that you were probably talking to your friends. We're making manicotti, but it won't be ready for another twenty minutes or so."

"I'm actually not that hungry," I say. "I'm going to go for a run."

My dad frowns. "After working all day? Rachael thought you'd be too tired to even stand."

"I have a lot of nervous energy, I guess." I shift my weight from one foot to the other. "I promise I'll eat something when I get back."

"All right," Dad says, but I can see the worry in his eyes.

I head out the front door and turn toward the park without even thinking about it. The soles of my Nikes pound against the concrete. My heart beats in my ears as I run. Pieces of the online articles flash in my brain like billboards. Freeman said he wasn't driving under the influence. Freeman is blaming me for the accident. Strangers are trying to get him fired. He needs his job.

It's a little past seven p.m. when I reach the entrance to Zion. It'll be getting dark in the next hour or so—not exactly enough time to go on a hike or anything. I could keep running. Just going and going until it all makes sense. That was my original plan. But that crushing feeling is back in my chest and my breath is coming in sharp shrill gasps. I'm not sure how much farther I can make it without collapsing onto the warm pavement. I turn toward the Visitor Center. They closed about fifteen minutes ago and the area is mostly deserted. I get a drink from the fountain, the water cool against my sunburned lips.

Then I lean back against the wall of the building and sink slowly to the pavement. *You. Are. Alone.* Normally I don't mind being all by myself, but this is different. I'm not just isolated physically. I'm emotionally alone too. There's no one I can talk to. The one person who would listen without telling me what to do—without judging me—is dead.

I bury my heads in my hands and start to cry.

The tears come hot and fast, the sobs shaking my insides. I'm not crying because of what Brad Freeman said in the article. Well, no, that's a lie. I *am* crying because of that, but not because he's taking advantage of my head injury to prove his innocence. I'm crying because Brad Freeman is right. I did cause the accident.

I'm the reason Dallas is dead.

I remember everything now.

CHAPTER 18

MAY 12

I sat in Dallas's car for what felt like forever, waiting for him to make his rounds and say his good-byes. It was almost midnight by the time he showed up.

I gave him a look as he slid into the passenger seat, but I didn't say anything.

"Sorry," he said. "A lot of those people supported me even back before I made the album. I didn't want to be rude to them."

"Just to me, huh?" I said snippily, immediately regretting my words.

"You could've waited inside," Dallas reminded me.

"I know. I'm sorry. Let's just get out of here."

I started the car and pulled away from the curb in front of Tyrell's house. His neighborhood was dark and quiet. Next to me, Dallas reclined his seat, his eyes drifting shut.

Ass, I thought, as I twisted and turned through the Central West End and merged onto Forest Park Parkway. *Must be nice to have millions of people fawn all over you, to have local celebrities throw you parties where they serve you alcohol even though you're underage, and then to have your girlfriend as a handy designated driver.*

I realized I was going fifty-five in a thirty-five and hit the brakes. I glanced over at Dallas. He was snoring softly. I considered waking him for a second to ask for help setting the cruise control, but then I decided just to let him sleep. At least we weren't fighting for once.

I merged onto Interstate 170, which was also mostly deserted at that time of night. Keeping a careful eye on the speedometer, I headed north, away from the city. I probably should've taken Highway 40, but I grew up listening to my parents talk about how many accidents happen on that road. Dallas usually drove when we went someplace, so I'd never taken 40 anywhere and that night didn't seem like the night to try something new.

A big eighteen-wheeler truck blew past me on the left and cut back in front of me. I slowed slightly to reestablish a space cushion like I learned in Driver's Ed.

Dallas's phone buzzed in the console. I turned my head just enough to see it in my peripheral vision. I wondered who was texting him so late. Was it her? It had to be her. Even though I had once told Dallas I didn't want to know, I was suddenly overcome by the need to find out her identity—what girl had screwed up everything so royally between Dallas and me? I reached down for his phone with one hand while keeping the other one on the wheel.

Suddenly, his eyes flicked open. "Genna, what are you doing?"

"I, uh, was wondering who was texting you this late," I admitted.

Dallas removed his phone from my hand. He tapped in his pass code. "It's Tyrell," he said. "Music stuff. Want me to show you?"

I shook my head, tears welling in my eyes. Somehow I'd become someone I didn't even like—a girl who thought it was okay to snoop through her boyfriend's phone. A girl who didn't respect other people's right to privacy. "I'm sorry," I said hoarsely. "I don't know what my problem is."

"It's okay," Dallas replied. "I'd probably do the same thing if I were you." He paused. "Look, do you want me to just tell you who it was?"

"You don't have—"

"It was Annika. And before you ask, I haven't seen her or texted her since the night it happened."

"Annika Lux?" My voice squeaked. "The model who replaced me in your video shoot?"

Dallas swallowed back a yawn. "Yeah."

"Perfect," I said. "So I guess you can even blame me for your cheating. I mean, you probably wouldn't have met her if I hadn't bailed on you."

"That's bullshit, Genna. You know I don't blame you," Dallas said. "I just thought maybe knowing would help."

A tear made its way down the left side of my face. How could he think knowing he hooked up with a Swedish model would *help* me? I lifted my hand and quickly brushed the tear away. "You know what? Let's just drop it for now. Go back to sleep."

"Fine." Dallas tucked his phone in his pocket and reclined his seat back, shrugging out of the shoulder strap.

Trying not to think about Annika Lux, I exited from 170 to 70 and started the long journey west to Lake St. Louis. The dashboard clock read 12:20. It'd be after one a.m. by the time we got home. On cue, drops of rain plinked hard against the windshield. It took me three tries to find the windshield wipers. I slowed down to be able to better navigate Dallas's car on the slippery roads.

I knew I should pull over and text Shannon, tell her I'd just come over tomorrow. But pulling over meant getting off the highway, and that was another skill I wasn't all that good at. I mean, sure, I knew how to take an exit ramp, but finding my way back onto the road in the right direction could be tricky. I decided to just text her when I got home. She was probably asleep already anyway.

I yawned just thinking about sleep. I had shut the windows when the rain started and the car was kind of stuffy. I reached down and fumbled for the air-conditioning, but Dallas stirred as I turned on the fan and I didn't want to disturb him again.

I fought the urge to fall asleep for the next thirty miles. *You're almost there*, I kept telling myself. St. Charles. O'Fallon. When the exit for Lake St. Louis popped into view I could hardly believe it. And then I remembered that I had to bring Dallas home.

I pushed onward to Wentzville, taking the exit for Highway Z. I navigated the wet road carefully, squinting to see in front of me since I didn't know how to turn on his bright lights. I yawned again. *Just a few more miles,* I told myself. *Just three more neighborhoods and you'll be there.* I bit my lip to focus. From around a curve, I saw the soft glow of approaching headlights.

I yawned again.

I blinked hard.

Just one more subdiv—

A horn honked. Someone screamed. My eyes snapped open.

"Genna, what are you doing?" Dallas shouted.

A pair of headlights were coming directly at me. I had drifted over into the left lane. I lunged for the steering wheel, but it was too late.

There was a shriek of brakes and a sickening crunch of metal on metal.

And then, after that, there was nothing.

CHAPTER 19

I can't believe I fell asleep driving. I've seen stories about that online, and I even know one girl at school whose dad fell asleep on the way home from a hockey game and rear-ended their neighbor's car. But when it happens, it's always some older person who's been working or partying all night. It's never anyone I know. It's definitely never a *teen*. I don't even remember if we covered the danger of falling asleep driving in Driver's Ed class. Texting and driving? Yes. Talking on the phone? Changing the radio station? Applying makeup? Eating or drinking? Yes, yes, yes, yes. But falling asleep? Even though I struggled to stay awake that entire drive, it never occurred to me that I would *really* fall asleep.

Until it happened.

My stomach lurches and I nearly throw up all over the pavement outside the ladies' room. Struggling to my feet, I lean my head over the trash can for a few minutes until my nausea subsides. I remember how I felt sitting there in Dallas's car waiting for him, listening to his satellite music, watching the clock on the dashboard tick off minute after minute. At one point I was positive he was being slow just to punish me for wanting to leave. If only I hadn't been so angry. If only I had stayed home in the first place. If only we'd spent the night at Tyrell's like Dallas wanted. If only I had pulled over when I started to get tired, Dallas might still be alive today. I screwed up so many times that night.

I killed my boyfriend.

I can't even be bothered to try to stop the tears. There are too many—whole weeks' worth of tears. Tears for Dallas, for a life cut short. Tears for myself, because I did something stupid and someone ended up dead. Tears for Brad Freeman because he's being blamed for something he didn't do.

Just when I think today can't possibly get any worse, I see a guy in an NPS uniform striding toward the men's room. Elliott.

It's too late for me to run away or hide in the bathroom. He's definitely seen me. I wipe hurriedly at my eyes and suck in a big gulp of air. I grab my foot and fold it back behind me, pretending to be stretching my quadriceps.

"Jen?" he says as he approaches. "What's wrong?"

Everything. "Nothing."

It's such an obvious lie that for a moment Elliott just stares at me, like he can't even believe his ears. Then he shrugs. "Ooookay."

"What are you doing here?" I switch legs and stretch my other quad.

"Um, what most people do here?" He glances up at the sign that reads Restrooms.

"No, I mean, I thought you went home at five."

"I work longer shifts sometimes," he says. "I was helping one of the rangers out with a project, but I'm getting ready to leave." He strokes the black cord around his neck as he gives me a long look. "Are you sick or something?"

I shake my head.

"You look like you're about to pass out. Do you want me to call Rachael for you?"

I shake my head again. "I'll be all right."

"You don't look all right." Elliott's dark eyes take in my tearstained face. "Whatever it is, do you want to talk about it?"

"Why would you even offer?" I ask, half wondering if maybe he's figured out who I am and is hoping for a scoop to sell to the media. "You hardly know me."

"True, but you remind me of someone I used to know." He looks past me, off into the distance. Sadness flickers in his brown eyes.

"Who?"

He returns his gaze to mine. "Someone I wish I'd listened to."

A moment of silence passes between us, and suddenly it hits me that I'm not the only one with a secret that's eating away at me. Maybe Elliott wants to listen because he also wants to talk.

I try to imagine spilling everything that's happened—everything that I did—to this boy I barely know. "I can't," I say. "But I appreciate the offer."

"Okay." He shifts his weight from one foot to the other. "Can I give you a ride home?"

"No. I think I'm going to run. It might help clear my head."

"All right," he says dubiously. "I'll see you bright and early tomorrow. And Jen? I hope you feel better."

"Thank you."

Elliott looks like he wants to say more, but then he jams his hands in his pockets and ducks into the bathroom. I dust off my T-shirt and shorts and turn toward the park's exit. Normally this would be one of those supremely humiliating experiences, but it's hard to feel embarrassed that a random guy caught me crying when I just found out I killed my boyfriend.

By the time I make it back home, it's after eight and Dad is in his study working on the computer while Rachael putters around the kitchen. I manage to choke down about three bites of manicotti, just so I can say I ate.

Rachael sets a white envelope with red and green lettering on it next to my plate. "Your mom forwarded some stuff from Wash U. I think it's a letter from your academic advisor or something."

I look at the envelope and frown. "Did you open it?"

"No. I think maybe your mom did that."

"Figures."

"She probably just wanted to make sure it wasn't anything requiring an immediate response."

I look up at Rachael. "Why do you stick up for her? She'd

never stick up for you like that."

"Because I know I hurt her," Rachael says. "I've got a lot to make up for."

"I don't think giving her the benefit of the doubt over a piece of mail is going to do much to make up for stealing her husband."

Rachael winces. "I guess not, huh?"

"Sorry," I say. "I didn't mean that the way it came out." I take my plate to the sink and rinse it off. Then I escape to the safety of my bedroom.

When I close the door, my laptop calls out to me. I know I shouldn't look, but I can't help it. I can still search Twitter, even without an account, so I type in the hashtag #BradFreeman and read down the column.

Tyrell James @RealTyrellJames • 3m

As a man who has been falsely accused of a crime, I beg you to reserve judgment and wait for the facts in the #BradFreeman case.

Kimmy Crook @kcrook1218 • 10m

#BradFreeman's mom took to her FB page to proclaim his innocence. She should've gotten an unlisted number first. Call her at 636-555-2245.

Reale News Now @RealeNewsNow • 11m

Pls think before you take justice into your own hands. Campaigning to get #BradFreeman fired has the potential to hurt more than just him.

Tyrell James @RealTyrellJames • 16m

We are allowed to demand answers. But please remember #DallasKade's friends & family when you are tweeting and commenting about #BradFreeman

Hate is Great @hateisgreat418 • 17m

Kill #BradFreeman.

Monkey Man @boxxofmonkees • 21m

Join the Fire #BradFreeman FB page. Boycott the New Melle Eight Ball Bar and Grill until they can his ass. bit.ly/1RkXpaS

Izzy Rocks @izrockin • 24m

#BradFreeman needs to go die already. This is how I know there's no God, because dirtbags like him are allowed to live.

Just A Troll @troll_lo_lo_lol • 26m

What's the max penalty for manslaughter? They oughta chop this #BradFreeman mofo up and send little pieces of him to all the Kadets.

Just A Troll @troll_lo_lo_lol • 26m

I want a necklace made out of this #BradFreeman's dude's teeth.

X Marks the Spot @xxspotxx • 26m

@troll_lo_lo_lol You are one sick bastard, but I like your style! #BradFreeman #KadetKorps

I can't believe some of the horrible stuff people tweet. And who starts a Facebook page just to get someone else fired? What is wrong with people? What is wrong with *me*? I shouldn't be online sifting through tweets about Brad Freeman. I should be on the phone to Detective Blake telling her I'm the one who caused the accident.

I reach for my phone. There's a text message from my mother:

Mom: If you haven't seen the latest news articles, just stay offline, please. This man and his lawyer are trying to manipulate you. Call me if you need to.

I swear under my breath. I could call her and tell her the whole truth, but I know it wouldn't change anything in her mind. Even if he wasn't wasted, Freeman was still drinking and driving. I wasn't. Freeman is a repeat offender. I'm her almost-perfect daughter. She would never want me to ruin my life to clear the name of some stranger.

But you don't have to listen to her. You're more than her almost-perfect daughter. You can make your own choices.

Once again, I imagine how the internet would respond if they found out I was the one who killed Dallas Kade. #Careless, #Negligent, #Guilty—the hashtags pile up on top of #ControlFreak and #JealousBitch. So many horrible labels I never would've applied to myself. So many horrible labels that I suddenly feel like I deserve.

A bolt of lightning flashes outside my bedroom window and one more hashtag flits through my head: #Murderer. With shaking fingers, I Google the motor vehicle laws in Missouri and find out that it's not a crime to fall asleep while driving. I'm not a murderer. It's not even manslaughter.

But is that how everyone else will see it?

Is that how *I* see it?

Thunder rumbles overhead, followed by the tapping sound

of rain falling against the roof. Streams of water run down the window panes.

I minimize my browser so I'm looking at the picture of Dallas and me again. "I did it," I tell him. "I killed you by being stupid, and I will never forgive myself. And no one else is going to forgive me either." Tears leak out of my eyes, almost hot enough to scald my skin. "I bet you don't forgive me either, do you?"

It was an accident, Genna. There's nothing to forgive.

"That's not true. I could've done so many things differently that night. I knew I was tired. I could've stopped. I should've stopped." My voice is racing now. "Everyone will blame me. They should blame me. I blame me. I am so, so sorry." I think of how quickly the world jumped on Brad Freeman, how they took what felt like it should be true and made it real, even though it wasn't real at all. I have to fix it, somehow. I have to tell the truth.

But then I think of the Fire Brad Freeman Facebook page. What would a bunch of angry strangers do to try to hurt *me*? If they knew I was volunteering at Zion, would they pressure the National Park Service to fire me? My eyes flick to the envelope from Wash U. What about college? If enough people complained to the university, would they give away my spot?

Or would the angry masses go after my parents—maybe tell people to boycott their offices until I'm properly punished? My mom gets so upset if she receives anything less than a five-star rating from a patient. And my dad's clients could decide to drive to Las Vegas or Salt Lake City for nonurgent procedures.

And what about my own future as a doctor? Would med schools be less likely to accept me after they Googled my name and found out my poor judgment killed someone? Once the truth gets out online, it'll be there permanently. It could haunt me forever. It could ruin my entire life.

The way it's ruining Brad Freeman's life?

I think back to the conversation I had with my mom: *He's the criminal, not you.*

But what if Freeman's telling the truth, that he *didn't* drink that much, that the blood test was wrong somehow? I know enough about medical stuff to know that's possible.

I need more information. I flip through all the recent articles, looking for new facts, but I don't find anything. I scan the comments looking for more by Brad Freeman, but there's nothing except for that single article, and the comments where he begs to keep his job.

Shutting my laptop again, I crawl into bed, even though it's only eight-thirty and I'm still sweaty from jogging home. I can't bring myself to shower or brush my teeth, to do anything where I might have to face my dad or Rachael in the hallway. I don't even want to look in the mirror right now. Above my head, the rain continues, rat-a-tat-tatting, a million tiny gunshots all aimed at me.

I have always believed in telling the truth. I got mad at my dad because he lied about his affair with Rachael. I stayed with Dallas because he told me the truth about cheating on me. I can't think of anything important in my whole life that I've ever lied about. And yet when I think about picking up that phone, about calling the police and confessing, I would almost rather die.

But when I think about *not* saying anything, about staying quiet and letting someone else take the blame for something I did, my whole body ignites with shame. #Hypocrite, #Coward. I add to my pile of hashtags. I have to figure out something, or I will never be able to face anyone ever again. There has to be some way I can help Brad Freeman without destroying my entire life.

CHAPTER 20

The next day, Rachael and I arrive at Zion Lodge a few minutes before seven a.m.

"Elliott is going to take care of you today. Just keep working on clearing the area for the trail," she tells me. "How are you doing after yesterday? Feeling sore?"

"You could say that." I woke up with a stiffness across my shoulders and entire back. Even my hands ache a little from gripping the Pulaski so tightly. "But it's okay. I kind of like it. Working hard clears my mind." Right now I want it to be as empty as possible. The hashtags are still tormenting me, burning themselves into my brain like digital scarlet letters. #TerriblePerson, I add to the pile. #Criminal. Maybe falling asleep driving isn't a crime, but staying quiet about my part in Dallas's death surely is. Every moment I don't tell the truth makes me more #Guilty.

"Well, according to Elliott, you excel at it, so I'm delighted to have you help out, but just don't overdo it, okay? Take breaks and stay hydrated. Your dad would never forgive me if anything happened to you."

"I'll be fine, I promise." #Liar, I balance on the top. I will never be fine again.

Elliott hops out of his truck when he sees me arrive, but Halley is nowhere to be found. Rachael drives off in a cloud of red dust.

I look around. "Where's Halley?"

"She doesn't work on Sundays."

"Ah," I say. "Church thing?"

"Yep."

"So I guess you're not a Mormon?"

Elliott snorts. "No. Most definitely not."

I sense there's a story there, but I'm not one to push people, especially not today. I take the Pulaski from Elliott's outstretched hand and get to work. The dirt is soft from last night's rainstorm and I make quick and steady progress. There's just something about repeatedly punching the crap out of the world with a badass tool. After about thirty strikes I almost feel like someone else—someone who is strong and capable. Someone who is not a #TerriblePerson.

Elliott's walkie-talkie crackles with static and I pause, mid-swing, to watch him answer it.

"What are they doing up there this early?" he asks to the person on the other end. I can't make out the response. "They must have started before sunrise. Fine, I'll check it out." He slips the walkie into the side pocket of his pants and turns to me. "Have you been up Angels Landing yet?"

I shake my head. "I haven't done much hiking here," I hedge. Or anywhere.

"It's the best trail in the park. You want to see it?"

"Uh . . . sure, I guess."

"Are you afraid of heights?"

"No." I don't think so, anyway. St. Louis is pretty flat. I haven't exactly tested this fear.

"And you've got water?"

I hold up a blue water bottle that Rachael gave me.

"All right. Come on."

I follow Elliott across the grassy area in front of Zion Lodge and over to the parking lot. I set my Pulaski in the back of his truck and hop into the passenger seat. Elliott turns out of the lodge parking lot and onto Zion Park Boulevard. Small hills of red dirt dotted with green vegetation rise up on the left side of the road. Behind them are the towering red rock cliffs that Zion is famous for. On my side, cottonwood trees provide the occasional slice of shade and the Virgin River twists and flows around pockets of high grass and sagebrush. It's still early, and there's no activity in sight.

"It feels like another planet to me," I say to Elliott. "Or a prehistoric world."

"It kind of does," he agrees. "Sometimes I think the people who grew up here take it for granted, like maybe you can only be around something so beautiful for so long before it starts to lose its appeal."

I don't respond, but I mull the idea over in my head. Do the laws of supply and demand doom us to underappreciate things that are plentiful?

Something moves in the foliage along the side of the road. I lean halfway out my window to get a better look. There is a flash of gray and white and then long spindly legs disappearing into a grove of trees.

"What did you see?" Elliott asks, without looking away from the road.

"A deer, I think."

A smile plays at his lips. "There are a lot of bighorn sheep in the park too, but mostly on the east side. Sometimes you'll see a whole herd of them right on the road."

"I don't even know what a bighorn sheep looks like."

"Kind of like a sheep with big horns." Elliott chuckles. "Nah, I'm kidding. They're not wooly like domestic sheep. Some people say they look more like goats."

"What other animals are here?"

"Well, there are over two hundred species of birds, and loads of lizards and small reptiles. As far as mammals there are the sheep and deer, foxes, coyotes, bats, porcupines, the occasional bobcat or mountain lion." He pauses. "Lots of rodents, too."

"Wow."

"Yeah. It's a pretty cool place." Elliott pulls the truck into a parking lot marked as Grotto Picnic Area. There's a set of restrooms and a shuttle stop marked Zion Canyon #6. We hop out and cross the road to a sign that reads The Grotto Trailhead.

Elliott drapes yellow caution tape across the sign and puts up a smaller sign that says: Angels Landing Trail temporarily closed. The NPS apologizes for the inconvenience. Please check with the Park Info Desk in the Zion Canyon Visitor Center or call 435-555-7275 for more information.

The two of us set off down a wide dirt trail that follows alongside the Virgin River. As we wind around several rock formations, the trail grows steeper. The canyon stretches out below us, cottonwoods, fir trees, and sagebrush painting the banks of the river in a rainbow of greens. I stop a few times to photograph the views with my phone and Elliott waits for me, but otherwise we hike in silence. I'm starting to feel the change in elevation, my calves aching, my breaths more labored.

"You really *don't* talk much," Elliott says. "I thought maybe you just couldn't get a word in edgewise around Halley."

I lower my gaze to the ground. Right now I'm pretty sure if I open my mouth the only thing that's going to spill out is a horrible story about how I killed someone and am currently letting someone else take the blame. "I guess I don't have that much to say," I murmur.

"I doubt that," he says. "But I like that you're quiet."

I shrug in response, and we continue down the trail for a few yards. Then he says, "Was that offensive? I think my dads would have yelled at me for that, as if I'm implying all women talk too much." He pauses. "Which I'm not. I guess I'm just easily distracted and sometimes I'm having these internal conversations with myself or trying to embrace nature and—"

"It's fine," I say. "I'm not offended. So, your *dads?*"

"Yeah. I have two dads. Is that unheard-of or something where you came from?"

"No, I guess I just figured it might be unheard-of here."

"Well. The LDS church is not exactly down with it, but there's a decent gay scene in St. George where I go to school."

I nod. Part of me wants to ask Elliott questions about his life. Does he like college? Where is he from? What was it like to grow up with two dads? But if I do that, he'll ask me about my school and my parents and where I'm from, and I don't want to lie to him. Plus, he just said he likes quiet. I turn my eyes away from his rugged frame and try to focus on the beauty of my surroundings.

Towers of rock rise up on either side of us, a metropolis of natural skyscrapers. Trees sprout from the tops of the cliffs, their leaves a vibrant green against a swath of white clouds. The sun is muted today, but the temperature is steadily rising and I'm grateful each time we turn a sharp corner on the trail and find ourselves in a pocket of shade.

The trail flattens out for a bit and lush foliage crowds the path. Beyond it, water seeps from the rocks in various spots, creating miniature waterfalls.

Elliott waits as I snap a picture of one. "From last night's storm," he explains. "The rain soaks into the tops of the cliffs, but the rock can only hold so much moisture."

We continue onward and the path beneath our feet becomes fragmented in places, reddish sand peeking up through cracks in the concrete. The trail gets steep again. I blot the sweat from my forehead and then pause for a minute to drink from my water bottle.

"Good plan." Elliott grabs his own water bottle from his backpack and takes a long drink. "Shit's about to get real."

I start to ask him what he means, but then I don't have to. In front of us, a series of steep switchbacks looms, like we're going to zigzag right up the side of the cliff.

"Holy crap," I say.

"Take it slow and steady," Elliott advises. "The change in elevation from this point forward is going to be intense. We're in no hurry."

"Won't Rachael be mad that we didn't make more progress on the touch trail?"

"She's expecting the touch trail to take all summer. The hope is that it'll be ready for Labor Day. This is a more pressing matter."

"What's so pressing?"

"The final ascent of Angels Landing is a half-mile climb over extremely rugged terrain with sheer drop-offs on both sides. Apparently a tree fell across the path last night, making part of the trail impassable."

"Got it."

I take another gulp of water before we start on the switchbacks, which Elliott tells me are called Walter's Wiggles, after the first superintendent of the park, who helped engineer them.

They don't look like they'll be that bad. I mean, they're steep, but they're also wide and well paved. But after completing the first ten or twelve, I need another break. Bending over, I rest my palms on my thighs. My breath whistles in my throat.

"You okay?" Elliott stops at the next switchback to check my progress. His voice is completely level, his breathing not even slightly labored.

I'm relieved to see he's at least broken a sweat. "I'm good," I say.

"You can stop if you want. You're a volunteer, remember? You don't have to kill yourself for me."

I reach up to wipe the sweat from my brow again. The headband I wear to cover my craniotomy scar is completely damp. "It actually feels good to be out here like this," I say. "I used to run a lot but I haven't exercised much in the past few weeks." Too late, I realize my mistake.

"Why not?"

"Focusing on schoolwork, I guess." I start walking again before he can ask me more questions.

Elliott lets me take the lead until we come upon a pair of hikers also on their way up the trail—a girl and a guy dressed in casual clothing and Birkenstock sandals.

"Excuse me," Elliott says. "I'm with the National Park Service. I hate to do this, but the trail is closed for the morning, possibly the whole day. I'm going to have to ask you to go back down."

"What?" the girl barks. She looks a couple of years older than me, with streaks of pink in her black hair and a sleeve full of tattoos. She adjusts the bandana she's using to tie back her hair as she looks incredulously at Elliott. "I just went up all of that." She points at the steep switchbacks below. "And now you're telling me to turn around?"

I retreat a few feet and pull a granola bar out of the back pocket of my jeans. I wolf down the bar in about three bites while Elliott talks to the hikers.

"I'm sorry," he says. "You can go up to Scout Lookout if you want. There are some nice views from that area. But there's a fallen tree blocking part of the path leading to the summit. I need to go clear it and make sure everything is safe before I can reopen the trail." Elliott pauses. "I'm sure you're aware people have died on this hike."

"Yeah, but like old out-of-shape people, right?" the guy says. He hooks his thumbs through the loops on the waistband of his long shorts. "My girlfriend and I are expert hikers. We won't fall. Right, Lola?"

Lola lifts her chin. "We sure as hell won't. We've done way harder hikes than this."

Elliott glances down at the guy's sandals and back up at him. "I'm sorry. I'm telling you to stop, and if you continue against my order then I have to report you."

"And then what?" Lola scoffs. "You gonna put us in Zion Jail?"

"Then I'll call a ranger and you'll both be fined for disobeying a direct order from a park official."

I'm impressed by his composure. These people aren't much

older than him but they're treating him like he's a dumb kid and he's not letting it get to him.

"Fine." Lola tugs on her bandana again. "When do you think the trail will be open again?"

"Possibly this afternoon," Elliott says. "Check with the Park Information desk in the Visitor Center or the hiking conditions link on our web page for the most up-to-date information."

"Whatever," the guy says. "This is totally bogus, man. If you guys get to go, we should get to go too."

"One of the benefits of working for the NPS." Elliott smiles tightly. "We get to risk our lives so that park visitors don't have to."

This seems to satisfy—or at least quiet—Lola and her boyfriend, who both utter huge shoulder-slumping sighs before turning back the way they came.

I shove the granola bar wrapper into my back pocket as Elliott gestures at me to come on.

"Nice job," I tell him. "Are you going to be a park ranger someday?"

"Probably not," he says. "I think I want to be a veterinarian, but one of my dads is always telling me I need to line up a fallback career, because vet school is even harder to get into than med school, especially when you're applying as a nonresident."

I'm planning to go to med school someday. My parents are both doctors. More words swallowed back in the name of staying anonymous, of hiding who I am and what I've done. "If you want it enough, you can make it happen."

Elliott smiles. "That's what my other dad says, that just because something is really hard doesn't mean I shouldn't do it."

We reach the top of the switchbacks and I gasp at the view. We're standing atop one of the red rock peaks and are surrounded by other peaks off in the distance. The ground is level here, made of sand and flat pieces of rock, the trail dotted with sagebrush and desert shrubs.

My gasp attracts the attention of a second pair of hikers standing just off the path. They're posing for a selfie together, the vast canyon, river, and red rock cliffs as their background. The boy abruptly puts his phone back in his pocket as Elliott approaches him.

Their faces fall as Elliott gives them the bad news, but unlike the other hikers they don't protest.

"We'll be back," the girl declares.

"Enjoy the rest of the park," Elliott tells them. He turns to me. "Now. You."

"Hmm?" I'm watching the hikers start down the series of switchbacks.

Elliott takes me gently by the shoulders and turns my body so that I'm facing one of the many peaks. He points out in the distance, at an impossibly narrow ridge of rock that seems to connect where we're standing to another, even taller, summit. It slopes up and then down and then back up again.

"That's where I have to go," he says. "A lot of people stop here, at Scout Lookout. The views are great. You could snap some pictures, hang out, and wait for me. Or you can head back down on your own if you get bored."

"You're going out there?" My voice is sharp. The path Elliott is pointing at looks like a steeply inclined balance beam, with deadly consequences if you stumble.

"It's not as bad as it looks," he says. "But it's not easy, so maybe it'd be better if you waited here."

Something sparks inside me. Do I need things to be *easy*? I know Elliott's words aren't meant to be hurtful, but lately I can find a way to make everything cut. I stare out at the path. What's the worst thing that could happen? I die? Maybe that's what *should* happen. I bet Dallas would've told the truth if he had fallen asleep and I had died. Maybe I deserve to fall for being such a coward.

"I'm game," I blurt out. "Let's do this."

"All right," Elliott says. "But first let me see your water bottle."

I hand him my bottle and he attaches a small metal clip to it. He turns to attach the bottle to a loop in my jeans, but I step back without even thinking.

"Sorry," he says. "I was just, uh, you should clip this to your-self in a place where it doesn't restrict your mobility. You'll want to have both hands free for the rest of the trail."

I nod, clipping the bottle to one of my side belt loops. I blush and look down for a second as I think about what would have happened if I had let Elliott clip it for me, the idea of his hand on my waist or my hip.

He clears his throat. "You ready?"

"Ready."

The next half hour is an exhilarating—at times, excruciating —scramble up and down sandstone boulders and natural steps cut into the rock. In places the path feels reasonably safe despite the drop-offs, with several feet of clearance and sturdy footholds carved into the stones beneath my feet. In other places, I am crouched low and crawling my way up rock formations with nothing but a thick silver safety chain to keep me from falling to my death if I slip.

We reach a spot that's flat, with a lone fir tree providing a bit of shade and I drop to a seated position. I adjust my headband and pull the ponytail holder out of my hair, letting it fall around my shoulders in sweaty clumps.

"You can keep going if you want," I tell Elliott. "I just need a couple minutes."

"No worries." He sits next to me and pulls his water bottle out of the side pocket of his pants. He takes a long drink. "You're doing great by the way."

I twist my tangled hair up into a bun and secure my ponytail holder around it. Elliott reaches over and pours a few drops of water on the back of my neck.

"Hey," I say in protest. But the cool water feels wonderful.

"Hey what?" He splashes his own neck with water. "I hope you remembered sunscreen there. You're looking a little pink."

"I did, but I probably sweated it all off," I say.

Elliott reaches out and touches the scar on my cheekbone.

I'm sure I sweated off all my makeup too. "What happened here?" he asks.

I flinch. His touch is softer than I imagine. "Mountain lion attack," I tell him with a straight face.

"Oh yeah?" He smiles. "Good thing it didn't get your neck."

"Yeah. That's what I get for not heeding your warning about jogging alone."

He stares at me for a second. "You're not going to tell me, huh?"

I imagine telling Elliott how I forced Dallas to leave his own party and then fell asleep driving him home. Maybe he'd be so disgusted that he'd leave me out here. Or if not, I could always give him the additional info that I'm letting someone else take the blame for the accident. Surely that would be enough to drive him away.

I bite my lip. "It's not a very good story," I say finally.

"Fair enough." Elliott slides his water bottle into his backpack. Rising to his feet, he turns to offer me a hand but I'm already up and ready to go.

We continue until we reach a place where a small tree is lying across the path, covering a couple of footholds in the rocks and making the safety chain hard to manipulate. The tree is blackened at the base, like maybe it got hit by lightning.

We're in kind of a precarious spot, so I start to back up to give Elliott room to work, but he shakes his head. "The summit is right ahead, maybe ten minutes more. Go ahead and pass me if you want. That way you can enjoy some time up there while I deal with this. I'll join you when I'm finished."

"Are you sure?" Passing Elliott on this narrow section of trail would be tricky, even before adding in the extra obstacle. "Aren't you just going to toss the tree off the edge?" The trunk is only about as wide as my arm. I'm quite sure Elliott could pick it up and throw it like a javelin if he wanted.

"No, because it could end up on a ledge somewhere and fall at some later point and kill someone." I wince, but he doesn't seem to notice. "I've got a handsaw in my backpack. I'm going to cut it down so there's no danger of it blocking the path again."

"Okay. So how do I get past you?"

Elliott grabs the fallen tree and pulls it to the far side of the path. He anchors one foot behind a rock poking out of the sandy soil and leans his weight against a massive boulder. "Give me your hands."

I reach out and he wraps his fingers around mine. His hands are warm, almost hot, his grip secure without being too tight. Our eyes meet for a second and then we both look away simultaneously. I blush.

"Lean toward me." Elliott clears his throat. "Now step forward with your right foot, then your left."

I follow his careful instructions, my body wobbling slightly on the narrow path.

"I got you," he murmurs. "You're doing fine. Right foot again. One more step. Then let go of me and grab the chain."

Slowly, I navigate my body past his. There's a moment where my face ends up pressed against his chest and I can't help but think about how muscular he is for someone our age. I can smell the sharp wintergreen scent of his deodorant and something softer mixed in—detergent maybe.

"Sorry if I'm all sweaty," he says after I'm safely past him. "I know I about smashed your face in my armpit there for a second."

"It's okay," I say. "I mean, you actually smell kind of nice." I blush even hotter. Good thing it's turning into another sweltering day.

"Good to know." Elliott laughs and some of the heaviness inside me is lifted. I cling to the sound for a second, as if it's a magic phrase that's unlocked a secret, happier part of me. I can't remember the last time I laughed. I'm not sure I ever will again—I think that part of me might be broken. Still, it helps to hear someone else doing it.

He digs in his backpack and comes back with a set of safety glasses and a saw. "Enjoy the view, Jennifer. I'll see you soon."

The heaviness crushes down on me again as I turn away. The moment is ruined when Elliott calls me by the wrong name. Ruined because I once again remember that I'm a liar.

CHAPTER 21

You'd think that knowing the end of the trail is close would make finishing it easier, but each move is even scarier without Elliott in front of me. I hadn't realized just how carefully I was copying his every step, putting my feet where his feet went, reaching out for the same holds that he gripped with confidence.

When I finally reach the summit, the view is even more breathtaking than at Scout Lookout. Instead of being surrounded by the other peaks, I'm above most of them, looking down. One of them—I think it's called the Great White Throne—glistens almost silver in the bright sun. I see the twists and turns of the Virgin River, the dark asphalt of Zion Park Boulevard. The view stretches off for miles in the distance, bands of sandstone and red rock speckled with green, the perfect blue sky bleeding into forever.

For the first time in a long time, I feel free. My eyes water. A single tear runs down my cheek. Standing here, looking out at all this, I wish I wasn't an atheist. I want to believe there's something more.

I want to believe there's someone listening.

Someone with the knowledge to guide me.

Someone with the power to forgive.

I walk along one side of the cliff, certain death just inches away. My heart pounds hard in my chest, as if it's trying to escape the prison of my rib cage. I look up at the sky. "Are you real?" I ask. "Because if you are, if there's *really* someone listening, then I could use some help." My words come out fractured and breathy. As expected, no one answers.

The vast open expanse of Zion Canyon looks back at me, waiting to see what I'll do next. A bird soars through the sky, and then stops, hovering on a current of air. It's like everything is frozen, like the world is holding its breath.

The wind blows and I reach out with one hand to stay balanced. Slowly I lower myself to a seated position. "If you are real," I continue my conversation with an invisible deity who may or may not exist, "you should know I'm pretty pissed at you. I mean, why would you take Dallas? He was going to touch so many people with his music." I pause. "And why let *me* live? Especially since I'm the one who killed him."

Another tear falls. My breath sticks in my throat. I lift a hand to my chest. "It hurts," I say. "It hurts to accept that I killed him. And it hurts even more that I haven't told anyone the truth." I pause. "Until now."

The tightness in my chest loosens ever so slightly. "I killed him," I say again. "It was my fault. Some people might say it was your will, or that it was destiny or something, that I couldn't have prevented what happened. But I don't think that way, you know? I wasn't raised to rationalize my mistakes by denying the existence of free will. I made choices that night. Choices that had deadly consequences. And now I have to take responsibility for it." My voice cracks. "And I will—I promise you. I will take responsibility."

I feel a buoyancy, a lightness in my heart.

And then I see a shadow move behind me.

"Take responsibility for what?" Elliott asks.

CHAPTER 22

I spin around and the shock must be written all over my face, because Elliott quickly steps back. "I was just kidding. It's none of my business."

I wipe hurriedly at my eyes. "God. You must think all I do is cry."

"I'm sure you have your reasons."

"Yeah. Maybe. Sorry. I was just . . . having a moment with the universe."

"Don't apologize. I bet half the people who make it up here are reduced to tears by this amazing view." He comes to sit next to me. "And the other half are reduced on the inside, they're just not in touch enough with their emotions to let the tears out."

"Which half are you?"

"I might have sniffled a little," he says with a grin.

"So what's the story with the tree?" I ask.

"It's good to go." Elliott pulls his water bottle from his side pocket. "Oh, and I radioed Rachael and let her know I cleared the path and she said she was looking for you. I told her you were up here with me and she screamed at me for a few minutes for bringing you, so be prepared to hear about that later."

"Well, no hurry to get back down then." I sit next to Elliott. "I feel . . . lighter up here. Thank you for bringing me."

"Technically, you are lighter, a little bit. Weight actually decreases directly with—"

"Gravitational pull," I finish. "Right."

"You took physics in high school?"

"Yeah. It was one of my favorite classes. You too?"

"I'm not sure I would go that far, but I have to take a lot of science classes as a pre-vet student." Elliott pulls an apple out of his backpack and polishes it on his shirt. He bites into it with a loud crunching sound.

"Wow," I say. "Noise pollution alert."

"Crisp," he agrees. He holds the apple out in my direction. "Want a bite?"

I start to decline, but then my stomach growls audibly. "I guess I do." I bite into the other side of the apple and hand it back to Elliott. We pass it back and forth for a few minutes. "I've never shared an apple with anyone before," I say.

"Me neither. It's rather biblical, huh?" He gestures around. "It's not like we'll get much closer to the Garden of Eden."

"I think this is the closest I've ever gotten to believing in God."

"You don't believe in God?" he asks. "I figured that's who you were talking to."

"I was, I guess, but it was just a weird, random impulse," I say. "Both my parents are atheists. I was raised to believe that religion is a psychological coping mechanism."

Elliott nods. "I don't belong to an organized religion, because so many of them seem to have rules and regulations that serve to ostracize or separate, and I think religion should be about bringing people together. But I believe in something." He points at the majestic view. "I mean, how can all this just be random?"

"Yeah." I try to regain the feeling I had before Elliott arrived, the sense that maybe a higher power was guiding me. But it's gone now, and I'm starting to wonder if I imagined the whole thing. I don't think you can just choose to believe in God. You either do or you don't, and no matter what camp you're in, it would take something life-changing to truly lead you into the other one. I think of my dad's glance heavenward, the mini-prayer he said in my hospital room. I like the idea that my accident might have helped him find faith.

Elliott finishes off the apple while I walk along the edge of the clearing, taking photos with my phone. I discover a trio of curious chipmunks at the far end of the summit.

"How did these little guys get up here?" I ask.

"They live up here." Elliott watches the chipmunks scamper around for a few seconds.

"I wish I had another granola bar," I say. "They look hungry."

"You can actually get fined for feeding the park wildlife," he says. "I know they're cute, but the more they get fed, the less afraid they become of humans. And then some idiot decides to try to pet them and gets bitten and . . ." He turns to me. "Not that *you're* an idiot. Just that I've seen a lot of wildlife incidents that could've been prevented if people followed the rules."

I like the way Elliott just sort of says what he's thinking and then clarifies and softens afterward if it comes out wrong. I'm the exact opposite these days. I feel the need to mentally rehearse every line three times before I say it to make sure I'm not giving away too much information, and then half the time I decide not to say anything after all.

"I never thought about it like that." I snap a picture of the chipmunks, thinking of the countless times I've fed wild animals. "I'm glad I got to see them up close, anyway. This day has been just what I needed. Thank you."

"You're welcome." Elliott reddens slightly at the praise. "We should head down soon so Rachael can stop worrying about you."

"Can I have another minute?" I ask.

"Sure. I should probably take another minute too. This is one of the most popular trails in the park. It's not very often I get to be up here without a crowd." Elliott turns away from me and walks to the other side of the summit.

I stand looking out at the scenery again. I close my eyes and once again try to find that sense of something more. But all I feel is the hot sun and the sweat starting to bead up on my lip.

Still, I remember that moment of lightness when I admitted the truth, that temporary buoyancy when I resolved to do the right thing.

I *want* to do the right thing. I want to tell the truth.

CHAPTER 23

I feel like it should be easy to tell the truth, now that I've made the decision. But later that night in the safety of my room, I can't find the words again. I keep imagining how it would feel to have the whole world hate me.

"Okay then," I say to myself. "I need help." I grab my laptop and set it up on my desk. I sit down and very purposefully type "how to tell the truth" into the browser search box.

There are about twenty million possible web pages for me to look through. The ones at the top of the list belong to a popular national blog, a wikiHow, and a relationship expert. I skim through all three of them, but it's mostly common sense. There are no magic solutions to make what I have to do any easier. It occurs to me that I'm living with an expert in telling the truth when it's ugly and difficult and you've been hiding it for a while. Dad and Rachael were having an affair for over six months before he came clean to my mom.

It's surreal, the thought that maybe my dad typed these very same words into his iPad one day, looking for some advice from strangers about how to do the right thing.

But Dad only had to worry about Mom turning on him; okay, and me, and maybe some of Mom's colleagues at the hospital. But then he moved away from all the people who judged him and basically started over. How am I supposed to escape an entire internet full of judgment and threats? Are there even places left on the earth with no web access at all?

Sighing, I push my laptop back and rest my head on my desk.

My phone buzzes with a call and I'm grateful for the distraction. I'm surprised to see an unfamiliar local number pop up on the display.

"Hello?" I say warily.

"Hey, it's Elliott." He continues before I can even respond. "So I know it's a bit creepy to call you like this, but you're new in town and don't know that many people so, uh, I was wondering if you wanted to hang out?"

Definitely a weird development, but I could use something to take my mind off figuring out how to tell the truth. I don't think I'm going to solve that problem tonight. Still. It feels . . . unnatural to go somewhere with a boy who isn't Dallas.

"What do you mean by hang out?"

"That is when two friends spend time in the same location." He pauses. "Unless you don't want to be my friend."

It's strange to hear someone call me their friend. I did not expect that to be part of my Springdale, Utah, experience. "Where would we go? It's after ten p.m. I thought everywhere

here closed by six, especially on a Sunday."

"Not everywhere." He laughs lightly. "It's a surprise."

"How'd you get this number?" I'm stalling because I'm still deciding if I want to go.

"Rachael added it to the volunteer database at work." He pauses. "I bet you're bored right now, aren't you? I can fix that. There's something I want to show you. Just say yes and I'll be at your house in two minutes."

"How do you know where I live?" I ask, my voice rising in pitch.

"Rachael had a Labor Day barbecue for all the staff last year. I not only know where you live, I've peed in your bathroom."

"Lovely," I mumble. "I'll be sure to think of you when I'm brushing my teeth later."

Elliott laughs again. "So are you in, or what?"

"Maybe. Hang on." Slipping my phone into the pocket of my jeans, I stroll down the hallway to the living room. Dad and Rachael are both on the sofa, watching the end of a movie. Leaving the house at this hour is going to involve a lot of explaining. I'm not in an explaining kind of mood.

But I'm definitely in an escaping kind of mood.

"You okay, hon?" Dad asks.

"Yeah. Hey, can I go hang out with a friend for a while?"

Dad glances at the clock. "It's kind of late, isn't it? What friend?"

"His name is Elliott. He works for Rachael." I look back and forth between her and my dad.

"Elliott, huh?" A smile plays at Rachael's lips.

"Ah," Dad says. "I think I met him at some point."

"You met him at last year's Labor Day barbecue," Rachael says. "Elliott Helberg. The kid who wants to be a veterinarian. He and Gen have been working on a trail project for me."

My eyes flick to the front window. A white truck pulls up across the street from the house. "So can I go or what?"

"What did you say you guys were going to do at this hour?"

I start to blush for some reason. Leave it to my body to betray me at the worst possible moments. "I—I think just go for a drive. He said he had something he wanted to show me."

"Oh, is that what he said?" My dad makes a noise between a cough and a snort.

My face gets even hotter. "Jeez, Dad. Not like that. I've only known him for a week. We're barely even friends."

Rachael rolls her eyes at my dad. "He's a good guy. Let her go."

"All right. But be careful," Dad says. "I know you're vulnerable right now and I don't want to see you get hurt."

I lean over to give my dad a kiss on the cheek. "It's not a date or anything. No one is getting hurt, I promise."

My dad nods, but he doesn't look convinced. "And next time he picks you up at a reasonable hour and comes to the door like a gentleman. And you need to be home by twelve-thirty."

"Aye aye, sir. I will relay the messages." I give my dad a mock salute and then hurry out the door before he can change his mind. I cross the lawn and the street to where Elliott is waiting for me in his truck. He leans over and opens the passenger door for me.

"Hey," he says. "I wasn't sure you were going to make it. Seemed to be quite a discussion going on."

I pull my phone out of my pocket as I slide into the truck. "Ugh. You heard all that? I saw your truck and totally forgot you were waiting on the phone."

"No worries. It was just a lot of muffled talking."

"Mostly Rachael telling my dad that you're a good guy."

Elliott snickers. "It's true . . . for the most part."

As we turn onto the main road, the streetlamps illuminate the cab of the truck and I get my first real look at Elliott out of his uniform. It's probably a longer look than it should be. His black hair is kind of disheveled, but purposefully so, like he put wax or pomade in it. His T-shirt hangs on his body in a way that emphasizes his pecs and abdominal muscles without making him look like one of those bulked-out bodybuilders who live at the gym. Tanned arms emerge from his shirtsleeves, the outline of his biceps and triceps visible through his skin.

"You're staring at me," he points out, before my eyes get a chance to drop below his waist.

"Sorry. You just look different out of uniform." Even though this is absolutely not a date, I can't help but compare Elliott to Dallas. Physically, they're complete opposites. Dallas was tall and pale and blond. Even with his styled hair, Elliott is definitely a lot more casual—Dallas wasn't one to wear tennis shoes or track pants outside the gym.

Elliott gives me a sideways glance as he continues down the main street of Springdale. "Different how?" His lips twitch like he's fighting back a smile.

"You know . . . sportier? More laid-back?"

"Sportier . . . Thanks, I guess."

"Except your hair. Did you put some sort of product in it?"

"Maybe. Is that okay?"

"Yeah. It looks nice." Even as I say the last word, I regret it. Dallas and I might have broken up by now if he had lived, but it still feels wrong to be telling some other guy he looks nice.

Elliott loses the smile battle as his lips curl up into a grin. "I'm glad you like it."

I slouch down in my seat as we pass by the businesses of Springdale—all closed at this hour—in rapid succession. I try to push thoughts of Dallas out of my mind, not because I don't want to think about him, but because I don't want to start crying again on Elliott.

I give him a quizzical look when he slows down at the outskirts of town. He pulls the truck into the parking lot for something called Zion Outdoor Experts.

"Are we breaking into a sporting goods store?" I ask.

"My dads own it," Elliott explains.

"You're taking me shopping?"

Elliott parks the truck and then hops out into the parking lot. "No, but I can get you a thirty-percent-off discount during normal business hours if you're interested."

"So then what are we doing here?"

"Nothing." Elliott strides across the gravel lot, passing up the entrance to Zion Outdoor Experts and stopping in front of the next shop, which has no sign. Boards have been pounded across the window so no one can see inside.

"Look. I'm not really into . . ." I trail off, unsure exactly where Elliott has brought me. Maybe this is where he and his friends bring girls or get drunk or something. I glance around the darkened parking lot, suddenly realizing I don't know very much about this guy.

Elliott is flipping through a bunch of keys on his key chain, but he pauses and looks up, a bemused smile on his face. "What, Jen? What aren't you into?" His dark eyes study me curiously.

I realize he has a key to unlock the front door. "Oh, your family owns this too?"

"Yep." He smirks. "And don't worry. We keep our crack house and our brothel on the other side of town."

"Sorry," I say. "It isn't that I don't trust you. It's just—"

"That you don't trust anyone?"

"Something like that."

"Well, prepare to be surprised." Elliott unlocks the door and pushes it open.

CHAPTER 24

We step inside the shop and he flips on the lights as the door falls closed behind us. I don't know what I was expecting, but it wasn't this. My eyes trail across the ropes and nets and obstacles that take up every inch of space in the building. "What is all this?"

"It's our Ninja Warrior gym," Elliott says proudly. "My dad Garrett competes every year, so we built it for training purposes, but now my parents are thinking of running training camps for all ages during the warmer months."

"Your dad is on TV?" I ask. "On the real show?" I've seen clips of *American Ninja Warrior*, but only enough to know that the obstacles are really hard.

"Yep. Cool, huh?" Elliott says. "The contestants don't get paid, unless they win it all, which is why a lot of them are trying to coach aspiring competitors or open their own gyms. Dad fell in the qualifiers this year, but last year he made it to the third round in Vegas—his best showing yet."

"Wow. He must be really strong."

"He is," Elliott says. "But this stuff is about a lot more than strength—you need flexibility, balance, and mental toughness. Garrett credits his success to rock climbing, triathlons, and yoga."

I arch an eyebrow. "Yoga? Seriously?"

"Seriously," Elliott says. "Now, where do you want to start?"

I look warily at the different stations. There's a log bridge, a series of cargo nets hung at different angles, a trampoline, some kind of extreme monkey bars, and a warped wall made of plywood, with rock-climbing holds bolted into one side of it. And that's just the first quarter of the gym. I shake my head. "I don't think I can do any of this."

"No one can do this stuff without practicing," Elliott says. "Rachael said you liked hard physical labor. It doesn't get much harder than this."

"True," I say slowly.

He tugs me toward the log bridge. "Let's see how your balance is on the Spinning Log. All you have to do is get to the other side without falling off."

"Okay." I step up onto a platform and look at the platform on the other side. It doesn't look that far away. Maybe ten feet or so. I reach out to test the log with one foot. It wiggles—a lot. "I'm going to fall on my face."

"That's why we have these big squishy mats on both sides," Elliott says.

I step one foot forward again and then pause. "I don't know.

I've had such a good day. I'm not sure I want to wreck it by failing miserably at something."

Elliott nods. "You don't have to if you don't want to."

And then I feel bad. He brought me here trying to make me feel better. Who cares if I can't walk on a stupid log? Grown men have fallen off this thing on national television.

"Screw it, I'm going." I take off across the log at a fast clip, trying to keep my feet in the middle, one in front of the other. I make it about three-quarters of the way before I slip off and land on the mat. "Oof," I say.

Elliott reaches down and helps me to my feet. "Pretty impressive for your first try. You want to go again?"

"Let me watch you."

Elliott grins and I can tell I'm about to get massively schooled. He leaps up onto the starting platform without even using the built-in steps. He races across the log in about three strides, flinging his body toward the mat at the end once he's past the midway point. "That's one way to do it," he says. "It's not pretty but it gets the job done." He rises from the mat and turns back toward the starting platform. "Or you can take the slow and steady approach, which is a lot harder." He inhales deeply, and extends his arms out to his sides. Then he turns to the left and crouches down like a surfer. Slowly but surely, he sidesteps his way across the log. It barely even moves.

I clap my hands together as he jumps down. "That was amazing. I bet you can do this blindfolded, can't you?"

"Nah," he says. "But thanks. Want to try again?"

"Definitely," I say. This time I try the three-steps-and-leap-to-the-mat strategy. It takes me four more attempts to make it across, but I am so amazed to hit the mat at the end without falling that when I hop down to the floor I give Elliott a somewhat sweaty hug. "Thank you," I murmur into his -T-shirt. "Normally I don't even try stuff unless I'm pretty sure I'll be good at it." Yet another bad habit I picked up from my mom: If you're going to do something, do it better than everyone else. Or don't do it at all.

"You're welcome." He squeezes me gently. "And we're going to have to get you past that frame of mind, or else you're going to miss out on a lot of fun stuff."

I look around the gym. "What's next?"

He grins. "You tell me."

I point at a set of angled platforms pushed against one wall of the gym. "What are those?"

"Quintuple Steps. Probably not the easiest thing to do in jeans, but you can try." Elliott arranges the platforms and shows me how to jump from one to the next. For being a stocky guy, the hang time he gets between leaps is amazing. "Now you," he says.

It takes me a few minutes to work up the nerve to make the first leap, but once I do, I manage to complete all four jumps with varying degrees of gracefulness. My palms get scraped up and I'm probably going to have a bruise on one knee, but I'm still surprised at how well I did. "That didn't seem hard enough."

"Well, I might have put them a little closer than regulation for you," Elliott says. "But yeah, these used to be the first obstacle on the show. Now they're using something a little harder."

"Give me something really hard," I say.

"That's the spirit." Elliott leads me over to the Warped Wall. "If you've seen this before, you know it's extremely challenging, especially for shorter competitors. Being successful requires both strength and timing. You want to build up as much speed as you can in your approach and take about three steps on the wall before you go for the top. The trick is converting your horizontal momentum to vertical momentum in the right spot."

I've seen people make this look easy on TV, but in real life it looks impossible. I exhale deeply and then run full speed at the wall, making it about halfway up before I tumble back down the curved surface to the bottom.

"Not bad, not bad," Elliott says. "But don't lean into the wall, because then you run out of room. Try to lean back a little."

I try a second time, this time making it farther up the wall, but still nowhere near the top.

Elliott arches an eyebrow at me as I hop to my feet again. "In competition, you get three tries."

"I'm not sure a million tries would be enough," I say, but I tilt my head from side to side to crack my neck and then face the wall once more. After the third time of leaping toward the top only to end up tumbling back to the bottom, I lie on the mat and wave one hand in front of my face. "I'm hot."

"Yeah, maybe," Elliott says with a grin as he helps me to my feet.

No guy besides Dallas has ever called me hot and I'm completely unprepared for how to respond. I open my mouth to mumble a classic "Funny," when I see the serious expression on Elliott's face. He's staring at me. I lift one hand and realize my headband slipped off during that last fall.

"That mountain lion got you good, huh?" he says quietly.

Bending down, I snatch my headband from the mat and put it back on, adjusting it to cover my bald spot and scar. I concentrate on the floor of the gym. "I should probably go soon. It's getting late."

"It's about eleven-thirty," Elliott says. "I'll take you home if you want. But do you want to see the best part of this place before you go?"

I shrug. "Okay."

Elliott ushers me past several more obstacles to a door at the back of the gym that opens out into the alley. There's a ladder connected to the building, with rungs leading up toward the roof. "Your next challenge is this very technical ladder."

"Is it going to start spinning or twisting or something?"

"No, but there's a nice view at the top. Take your time. My dads will kill me if you fall."

I follow Elliott up the ladder and onto the roof. This building is taller than the fluorescent lights that illuminate the parking lot, and if I cup my hands around my eyes, I can blot out almost all the lights from Springdale. There are more stars than I ever knew existed.

I can't believe I've been living here for almost two weeks and

I've never even gone outside to appreciate this. The only time I've even been outside when it was dark is when I went running at six a.m. It must've been cloudy that morning.

I gesture at a rolled-up sleeping bag that's tucked against an air-conditioner unit. "Do you sleep up here sometimes?"

"Nah. It's kind of hard for that, though I suppose I could bring a sleeping mat up here." He looks thoughtful. "I usually just hang out and watch the stars. I guess I could go get a second bag. I've never brought anyone else here before."

"We can share." I grab the bag and unzip it into a big square. Together Elliott and I lay it out on the concrete roof. Reclining back on the quilted fabric, I marvel at the night sky. It's a mix of black, blue, and purple, with millions of pinpoints of light scattered across it. I've seen pictures like this on websites and in museums, but I always thought they were taken with special cameras or heavily edited. It never occurred to me that the real sky could be this beautiful. "This is incredible," I say.

Elliott lies next to me, close but not touching. "Springdale has special lighting ordinances to help stargazers," he says. "Businesses turn off all the lights they don't need and outdoor fixtures are angled toward the ground to minimize scattered light. There are places in the park where you can sometimes even see the Milky Way."

"That's awesome." I stretch my arms over my head. "So why'd you bring *me*?"

"Hmm?" Elliott asks. I can hear the fatigue in his voice.

"You said you've never brought anyone here?"

"Oh, well, I've brought friends to the gym, just not up here. This is kind of my spot to get away from everything, but it seemed like maybe you needed a spot too. You can feel free to sneak up here even if I'm not around. Just be extra-careful on the ladder. Ezra keeps saying we need to get a lock for it so no one falls and sues us."

"Ezra is the practical dad, huh?"

"They're both practical. Ezra is just more of a worrier."

"I bet he's the one who told you that you need a fallback career."

"Yep."

"You don't need a fallback career," I say. "You're going to be an amazing vet."

"Says the girl who's never seen me with an animal."

"Sometimes you can just tell," I say, thinking about the way he's treated me. Kindness. Compassion. Add that to brains and hard work and I have no doubt that he'll succeed.

"Thank you."

"You're welcome." I pause. "Don't you sort of have a fallback career anyway? Working at the store?"

"Pretty sure my parents want me to have a career I'm passionate about. The store is okay and I'd never turn down a job there if I was desperate, but I like animals, and the outdoors."

"And people?"

"I could take 'em or leave 'em." Elliott laughs lightly so I know he's kidding. He nudges me gently in the ribs with his elbow. "I like some more than others."

My face goes hot as I try to decide if he's flirting with me or just being nice. "Thanks for tonight," I say. "And thanks for not asking."

"About your mountain lion?"

"Yeah."

"We've all got our mountain lions." He props himself up on one elbow and looks over at me. "Just promise me you'll talk to someone if shit gets too hard. It doesn't have to be me."

"I will," I say. "I think it might be getting a little better." Deleting my social media accounts has made it possible for me to distance myself from all the online hate. And now that I've vowed to tell the whole truth, I just need to figure out who to tell first and how to work up the nerve to do it.

"Glad to hear it," Elliott says. "But the offer for a good listener stands."

"Thank you. Even if I never take you up on it, knowing it's on the table helps."

We both fall silent as our eyes are drawn back to the sky. I almost ask Elliott if he knows anything about stars, but right now I don't care what the constellations are called or which of these points of light are actually planets. All I care about is the way I feel. Calm. Safe. I embrace the sensations and let the beauty of the night wrap around me. The stars twinkle and blur before my eyes. *How can all this just be random?* Lying here, I understand why Elliott believes in something greater than what we know. I also understand what Elliott meant when he said he was quiet sometimes because he was embracing nature.

There's no need to wreck this moment with words.

The wind blows across us, but it's a warm night for the desert, so it makes the hairs on my arms stand up without chilling my skin. As I lift a hand to my mouth to stifle a yawn, a streak of light arcs across the sky. I close my eyes for a second and make a wish: *Give me the courage to do the right thing.*

"Did you see that?" I say. "Shooting star."

Elliott doesn't respond. I look over at him and smile when I see that his eyes are closed. I try to match my breathing to the rise and fall of his chest. His dark eyelashes flutter slightly.

I'm not sure how much time passes, thirty seconds, a couple of minutes, maybe. I know it's intrusive and a little creepy to watch someone sleep, but it's also kind of soothing. The pendant he wears around his neck has slipped out of his T-shirt and I can see that it's some kind of deer carved out of dark rock. I'm just turning back to look at the sky when my phone buzzes in my purse. It's 12:15 and I have a text from my dad: Fifteen minute warning.

I text him back: Thanks. On the way.

Next to me, Elliott shifts in his sleep. I reach out and touch his arm, resisting the urge to trace the V of his deltoid with my fingertips. His eyelashes flutter again and then his eyes blink open.

He looks confused for a second as he sits up. "Did I fall asleep?"

"Yeah," I say. "I guess showing off downstairs must have worn you out."

His lips quirk into a smile. "What can I say? ANW is a pretty exhausting sport."

"I have to be home in twelve minutes or my dad is going to give me a lecture."

Elliott rolls his head around in a slow circle and then swallows back a yawn. "Guess we'd better get going then."

"Are you awake enough to drive?" I ask, that horrible image of Brad Freeman's headlights flashing through my mind. "I can always call my dad to come get me."

Elliott doesn't say anything for a few seconds and I wonder if he's thinking it over. "I'm okay," he says finally. "It's only a couple of miles and I'm not that tired. It's just easy to relax up here, you know?"

"Yeah," I say. "It is. I could totally fall asleep too."

Elliott and I make our way back down the ladder. From the ground I appreciate not only the stars, but also the silhouettes of the red rock cliffs towering beyond the buildings of Springdale, like the walls of a giant fortress.

"You'll have to show me more of the obstacles sometime," I say.

"Anytime. I work out almost every night."

We cut around the Zion Outdoor Experts building back to the parking lot. Elliott unlocks the door for me and I step up into his truck. He slides into the driver's seat, clicks his seat belt in place, and starts the engine.

"So are you training to be on *American Ninja Warrior* too?" I ask. "Like your dad?"

"It's a good question. By the time I'm old enough to compete, I'll probably be good enough to at least survive the qualifiers, and the show loves to spotlight families competing together. I like the idea of pushing myself to the limits and I love mastering the obstacles. But I don't think I want to be on TV." He turns out of the parking lot and onto the main road that runs through Springdale. "I could definitely see helping out in the gym as a coach, though, if we get it up and running. It'd be fun to work with wannabe ninjas, especially the kids."

I think about how shocked everyone was when I turned down the chance to be in Dallas's video. "I wouldn't want to be on TV either," I say. "The whole experience seems like it would be too stressful."

"Garrett says the crowd energizes him, but Ezra is more like me. We go every year and sit in the stands, and you can tell when the cameras are on you and it makes us cringe."

Elliott turns off the main street and pulls his truck over in front of my dad's house. The blinds are partially open, and the living room light is on. "Home right on time," he says. "When do you work next?"

"Tuesday."

"I'll see you then." Elliott pats me lightly on the leg and I open the door and step down from the truck. I turn and wave as he drives off.

My dad is on the sofa, looking at something on his iPad, when I enter the living room. "You're late," he says.

"One minute that it took me to walk across the yard," I say.

"You didn't have to wait up, Dad. I'm going to college in a couple of months. You're going to have to trust me to get home all right on my own."

He sets the iPad on the coffee table. "I suppose you're right, but that's not exactly easy given everything that's happened."

My face flushes just thinking about the accident. What would my dad think if he knew the truth—that my insecurity and carelessness got Dallas killed? What *will* he think, when I work up the nerve to tell him.

"I'm trying to do things better this time," Dad continues.

"I know you are, and I appreciate it." Somehow this tragedy has made Dad into a better person and me into a worse one. I bite back tears. I don't want to lose it on him, especially not this late. I'm sure he has to be up early for work. Desperate for a distraction, I gesture at the iPad screen. It looks like someone's CT scan. "What are you looking at?"

"Oh. It's actually pretty interesting. Check this out." Dad taps the screen and goes through various views of the CT. He points out certain areas on the screen. "This is a thirty-four-year-old woman. The body of this tumor is compressing her spine and threatening to rupture the aorta. There are offshoots invading the pericardium and left atrium."

"Holy crap. Do you have to remove that?"

"We're thinking about attacking it as a team—there'd be me and Dr. Kent from my practice, as well as a couple of vascular surgeons. And then a neuro guy from Salt Lake City would be in charge."

"Would you have to go to Salt Lake City to do the surgery?" I ask.

"Just for a day or two," Dad says. "Probably next month. Would you be all right with that?"

"Sure," I say. It would be strange to be here alone with Rachael, but I'm not going to keep my dad from participating in an epic surgery that could save someone's life.

"Right now it's all academic. We're formulating a plan of attack so we can share it with the patient and hopefully get approval from her insurance company." Dad yawns as he stands up from the sofa. "Did you have a nice time with your friend?"

"Yeah. It was cool."

"Good." We walk down the hallway toward our bedrooms together. He pauses in front of my door. "It's really nice to have you here, Genevieve."

"It's nice to be here," I say.

Dad gives me a quick hug and I slip into my room and get ready for bed, replaying the events of the evening in my head. I never would have thought I'd have fun messing around on a Ninja Warrior course, but Elliott is right about it demanding total focus. And I did better than I thought I would.

And then the stars. Lying out on the roof was so peaceful. The sense of calm that came over me there lasts until I fall asleep.

But then when I wake up the next morning, there's another text from Shannon. And my sense of peace goes right out the window.

CHAPTER 25

Shannon: Did you hear? I just wanted to make sure you're okay.

Me: ?

Shannon: They dropped the charges against #BradFreeman. Apparently the witness to the actual accident is a big fat liar and Freeman's hotshot lawyer got the BAC results thrown out.

Me: Why are you hashtagging him in a text?

Shannon: IDK. Habit, probably. Shit is blowing up everywhere. Everyone is pissed. They're calling for Dallas's parents to file a wrongful death lawsuit.

Me: Dallas wouldn't want that.

Shannon: I would if it were me. I don't care if he was officially drunk or not. His bad choices killed Dallas. He deserves to be punished.

I flinch. She has no idea how close to home she's hitting. Still, part of me is flooded with relief. Maybe this is a sign. If the charges have been dropped, maybe everything will finally go back to normal and I won't have to tell the world what really happened. Maybe no one needs to know I lied and have been letting someone else take the blame for it.

I've read so many stories online about how tragedy brings people together, how hard times encourage bravery and sacrifice, how a crisis can turn ordinary folks into heroes. But what about the opposite, when something horrible happens and it strips us bare, exposing weaknesses we didn't even know we had. What about when tragedy makes people worse?

I don't want to be that story.

For the next couple of weeks, I actually let myself believe things are getting back to normal. Shannon is busy at the pool during the day and has started hanging out with her sexy lifeguard partner Niko in the evenings. She still texts me most days, but finally seems to have gotten the hint that I don't want to hear about Brad Freeman or the possibility of a wrongful death lawsuit. Dallas's parents haven't contacted me about it. Mom and I talk every couple of days and she hasn't mentioned anything about a lawsuit either. She tells me how one of her scrub nurses convinced her to take a pottery class and that's she's enjoying the challenge. She sounds happier than she has for a while.

At Zion, work on the touch trail continues. On the weekend, Rachael has six Boy Scout volunteers and Elliott rustles up extra Pulaskis so everyone can chip in. By the end of the day on Sunday, we've completed the first stage of the trail—digging the trench.

Next we have to level the trail. Rachael says the natural

surface will work best if it's the same thickness all the way around, so Halley, Elliott, and I walk the trench and use shovels and trowels to even out any rough patches and fill in dips or divots.

It takes another couple of days to complete this. Elliott and I are friendly at work and often eat lunch together—sometimes with Halley too—but he hasn't invited me back to his Ninja Warrior gym and I kind of miss it.

It takes me until Friday, but I finally work up the nerve to ask him if I can come by the gym at some point on the weekend.

"What are you doing later tonight?" he asks.

"No plans," I say.

"I'll pick you up at eight."

"Maybe I should just jog down to the store," I say, thinking of my dad's insistence that Elliott come inside and pick me up properly.

"I'm not afraid to get grilled by your dad," Elliott says with a grin. "Besides, what kind of friend would I be if I let you go running around by yourself in the dark? It's dangerous."

"It won't even be dark yet. And did you actually say dangerous?" I snort. "When's the last time this place had any actual crime?"

"Does parking in a no-parking zone count?" Elliott asks. "If so, yesterday. But still. You could trip over a rock squirrel, maybe fall into a cactus."

"Okay. I'm convinced. You can pick me up." A tiny smile forms on my face. "I'll be ready at eight."

• • •

True to his word, Elliott comes to the door right at eight and knocks sharply. My dad is in his study reviewing some surgical case notes while Rachael putters around the kitchen, cleaning up after dinner and loading the dishwasher.

"I'll get it," I say, hopping up from my spot on the sofa.

Dad appears in the doorway behind me. "Well, don't you look . . . sporty."

I'm dressed in capri-length exercise pants that hide my leg scar and a hot pink running shirt, a zip-up hoodie open over my shirt just in case Elliott and I decide to go back on the roof. My hair is twisted into a braid, my now-standard wide headband fastened in place with a handful of bobby pins.

"That's because we're going to work out." I give my dad a look. "This is not a date," I hiss before opening the door.

Elliott stands on the porch in black-and-white warm-up pants and a Zion T-shirt. His hair looks damp, like maybe he just got out of the shower.

"Well, don't just stand there," Dad says. "Invite the poor boy in."

"Come on in," I say through gritted teeth. "Your turn to be tortured."

Elliott laughs. "It's good to see you again, sir," he says. "I'll be sure to have Jen back by her curfew."

"What are you guys planning to do?"

"Dad! I already told you all this," I mutter.

"It's fine," Elliott says. "I'm not sure if you know, but my dad

Garrett competes every year on *American Ninja Warrior*. He's built himself a practice gym that we might turn into a summer camp for aspiring competitors, but right now it's just a bunch of random obstacles. Jen and I are going to get our ninja on for a couple of hours."

My dad clears his throat. "Is it safe?"

"It's pretty safe. We've got mats everywhere. The worst she'll end up with is a few scratches and bruises."

"I did it before, and look, I'm fine," I point out, before my dad can object. "Is this interrogation almost over?"

Rachael hollers something from the kitchen about making ice cream sundaes and my dad decides to let us leave. "Have her back with minimal scratches and bruises, please."

"I'm not a porcelain doll," I say.

My dad sighs deeply and I can tell he wants to make a comment about how I'm breakable, but he's promised not to talk about the accident. "Just be careful," he says finally. "Both of you." He turns toward the kitchen and Elliott and I head outside.

"Jeez," I say after the door closes behind us. "Sorry about that."

"I don't mind." Elliott grins mischievously as we both hop into his truck. "I might have forgotten to mention that you have to meet my dads, too."

"What? Why?"

"Because they're both at the gym tonight."

Immediately I pull my phone out of my purse and start

fussing with my appearance, tucking wispy pieces of hair back into my braid and wiping away bits of smudged eyeliner.

Elliott glances at me out of the corner of his eye. "You look fine." He coughs. "I mean, you look great. But they're not going to care about your appearance."

I put my phone away. "Sorry, whenever I meet parents, I always imagine it'll be like someone meeting *my* mom. And then I get nervous."

"Your mom would care what I look like?"

"My mom cares about everything. She'd draw conclusions based on your hairstyle and the condition of your shoes."

"Yikes. I guess that explains why you always look so put together."

"Perfect on the outside, a complete mess on the inside," I say.

Elliott grins. "Let's get your insides fixed up then." He pulls into the parking lot in front of Zion Outdoor Experts and we head into the gym.

CHAPTER 26

Elliott's dads are at the far side of the gym, but they both turn abruptly at the sound of the door.

"Ellie!" A lanky blond guy with a loose ponytail that hangs past his collar jogs over. His long shorts sit low on his hips, exposing a bit of tanned skin with each stride. I catch a glimpse of a tattoo—some kind of script writing peeking out from beneath the hem of his Patagonia T-shirt. As he gets closer, I can see lines around his eyes and bits of gray in his hair, but from a distance he didn't look much older than Elliott. He spends a few seconds taking me in before he holds out his hand. "Garrett," he says. "So you're the girl Ellie can't stop talking about."

"Dad." Elliott gives Garrett a look.

Garrett laughs. "He told me you were a natural on the Quintuple Steps and the Spinning Log."

"I don't know about all that." I reach out to shake his hand and nearly double over from his strong grip. "Nice to meet you," I say. "I'm Jen."

"Don't break her hand, Dad," Elliott says. "She's going to need both of them for the Salmon Ladder."

"Salmon Ladder! Hard-core. High five!" Garrett holds his palm out toward me.

I slap it. "I've seen that one on TV. I'm not sure if I can even do a pull-up, but I'll give it a try."

Elliott's other dad chuckles. "I'm still working on my first pull-up." He runs a hand through his thick black hair. "I'm Ezra Helberg. Welcome to our playground."

"Jen." I extend for another handshake, this time one that doesn't make my eyes water.

Ezra nudges Garrett with his elbow. "Go ahead and show off for the pretty girl. You know you want to."

Garrett grins as he bounces up and down on his toes. "Which obstacle do you want to see me do?"

I look around the gym and point at a series of narrow ledges nailed to a flat wall. "What's that one?"

Ezra groans. "Not the Ultimate Cliffhanger."

"Dad's a rock climber," Elliott explains. "The Ultimate Cliffhanger is pretty easy for him."

"How about I show you proper form on the Salmon Ladder?" Garrett says.

"Sure," I say.

The four of us walk over to the Salmon Ladder. It looks like a standard pull-up bar that's been fit into an angled slot. There are five more slots above the starting one and you're supposed to jump the bar from the bottom to the top in a series of pull-up moves. Like the Warped Wall, I've seen it on TV. And like the Warped Wall, it looks impossible in person.

"Do you know why it's called the Salmon Ladder?" Ezra asks me.

"Because the angled rungs look like fish bones?" I guess.

"Close," he says. "The act of jumping the bar from rung to rung mimics the movement of salmon swimming upstream."

"The first thing you need to do is get a good jump off the mini-tramp so that you're positioned in the middle of the bar. Like so." Garrett takes a running jump and hits the trampoline directly in the center. He flies through the air and grabs onto the bar. He checks his hand positions and moves his right hand slightly outward. "Next you want to make sure you don't favor one side or the other when you're transitioning from rung to rung."

"Alternatively, next is when you dangle helplessly from the bar while your husband laughs at you," Ezra says.

I smile. "I'll probably be right there with you."

Garrett jumps the pull-up bar up the rungs of the Salmon Ladder with ease.

"You look like you're defying the laws of gravity," I say.

He releases his hold on the bar and falls down to the thick mat beneath it. "You should see Ellie. The kid has wings." He turns to Elliott. "Show her."

"Nah." Elliott shakes his head. "She didn't come here to see that." He arches an eyebrow at me. "Want to show them your mad skills on the Spinning Log?"

I blush. "I only made it across once, and it's been a couple weeks."

"Whose fault is that? I told you that you could come by anytime you wanted. I would've given you the key even if I couldn't stay and play."

"I know. I just didn't want anyone to catch me and think I was a burglar."

"That'd be the biggest news story this town has had in months," Garrett says. "Come on, sister. Let's see what you got."

"Jen. Jen. Jen," Ezra chants.

"I don't know. I might—"

"Jen. Jen. Jen." Garrett adds a clap to the chant.

"Make it across the first try and I will cook you dinner," Elliott says.

"Ooooh. Now there's motivation." Garrett hoots. "Ellie cooks like a dream."

"That's because I taught him," Ezra says.

I hold up a hand. "All right, all right. I'll do it." Muttering something about peer pressure under my breath, I cross the gym and step up onto the platform by the Spinning Log. I am acutely aware of Elliott and his dads watching me. Inhaling deeply, I close my eyes for a second and envision the way I crossed the log last time.

I shake out my arms and then, without any warning, I dart across the log, trying my best to keep my feet exactly in the middle, exerting a direct downward force to minimize rotation.

One. Two. Three. The log spins beneath my feet, but I leap to safety, hitting the mat with my right shoulder..

"Woohoo. That was show-worthy." Garrett gives me a slow clap.

"Impressive," Ezra agrees.

"Thanks," I say. "I fell off about twenty times before I made it across the first time."

"You and me both, sister," Garrett says.

Everyone laughs and then it gets quiet. There's an awkward moment before Garrett says, "We'll get out of you kids' hair. I trust you won't let her get hurt, Ellie."

"We'll be safe," Elliott promises. "But don't let her small size fool you. She's a tough chick."

It's a nice thing to say, especially after he's caught me crying multiple times. "We'll be careful," I agree. "It was nice to meet both of you."

"Likewise." Ezra surprises me by leaning in for a hug. I pat his back awkwardly. "Elliott doesn't ever bring girls around, so you must be special," he whispers in my ear.

"Dad," Elliott says. "Not everyone likes to be hugged."

"It's okay." I smile shyly at Ezra. "It was nice."

"See. Nice." Ezra winks at Elliott. He slings an arm around Garrett's waist as the two of them head for the parking lot.

When the door closes, Elliott turns back to me. "That wasn't so bad, right?"

"They seem really great," I say.

"They have their moments." Elliott arches his eyebrows.

"And hey, now you can say you know someone famous."

I laugh weakly. If he only knew.

Elliott gives me a lesson in using the mini-trampoline and some tips for how to climb ropes and cargo nets in the most efficient way. We fool around on one of several rock climbing walls and he explains to me how various skills combine together to equal success on different obstacles.

Then we go from obstacle to obstacle, Elliott showing me how it's done, me trying my best to copy him. Some of the things are completely impossible for me to even try, like the Ultimate Cliffhanger. I just don't have the grip strength to hold on to the tiny wooden ledges. I also can't do the Salmon Ladder, but Elliott is impressed that I can even do a pull-up and he helps me go up a couple of rungs by holding my legs while I attempt to jump the bar.

After my arms give out, I drop to the ground. "Show me how it's done," I say.

"If you insist." Elliott grins. He gets a great jump off the mini-trampoline and goes straight up the Salmon Ladder in five easy pull-ups. The total elapsed time is less than twenty seconds.

"Holy shit," I say. "You rocked that even harder than your dad."

Elliott's eyes widen. "Do not ever say that in front of him or I'll never hear the end of it." He checks the time. "It's ten-thirty," he says. "You want to go hang out on the roof?"

"Sounds good." I follow Elliott up the ladder and we grab the sleeping bag we sat on last time we were here. I tug the ponytail holder out of my hair and undo my braid with my fingers. The breeze is cool against the dampness at the nape of my neck.

Elliott sits across from me, his broad shoulders backlit by the starry sky. Being face to face with him feels strangely intimate.

"Another gorgeous night," I say, my mouth going dry. I lie back on the blanket and look up at the stars.

Elliott reclines next to me. "Do you know what would make this moment perfect?" he asks.

"No," I say, a little afraid of the answer.

"Cactus Cooler."

I snicker. "We can go get something to drink somewhere if you want."

"Nah. I can live." Elliott looks over at me. "I don't really want to move right now."

"Me neither." It's a perfectly clear night and if I had to count the stars, it would take me hours. "Do you know anything about the constellations?"

"A little bit," Elliott replies. "Garrett is kind of a star nerd." He points up almost straight above us. "So there's the Big Dipper, which you can probably find."

"Yes, but I'm not sure I've ever found the Little Dipper."

"Straight across from the far top star in the cup part of the Big Dipper is the cup part of the Little Dipper."

"Cup part? Is that a technical term?"

"Bowl? Ladle?" Elliott offers. He scoots closer to me on the blanket and then holds up my hand toward the sky. "Right there," he says. "Do you see?"

"Uh-huh," I say, even though I can't focus on the sky when he's touching my arm. I can't focus on anything when he's so close to me that I can smell his wintergreen deodorant and the faint scent of his sweat beneath it.

"And there's Cassiopeia." Elliott moves my hand slightly. "Those five stars right there. If you connect them they make an M-shape."

"Holy crap. I can actually see it." I grin. "That's awesome."

"This whole night has been awesome," Elliott says, his hand still on my arm. "I'm glad you're here."

I swallow hard. "So tell me about your dads," I say, trying to get my mind off the warmth of Elliott's hand, off the solidness of his form now pressed up against me.

"My dads. Let's see." Elliott takes his hand back and threads his fingers together behind his head as a pillow. "Garrett grew up in Fort Collins, so he's been climbing and mountain biking and snowboarding since he was a kid. He's got a degree in engineering, but he never really used it, unless you count designing and building all the ninja obstacles."

"He built all that by himself?"

"Well, Ezra and I helped some." Elliott grins. "You've seen how handy I am with tools. Ezra is a couple years older than Garrett. He's from Long Island. He worked as an ad exec for about ten years and now he's the creative guy for the store—designing window displays, coming up with advertising, overseeing the buyers."

"It sounds like they complement each other perfectly."

"Pretty much. One is analytical but free-spirited, the other is cautious and creative."

"How did they meet?"

"Garrett moved to Denver after college and ended up working part-time as a rock-climbing instructor and part-time as a bartender. Ezra used to go to Denver on business, and I guess he struck up a conversation about how hard it was to find a good guy with the right bartender at the right time."

"Aww. That's a great story."

"It is, isn't it? Everyone always says you can't meet anyone quality in a bar. I'm glad it worked out so well for them." He pauses. "And me."

"So . . . you have Ezra's last name?"

"They adopted me as a baby and gave me Garrett's last name—Redmond—as my middle name and Ezra's for my surname. I don't know how or why they decided that. Maybe they didn't want me to be the only kid in kindergarten with two last names." He smiles. "They've always been overprotective of me. I've been a total spoiled brat my entire life." Before I can ask Elliott if he has any siblings, he says, "Your turn. Tell me about your parents."

I make a face. "My parents are not as awesome as yours."

"Said pretty much every kid, everywhere, throughout all of time."

"No, seriously," I protest. "So they're both cardiac surgeons, but—"

"Yeah, they sound all kinds of lame." Elliott elbows me in the ribs.

"I wasn't finished." I elbow him right back. "I guess you could say they've had really high standards for me my whole life. I was expected to be exceptional at everything."

"And if you weren't?"

"Then I either got private lessons or I quit doing it."

"I see."

"I mean, they're nice people. Well, my dad is, anyway. My mom is kind of . . . intense. I know they love me, but they never showed it much growing up. Just watching you with your dads tonight—I feel like you probably grew up with a lot of affection."

Elliott coughs. "Are you saying you're starved for affection? Because I could probably help with that."

I roll onto my side to see if he's kidding. "Oh yeah?" I say wryly. "That's awfully kind of you."

He blinks innocently. "Public service—it's just who I am."

"Right." I smirk. "Remember the day we met and you threatened to give me a ticket?"

"Oh yeah. Little Miss Sneak In Without Paying." Elliott laughs lightly. "You're a bad influence."

The last word catches in his throat and we stare at each other awkwardly for a few seconds. My eyes are drawn to his long eyelashes, to a tiny constellation of freckles under his left eye. For a second I imagine reaching out and touching him.

"Anyway," he says. "We can both agree you have an awesome stepmom."

"True. I was kind of a bitch to her from the moment I found out she existed. But she's never been anything but nice to me."

"I've never seen Rachael be mean to anyone," Elliott says.

Well, she did steal my dad away from my mom, I think. But I don't say it. Because maybe you can't steal someone away if they're where they want to be. Who knows how long my dad had been unhappy? Plus, maybe there's someone better out there for my mom—someone who can match her intensity and challenge her instead of just letting her win until they get tired of losing.

I lie flat so once again we're both looking up at the stars. The night breeze cools my skin. A bit of white fluff floats past me—cotton from one of Springdale's many cottonwood trees. "This is not how I imagined the desert."

Elliott laughs lightly. "Not enough camels?"

"Not enough cacti," I say.

"We've got prickly pear everywhere."

"True, but there are so many other plants. There are pine trees here!"

"It's unique geography, to be sure." Elliott swallows back a yawn.

A comfortable silence falls over us. I realize I haven't thought about Dallas or Brad Freeman or the internet for hours. For once I don't feel guilty about that. Maybe I'm finally starting to heal. Or maybe I'm just getting better at denial.

"I wish I could stay here," I blurt out.

"You can."

"No, seriously. I wish I could capture this moment," I say. "Like a firefly in a jar."

"Fireflies kept in jars die eventually," Elliott says. And then he adjusts his body and his hand brushes against mine. At first I think it's an accident, but he leaves it there. And then when I don't pull away, he twines our fingers together.

A current of warmth moves through me, followed by a rush of guilt. I do the math in my head. It's been exactly forty-eight days since Dallas died. What kind of girlfriend develops feelings for some other guy in forty-eight days?

I didn't even know I *had* feelings until right this second.

Elliott lifts up on one shoulder and looks down at me. "That day by the Visitor Center when you were upset. What was that about?"

"I was thinking about my ex-boyfriend," I say. The half-truth doesn't feel any better than an outright lie.

Elliott reaches out and traces the scar on my cheekbone with one finger. A tremor races through me. "Did he hurt you?"

"No, no." I shake my head. "Not like that, anyway." *Not as bad as I hurt him.* "He cheated on me once, but we got past it."

"You're a better person than me. I don't know if I could get past that."

"No I'm not," I say, almost violently. "I mean, I don't know if I did the best job either. He confessed the whole thing and I could see he felt awful about it. And I appreciated that honesty, so I forgave him. But forgetting is harder than forgiving, you know?"

Elliott strokes my face again. He hooks one arm under my waist and pulls me close to him. "Come here."

I tense up as I feel his body against mine. His heat radiates through his clothes and my own. His forearms are still damp with sweat. I trace one finger along his ropelike veins and a yearning starts to build inside me. My hand finds the curve of his biceps. His skin goes taut beneath my touch. My fingertip falls into a groove between two muscles.

"Can you feel that?" Elliott asks.

"What? Your big biceps? Yeah, I feel them." I roll my eyes.

"No, I meant the way you're giving me goose bumps," he says.

Sure enough, the hair on Elliott's arms is raised and his skin is covered with tiny goose bumps. "Wow," I say.

"How about a taste of your own medicine," Elliott murmurs. He drags his fingertips along my inner arm. I close my eyes and focus purely on the sensation, the gentle stroking. He cups his hand around my biceps. "Flex," he says.

I bend my arm and flex, but I'm quite sure it's nothing close to his definition.

"Not bad," he says. "You know, for a girl."

My eyes flick open and I look up at him to protest, but his lips are quirked into a smile.

"I thought that might get you." And then he leans in and

brushes his lips against the scar on my cheekbone.

I take in a sharp breath, surprised by the warmth of his mouth and the current of heat inside me.

Elliott rests his forehead on mine. "Is this okay?" he asks. Gently, he traces the line of my jawbone with his lips, slowly making his way toward my mouth.

I don't answer.

I can't answer.

I should pull away.

I need to pull away.

But I also need to feel like this. Accepted. Wanted.

I blink back tears as I reach up and run my fingers through his short dark hair, feeling the contours of his skull beneath it. Elliott rests one hand on my waist and cradles my face with the other as he brushes his lips against mine.

His kiss is gentle, tentative, as if he's expecting me to push him away at any second. I feel the tears coming on again but I tamp them down. They're not allowed to wreck this moment.

I kiss him harder, my lips parting. My shirt rides up slightly and I guide Elliott's hand onto my bare skin. His fingers tentatively explore my rib cage and the small of my back. His tongue tastes my lips, but then my headband slips off and I flinch.

Disentangling myself, I quickly try to put the circle of cloth back in place, but one of Elliott's strong arms wraps around my wrist. "No," he says.

He tugs my body up on the blanket and turns my head so he can see my craniotomy scar and the new hair growing in around it. Gingerly, he traces the pink line with one finger. "Your roots are showing," he teases. "I think you're the only blonde I know who dyes her hair brown." Before I can even reply he leans in to kiss me again.

"Hold up," I say, scooting back away from him. "I can't do this. I'm sorry." Shame weighs down on me. Maybe it's all right if a day goes by where I don't think about the accident, but kissing another guy feels like cheating on Dallas. It's bad enough that I killed him. I don't want to add to my list of crimes.

"Do you still love him?" Elliott asks.

My gut instinct is to say yes. How can I say I don't love Dallas given what's happened? But every day I don't come clean about the accident makes it a bigger and bigger lie. I don't want to lie to Elliott about this too. "No, not the way that you mean, anyway."

Elliott brushes my hair back from my face. "I'm sorry he hurt you, but not all guys are cheaters."

"I know."

"Look. It would probably be stupid to start something," he says. "Since you're only going to be here until the end of the summer. But I can't help it. I want to. I want to be dumb for once." I can see the questions in his eyes.

"As someone who has done a lot of dumb things recently, I don't really recommend it," I say, a hint of bitterness leaching into my voice.

"So is that a no?"

I sigh. "I like you, but . . . I don't think I'm ready." I turn away from Elliott because it hits me that's just one more lie. I'm ready, I just don't deserve him. I don't deserve anyone. But I'm afraid to tell him any of that, because he'll ask why. And then I'll have to tell him the truth, about what I did. About what I'm still doing. And then I'll lose him from my life.

And that's what I'm really not ready for.

CHAPTER 27

Elliott drives me home and walks me to the door. We pause on the porch and I'm expecting this big awkward moment where he tries to kiss me again, but all he does is give me a hug.

He's not that tall—maybe five foot ten—but since I'm kind of short we still fit together perfectly, my head right beneath his chin. My face ends up pressed against his T-shirt, which smells like a mix of sweat and sand and desert air. "Thank you," I say.

"For what?"

"For being so nice to me. At least I didn't cry on you tonight."

"I don't know where you got the idea that crying is this horrible thing, but you need to get over that. Stop apologizing for your body's involuntary responses to your feelings. It's almost like me apologizing for how sweaty I am right now."

I pull back so I can look him in the eye. "I never thought of it that way. Growing up, I never saw either of my parents cry. Even after my dad left, if Mom did any crying it was in her bedroom late at night after I was asleep. I grew up kind of programmed to hide my tears."

"Well, don't be like that, okay? At least not around me."

"Okay." We stand, looking at each other for a few seconds. I struggle to fill the silence. "Also, thanks for showing me the stars and making me feel like a Ninja Warrior Girl."

He laughs. "I love watching newbies try the obstacles. Almost everyone does better than they expect on at least one of them, and it's like watching a flower bloom, you know? Seeing people awaken to their true possibilities."

"I needed that today."

"Just remember. It's never as bad as you think it is," Elliott says.

"Thanks." I hope he's right.

He leaps off the porch and lopes across our front yard. I check my phone and when I see that it's not quite midnight, I sit on the steps for a few minutes and gather my thoughts. It's a nice night and I'm not ready to go inside.

My dad ducks out onto the porch. "I heard your friend's truck leave," he says, slight emphasis on the word "friend." "Did you have a good night?"

"Yeah. It was a lot of fun."

Dad sits next to me, his feet crossed at the ankles. We both stare out into the yard for a few seconds. "If you like him, no one is going to judge you for that."

Ha. I'm quite sure a whole lot of people would judge me for that if they knew who I was. But all I say is "He's cool, but what's the point? In two months I'll be back in St. Louis and he'll still be here."

"You know you don't have to leave, right?" Dad says. "You'll be eighteen next month. You can do whatever you want."

"Dad." I turn to him, somewhat shocked. "I know you're not telling me to change my plans because of some guy."

"Of course not. But honey, life already changed your plans. You didn't plan for your boyfriend to die. You didn't plan to come here. You didn't plan to make friends. I'm just saying, it's okay to change your mind about what you want. Not because of Elliott, but for all I know you were just staying in St. Louis to go to college because you wanted to be close to Dallas." Dad pauses. "Plans are great, but they should never make you feel trapped. And if we're being honest, Rachael and I love having you around, and I'm already getting sad at the thought of you leaving. That's all I'm saying."

"Thanks, Dad," I say.

He clears his throat. "Listen, Genevieve. I talked to your mom tonight. The Kades paid her a visit earlier today."

"Oh?" The single word almost gets caught in my throat.

"Glen and Nora are leaning toward going ahead with the wrongful death suit against Brad Freeman. They've been getting a lot of pressure, not just from Dallas's fans, but also from drunk driving nonprofit groups who want to use this tragedy to lobby for a one-and-done law. They haven't made any definite decisions yet, but they feel like they'll appease the public if they at least take Freeman to court."

My blood accelerates in my veins. A roar builds in my ears. I force myself to focus. "Okay," I say. "Is there a time frame? I assume I'd have to testify." Maybe this is a good thing. I wanted to tell the truth anyway. A wrongful death suit would mean I have to.

"That's one of the reasons they haven't made a definite decision about pursuing legal action yet. Glen doesn't want to put you through more than you've already dealt with."

"That's nice of him, but I don't want to be the deciding factor in this." I gnaw on my lower lip.

"I figured you'd say that. His attorney said it'd be best if you testified in court, but there's also the option of giving a videotaped deposition. You'd still be under oath, but it'd just be you and the attorneys and judge present."

I nod. "Well, whatever they need to do, I understand." I look down at the ground. "I feel kind of bad, though, for Brad Freeman."

"Why is that?" Dad asks.

"Knowing that you hurt someone is kind of the worst punishment of all. It seems excessive to have to pay a lot of money on top of it."

"Ha." He ruffles my hair. "I wish your mom had felt like that a couple of years ago."

I turn to face my dad. "It must have been really hard to finally be honest with her." I've only had to confess a handful of minor misdeeds to my mom, but every time it was scary.

"It was. But it was worse with you. Your mom is a smart lady and she knew I was lying. But you didn't see it because you were young and you thought I was better than I am. You gave me the benefit of the doubt and I betrayed that trust. I just didn't want you to be disappointed in me." Dad shakes his head. "Maybe if you'd had some warning, the whole divorce would have been easier for you to deal with."

I doubt it, but it's nice to hear that Dad regrets lying to me. "How did you finally work up the nerve to tell us?"

"Well, part of it was Rachael. I knew I was going to lose her if I didn't eventually break things off with your mom. But I guess the other part was faith that the people who really mattered—you, my family, my close friends—would at least *try* to understand why I did what I did." Dad exhales deeply. "Not that you didn't have every right to be mad at me, because you will always have that right. I guess I was just counting on the fact that you loved me enough to give me a second chance."

"I forgive you," I say. "I don't remember if I ever told you that."

Dad looks away for a moment. When he turns back, his eyes are misty. "Thank you. Any particular reason why you wanted to know?"

"I guess I was just wondering what it was that pushed you to do the right thing."

Dad nods. "Is there anything else you want to talk about?"

It's the perfect opening, but I can feel the truth stuck way down inside me. It's not ready to come out yet. I shake my head. "I love you, Dad."

"I love you too." My dad rises to his feet and then reaches down to help me up. I go in for my second porch hug of the night.

I take a shower and crawl into bed, but I can't sleep. I keep going back to the conversation with my dad, wondering if the Kades are going to file a lawsuit. Grabbing my laptop, I Google "Brad Freeman lawsuit." The first thing that pops up is an article about the charges being dropped.

I notice right away that this post is using a different picture of Brad Freeman, what looks like an official photo from a driver's license or similar. Freeman is clean shaven, his chin raised, just a bit of a smile on his face. It doesn't even look like the same person as the photo I've seen on all the other blogs.

REALE NEWS NOW
A Closer Look at the Freeman Vehicular Manslaughter Case
CHRIS REALE, 5 days ago

Unpopular opinion time. Social media erupted in a rage when the Wentzville district attorney dropped the vehicular manslaughter and DWI charges against Brad Freeman, the man accused of killing Fusion Records performer Dallas Kade. From the point of the announcement onward, there has been a steady stream of demonstrations and angry online postings accusing local officials of protecting

Freeman because he used to be a paramedic and his dad was the sheriff. I'm not denying that the thin blue line has been known to protect its family members, but let's look at the facts:

- Freeman worked for St. Charles County, not Wentzville. It was Wentzville officers who arrested Freeman and it was a Wentzville officer who was first on the scene and reported that he smelled alcohol on Freeman. That doesn't sound like a cover-up to me.
- The witnesses have all been discredited. Two of them reported seeing Freeman's truck on a road where he could not possibly have been driving at the time they claim they saw it and the supposed witness to the actual accident admitted to lying after parts of her testimony were questioned.
- The forensic evidence at the scene was deemed inconclusive.
- Genevieve Grace suffered major head trauma and has reported that she can't remember the events leading up to the accident.
- Freeman has stated that it was Grace who was driving in the wrong lane, not him.
- According to blood tests done at the hospital, Freeman had a BAC of .083, which is over the legal limit of .08, but there are many DWI cases on the

books where BAC results done at a hospital were thrown out. The methodology isn't as accurate, and when you add in that the blood was drawn through an IV used to give other medicines and wiped with an alcohol swab, it's at least plausible this result was flawed.

- The bartender at Eight Ball Bar & Grill where Freeman worked said he drank two beers over the span of an hour and his credit card confirmed these charges.
- BAC tables show that a man of Freeman's weight (180 lbs) would probably need to consume at least 4 or 5 drinks in that time to reach a BAC of .083.

I am in no way disputing that Freeman exercised poor judgment when he got behind the wheel of a car after drinking, but two drinks in an hour isn't generally enough to put someone beyond the legal limit, and to prove manslaughter charges the prosecution needs to prove not just that Freeman exercised poor judgment, but that *his driving caused* the accident.

Without any concrete evidence or eyewitnesses, all the DA has to go on is Freeman's own testimony that it was Grace, not he, who caused the accident. Is it possible that he's lying to avoid a prison sentence? Certainly. But is it also at least conceivable that he's telling the truth and that Grace might have been responsible for the accident? This reporter believes that it is.

Therefore, the decision made not to bring Freeman to trial seems less like a gross miscarriage of justice as other sites have been reporting and more like a prudent decision to avoid further clogging up an already overwhelmed court system.

I understand how upset and angry people are over the tragic death of Dallas Kade, but your feelings are not enough to put someone in jail. I have heard rumors that the Kade family intends to file a wrongful death lawsuit against Brad Freeman. I would assume that any lawyer they retain would urge them not to pursue a civil suit unless additional evidence comes to light.

Recent Comments:

pxs1228: Why should we believe the bartender where Freeman works? Friends cover for each other all the time. Not to mention Freeman could've paid cash for some of his drinks.

> **charlotteincharlotte:** I think you mean where he USED to work.

Jude_Archer: Wow, Chris. You live in St. Louis, right? Is Brad Freeman one of your former frat bros or something? Quite the biased reporting. And how is it that you're the only one who knows how the eyewitnesses were discredited?

jenjennjenni: someone explain to me how a hospital nurse messes up a blood test worse than cops doing it.

CeliaRN0612: I don't have specific information about this case, but I know that most hospitals use a different method of testing than crime labs, and use only the serum part of the blood. This requires the results to be recalibrated in order to obtain a proper BAC and not everyone uses the same formula. Also, hospital tests don't always separate out ethanol alcohol (drinking alcohol) from the presence of other types, including the isopropyl that the nurse reportedly used to clean the IV port.

Out of curiosity, I do a search for "Chris Reale Brad Freeman" to see if maybe the Jude commenter is right and this blogger is someone who knows Brad Freeman. But there are no website hits except for articles about the accident.

This article should worry me, because if this Chris Reale guy thinks Freeman is innocent, that means he thinks I'm guilty. But instead of feeling worried, I feel comforted. Maybe there's someone else out there who knows my secret. For some reason that makes me feel a little less alone.

CHAPTER 28

At work on Saturday, Halley is burbling with excitement about rumors regarding this year's secret Fourth of July party.

The three of us are back in the small staff lounge on the first floor of Zion Lodge, brainstorming ideas for what type of educational material we could put on the individual display signs along the touch trail. While we're doing this, Rachael has hired a crew to come in and dig all the post holes for the handrail and the display mountings.

"I heard it's going to be back in the Narrows this year," Halley says.

The Narrows is a section of the park where the canyon walls rise hundreds of feet above the Virgin River. I remember reading somewhere that the hikes in that part of Zion are often closed due to the danger of flash flooding.

"In the river?" Elliott asks. "In the dark? Seems kind of dangerous . . . and wet."

"There are dry areas over there too," Halley says. "And if they wait to use the restaurant upstairs like usual, the party won't be able to start until after ten p.m. when all the customers are gone."

"What about a Narrows display?" I suggest, trying to bring the conversation back on topic. "Maybe we could build canyon walls that the kids could walk through?"

"That's a good idea," Elliott says. "Put it on the list."

Halley adds "Narrows walk-through" to the short list of ideas for displays. "All right, Jen, if you're going to make us work, do you guys care if I put on some music? I know it seems counterintuitive, but it helps me focus." Halley pulls a portable music player out of her backpack. "This is hooked up to my Pandora channels."

"Fine with me," I say.

Elliott makes a face. "I hope you like ear-bleeding, soulless pop music."

I shrug. "I can listen to whatever."

Halley swipes at her phone a couple of times and sure enough a recent dance hit starts playing. I go back to my internet browsing. We've already got ideas listed for the plants and animals in the region. I do a search for all the types of stone that make up the cliffs. It might not be interesting to everyone, but some kids would probably have fun touching the different rocks.

"What about constellations?" Elliott adds. "We could do a display that shows the different major constellations that are visible above Springdale in the summer."

"For little kids?" Halley asked skeptically. "What do you think, Jen?"

My brain flashes back to Elliott and me looking up at the stars from the roof of the Ninja Warrior gym. To him pulling me close. To him kissing me.

Halley clears her throat. "Jen?" she repeats.

"Hmm?" I look everywhere but at Elliott, hoping that my cheeks aren't red.

"Do you think a display with information about constellations would be too advanced for three- and four-year-olds?" Halley arches an eyebrow at me.

"Depends. Some kids are pretty advanced these days."

"We could just do the location of the Big and Little Dippers," Elliott suggests.

A fist clenches in my stomach as a few familiar chords emanate from Halley's music player. Dallas's label must have released the second single from *Try This at Home*. The song is called "By My Side." It's a rock ballad, a mix of him playing piano and guitar. He wrote it back when he was sixteen.

He wrote it for me.

"Ooooh, Dallas Kade. I love his whole album." Halley sighs wistfully as she turns up the volume on the music player. "I can't believe he's gone."

"Too loud." Elliott shakes his head. "The whole lodge can probably hear that."

"I'll be right back." Grabbing for my purse, I jump up from the table where we're working and dart out of the staff lounge, hurrying across the main room of the lodge to the restroom.

I lock myself in a bathroom stall and wrap my arms around

my middle. My whole body is shaking. I try to inhale but I can't get any air. It's like there's something stuck in my throat. My head starts to go fuzzy from lack of oxygen. *Calm down*, I tell myself. *Just breathe.*

I sink to the floor of the bathroom stall and sit sideways, my back up against the partition that separates me from the handicapped stall. I know I need to get back to the staff lounge before Halley and Elliott start to wonder about me, but I can't move. What I *need* to do is do the right thing and tell the truth. The problem with the right thing is that apparently the longer you wait, the harder it is to do. I thought I just needed a few days to work up the nerve. But now days have stretched into weeks and I still don't feel any closer to being able to admit what I did.

I imagine all those tweets, those blog posts, those death threats directed at me and my family. So what if I wasn't drinking? I still picked a fight with Dallas and made him leave the party when it was dark and I was tired. I caused the accident, and worse, I remained quiet and let someone else take the blame.

The door to the restroom opens. I struggle hurriedly to my feet.

"Jen?" It's Halley.

"I'm here," I say. "Sorry. I just felt sick to my stomach."

"Do you want me to call Rachael for you? I think she's down at Weeping Rock."

"No, don't bother her." I open the door to the stall so Halley can see I'm okay. Striding over to the sink, I splash some water on my face. I stare at myself in the mirror, waiting for my reflection to distort like a surrealist painting, to become someone I hardly recognize so my insides and outsides will match.

Halley's face is a mask of concern. She taps the toe of one of her cowboy boots and then reaches out to feel my cheek. "You're a little warm," she says. "Maybe you should take the rest of the day off."

"I'll be okay," I say. "I'm feeling better now. Sorry to run off like that."

Her phone chimes with a text. She glances down at it. "Elliott," she says. "He's worried about you too."

"Well, then let's get back there so he can see there's nothing to worry about," I say, my voice unnaturally bright.

Halley and I head toward the door to the restroom. "He likes you, you know?" she says.

"Yeah, he told me."

"I know you're leaving at the end of the summer, but he isn't the kind of guy I would push away." She puts her hand on my arm. "I'm not saying you ought to date him necessarily. Just that two months with Elliott might be better than years with other guys."

I smile. "Sounds like maybe *you* ought to date him."

Halley laughs. "Nah, he's like my brother." She wraps an arm around my waist and leans over to give me a half hug. "Sorry, I shouldn't make you talk boys when you're not feeling well. To be continued."

"To be continued," I agree. I catch sight of her black-and-white bracelet in my peripheral vision and my hands start to shake again. I tuck them deep into my pockets. *Focus*, I tell myself. I can fall apart later at home—in private, where no one else will see me.

I follow Halley back into the staff lounge, where Elliott looks up in concern. "Everything okay?"

"Yeah, I'm fine," I say. "Sorry for the dramatic exit." I clear my throat as I return to my seat at the table. "Where are we on ideas?"

"I think we've got everything we need," Elliott says.

"All right. So then what do we do now?" I ask.

"Something else we've been waiting for you to do." He grins. "Want to be one of the first people to officially walk the Zion Canyon Touch Trail?"

"You guys haven't walked on it yet?"

Elliott shakes his head. "Nope."

"Let's do it," I say.

Halley and Elliott have worked at this park for years. They're paid staff and this is much more their accomplishment than it is mine. But I am strangely excited about playing a role in the creation of a brand new trail, especially one for kids. It's a tiny flicker of brightness in an otherwise dark tunnel I can't seem to find my way out of.

The three of us walk the trail, and I can't believe how good it looks. The surface is set and has a natural-dirt look to it but the flatness and stability of asphalt. All the holes for the handrail have been professionally dug, and someone has laid out lumber along the side of the trail.

"This afternoon we're going to start building the railing," Elliott says. "Get ready to swing a hammer for the first time."

I force a smile. "I'm definitely ready for more hard physical labor." I hope swinging a hammer has the same effect on me that swinging a Pulaski did. Anything that will clear my head for a couple of hours is definitely welcome.

Halley has been quiet for most of our walk, but near the end of the trail she turns to Elliott and me and grabs both of our arms. "We totally need to celebrate. I know just the thing."

Elliott smirks. "Let me guess. A certain Fourth of July party?"

"It would be kind of perfect." Halley grins back at him. He rolls his eyes and she turns to me. "What do you say, Jen?"

"Count me in," I say. I'm nervous at the thought of being around so many people, but Halley has been an awesome friend, and I want to do this for her. Who knows? Maybe it'll actually be fun.

On Sunday, I text Shannon to fill her in on what I've been up to.

Me: Hey Shan. You would not believe how that trail project I've been working on for Rachael is coming along. It looks like a legit trail. What about you? How's life at the pool? More importantly, how's Niko? ;)

Her: Sweet. The pool is good. And Niko is fun, but I'd rather hang out with you.

Me: Wanna come visit? I did this amazing hike I could show you.

Her: I doubt my mom would let me, even if I could get time off
work. How about you come home instead? I can teach you how
to do a back flip off the diving board.

Me: Ugh. Waiting for stuff to calm down.

Her: You might be there forever then.

Me: What's that supposed to mean?

Her: Everyone is riled up waiting to see if the Kades are going to
file a lawsuit. Apparently there's some FB page with 25,000 likes
where people are asking for them to sue. And Freeman's mom is
too afraid to leave her house because people have been calling
and leaving death threats on her voicemail.

Me: That's horrible.

Her: Yeah. But it's also horrible that he might get away with killing
someone. The #KadetKorps needs #JusticeForDallas.

Me: I don't think a bunch of angry, emotional strangers without
all the facts are the best people to be doling out justice.

Her: Well somebody needs to do it.

Do they? I wonder when exactly the whole world decided
it was their responsibility to judge and punish total strangers.

Her: Are you mad at me for telling you?

My fingers are trembling on the screen of my phone, making it hard to type. I should just tell her, just type it out a letter
at a time: Freeman didn't kill Dallas. I did.

But I can't. Shannon wouldn't understand the secrets I've
kept from her—from everyone. There's a chance she might not
forgive me, and I can't lose anyone else right now—especially
not my best friend.

Me: I'm not mad. I'm just not feeling very well. I think I'm going to crash.

Her: Okay. Bye. All the hugs.

It takes me three tries to tap out my standard **All the <333** without messing up, because my hands are shaking so badly.

I drop my phone onto my nightstand and grab my laptop. I shouldn't do it, I know I shouldn't, but I have to see what's being said. First, I search Twitter using the #BradFreeman hashtag.

Siobhan @curlsinterupted • 8s

I just read over at @Celebrity_Watch that #BradFreeman's ex-wife filed for a restraining order! bit.ly/1XNNbr5

Tyrell James @RealTyrellJames •4m

Please do not harass the Kade family in this trying time. The decision whether to pursue civil action against #BradFreeman belongs to them.

Reale News Now @RealeNewsNow • 4m

How many of us make it thru a week without doing something someone else finds wrong? Who gets to pick whose lives get ruined? #BradFreeman

Justine @Kadet4Ever • 6m

Dear Mr. and Mrs. Kade. Please sue #BradFreeman for wrongful death. The #KadetKorps needs #Justice4Dallas.

Allie Cat @Allison_in_Hell • 6m

People need to stop weaponizing their social media. There is no proof #BradFreeman broke the law.

Allie Cat @Allison_in_Hell • 7m

Where does seeking justice end and seeking vengeance

begin? #BradFreeman

Monkey Man @boxxofmonkees • 9m

Boycott the Eight Ball Bar and Grill in New Melle, MO. They employ drunk drivers and killers like #BradFreeman

CharlotteinCharlotte @charlottecharl • 11m

What's the name of the District Attorney out there in Wentzville? Someone find a phone number so we can make some "concerned citizen" calls.

Patrick S @pxs1228 • 14m

Here's the Yelp link to that craphole where #BradFreeman works if anyone wants to leave them a review. bit.ly/1RkZzXQ @boxxofmonkees

Lyle Fritz @LyleFritzThird • 19m

Did you hear that douchebag #BradFreeman used to beat up his wife? Can't we put this asshole behind bars for SOMETHING?

Sighing, I click on the first link.

CELEBRITY WATCH

Brad Freeman's Ex-Wife Pursued a Restraining Order Against Him

DAVE CLINKER, 2 hours ago

Six years ago, just after Carly Freeman filed for divorce, she also asked her attorney about filing a restraining order against Brad Freeman. We reached out to her to inquire about what precipitated this and her comments were quite chilling. "I was afraid. He'd been coming around my office, asking to talk to me." When asked about his alcohol intake, Carly said: "Brad comes from a family of drinkers . . . he's been known to have one too many."

Carly Freeman declined to comment on whether she thinks Brad Freeman should be held accountable for Dallas Kade's death. A Sue Brad Freeman Facebook page has popped up to go with the Fire Brad Freeman page that now has over 25,000 likes. If the Kades do indeed file a lawsuit, it's likely that Carly Freeman will be called to testify.

Recent Comments:

Kadet4Ever: I hope the Kade family pursues the wrongful death lawsuit. The #KadetKorps needs closure!

lovemelongtime: Get over it, world. Dallas Kade and Tyrell James are both sellout wannabes. Kade's whole album sucks the big one.

Carly Freeman: [This comment has been deleted by an administrator.]

Carly Freeman: Fine, I'll try it again without swearing. This article took my words completely out of context. For anyone interested in the truth, it's over here: bit.ly/1qFdySJ

It feels weird to be reading words that Brad Freeman's ex-wife wrote. It feels weird that I know she's his ex-wife, as if he's somehow become intertwined with me, even though we've never even met. I skip over the rest of the comments to click on her link. A plain black-and-white blog site opens. There is only one post.

THE TRUTH ABOUT BRAD FREEMAN
BY CARLY FREEMAN

A couple of days ago I was approached by a blogger from the website Celebrity Central regarding the Dallas Kade accident. I was told that as one of the people who knows Brad Freeman the best, I deserved to have my story told.

But what appears on their website isn't my story. It's bits and pieces of my story, excerpted out of context and rearranged to fit the narrative that Brad Freeman is a terrible person—an abuser, an alcoholic, and a repeat offender drunk driver who is responsible for the accident that injured Genevieve Grace and killed her boyfriend Dallas Kade.

I'm not going to speculate about who's to blame for the accident, because I wasn't there that night. But I'm also not going to stand by and let my words be used to hurt a man I was married to for eight years, a man I still respect and consider my friend.

During the divorce proceedings, I inquired about a restraining order because I was afraid of both Brad and I getting into trouble at work since he'd been coming around my office between his paramedic calls, asking to talk to me. I didn't want either one of us to lose our jobs and I figured the easiest way for us to move on from the divorce would be if we minimized contact. However, my lawyer was quick to explain that a restraining order can only be filed if there is proof that someone has threatened or stalked a person. Brad Freeman has never threatened or stalked me.

About his drinking, what I actually told the blogger was, "Brad comes from a family of drinkers, but he's not an alcoholic. Like most of us, he's been known to have one too many occasionally, but nothing out of the ordinary."

I am so angry and hurt that my words were twisted in this manner. Please share the link to this page so that everyone can know the truth.

Recent Comments:

jenjennjenni: how do we know you're really brad freeman's wife?

Carly Freeman: I don't know. To be honest, I don't care. I just wish that all of you out there liking those mean Facebook pages and destroying a man's reputation without all the facts would stop and think about whether the media is giving you the full story.

Macon Bacon: Do you want to earn $4000 a month working from home? Now you can kick back from the comfort of your living room sofa and make enough money to support your whole family, just by reviewing products and service companies. More info: bit.ly/1VfNll0

pxs1228: I bet this post is from Freeman, pretending to be his wife. Hey Freeman, you need therapy, dude.

CharlotteinCharlotte: LULZ! I bet it is him. #Loser

Carly Freeman: I should have known some of you would think I'm Brad. I'm not going to waste time trying to convince you of otherwise, but the next time you decide to tell someone they need therapy, stop and consider whether your own actions have helped cause them to lose their job and their immediate access to mental healthcare.

Allison_In_Hell: I'm so sorry you had to create your own blog just to get the truth out there. There's no denying that our legal system is flawed, but holding individual people accountable is not fair or helpful. Even if Brad Freeman did cause the accident, what people are doing to him is the digital equivalent of stoning someone, and that is not okay.

Carly Freeman: Thank you, Allison. I agree.

Sarah Kwan: So Brad really lost his job?

Carly Freeman: Not just Brad. The restaurant where he works was vandalized. The owner can't afford to fix the damages so he's closed the place permanently, leaving about forty people without jobs. I also heard the nurse at the hospital who drew Brad's blood has resigned because protestors have been demanding to know her identity and she was afraid for her safety and for the safety of her coworkers. People think their anger is righteous and justified, but they can't see

beyond their target to all of the other innocent people
they are also hurting.

Tears burn my eyes. I read the last sentence over and over.
Carly Freeman might as well be talking to me. I wish I could
respond, but my mom would kill me. Of course I could always
respond anonymously. Half of these people are hiding behind
screen names and false identities.

But before I can come up with a name to use, I'm distracted
once again. An email notification has just popped up on my
screen.

I have a message from Brad Freeman.

CHAPTER 29

To say I'm terrified to open this message is an understatement. How did he get my email address? What could he possibly have to say to me? *Oh, maybe something like that you're a raging bitch for continuing to let him take the blame for something he didn't do.*

No. He doesn't know I know the truth. I can't believe his lawyer is letting him contact me. I stare at the screen for another whole minute, and then my curiosity gets the best of me. I click on the message.

Dear Genevieve,

I am terribly sorry for your loss and for everything you have gone through. I hope you are healing from the accident.

I'm not sure how much you know about what's been happening, but Glen and Nora Kade are going to file a wrongful death lawsuit against me. I don't know what they're hoping to accomplish, since I don't have much money to give them, but I don't want to put my family through six more months of this hell.

If by some chance you get your memory back, it would be really helpful if you could come forward and tell everyone I didn't cause the accident. I am not trying to blame you, and I promise I won't go after you for any money for damage to my truck or my medical bills. I just want to clear my name. I want my family and coworkers to feel safe again. As you can see below, things are getting out of hand. You're the only one who can help me.

Sincerely,

Brad Freeman

I swallow back a lump in my throat. I was stupid to think that after the charges were dropped things would get better for Freeman. Sure, maybe he's no longer looking at jail time, but what kind of life can he have with everyone gunning for him? How long will it be before people get tired of going after him? And what will be left of him when that time comes?

I click on the link he's provided. A YouTube video starts to play. The image is somewhat shaky but it's a building surrounded by a mob of people. I squint to read the words on the black sign in front of it: Eight Ball Bar & Grill. The camera angle switches and I watch a brick being thrown at the restaurant's front window. The grass cracks, but doesn't break. This must be the vandalism Brad's ex-wife, Carly, was talking about. A second brick flies through the air, and then a rock. All I can do is watch in shock as more people start throwing things. The front window shatters, shards of glass falling to the concrete sidewalk. And then just when I think it can't get any worse, it does.

A bottle arcs through the air. Not just a bottle, a Molotov cocktail. As I watch, the flaming vessel hits the broken front window and falls into the restaurant. The Eight Ball Bar & Grill begins to burn.

I feel sick inside. On the screen, there is shouting. The picture tilts on an angle. Sirens sing in the background. Someone mumbles something about getting the hell out of there. The video ends and the screen freezes on the last frame, a blurry, tilted image that somehow seems to mirror my life. How did everything get so messed up?

I stumble from my room to the bathroom and drop to my knees in front of the toilet. With one hand I pull my hair back from my face, but my stomach is empty and all I do is retch violently.

Gasping, I collapse to the floor and end up on my side. I need to talk to someone—anyone. No, I need to talk to Dallas, but I don't dare open my laptop so I can see his picture. I'm afraid Brad Freeman might send me another email. I wonder again how he got my address.

I close my eyes and try to imagine Dallas is in the bathroom with me, but the only images that come to me are ones of my ex-boyfriend in a coffin, of him being lowered into the ground forever.

"I don't know what to do," I say, tears pricking at my eyes.

This time Dallas doesn't answer. Maybe it's because I'm not looking at a picture of him. Maybe it's because he's dead. Or maybe it's because I *do* know what to do—I'm just terrified. Terrified of how the world will judge and punish me for the things I've done. Terrified no one will understand, everyone will leave me, and I'll end up completely alone.

CHAPTER 30

There's a sharp knock on the door. "Genevieve?" Rachael calls. "You okay in there?"

"Just a second." Using the bathtub for support, I pull myself back to my feet and hurriedly splash some water on my face. I open the bathroom door. "I'm fine. I just haven't been feeling very good today."

Rachael touches my face. "You don't look fine. Your skin is clammy and you're shaking all over. Did something happen?"

You mean like did I burn down a restaurant?

"No. I think I just ate something bad."

She frowns. "I ate the same food as you today. Maybe we should go to the urgent care."

"Really." I take a deep breath and let it out slowly. "I'll be okay. I need to talk to my dad about something, though. Do you know if he'll be home soon?" I fight to keep my voice level. As scared as I am, I can't let this go on any longer. No matter what the consequences are, I need to tell the truth before things get any worse.

"He's spending the night in Salt Lake City tonight, remember? He's got that tumor removal surgery in the morning."

Shit. I forgot about that. Dad is expecting to be in surgery at least ten hours, and then he'll be in Salt Lake City for an extra day just in case there are immediate complications.

"He'll be back on the fourth," Rachael says. "But if you need him, you can call him."

"That's okay." I need him, but I can't do this over the phone. I say a silent apology to Brad Freeman as I shake my head. "It can wait."

The next day is a haze. There's not much going on with the touch trail, so Rachael tells me I should take the day off and rest. I assure her I'll call her at work if I start to feel worse. Once she's gone, I crawl back into bed and try to go back to sleep. It doesn't happen, so instead I spend the day cataloguing all my sins: jealousy, selfishness, recklessness, cowardice, lying, more lying, still more lying. I think about every single thing I've done in the past few weeks and stick mental pins in all the places where I made terrible choices. It's like a road map of destruction leading from my house to Tyrell James's house to Wentzville all the way to Utah.

Elliott texts me at lunchtime but I can't bring myself to read it. I can't bring myself to do anything. I don't shower. I don't eat. I don't even change out of my pajamas until right before Rachael gets home.

After I'm dressed, I venture just far enough outside to get

the mail. As I head back to the house, I catch sight of the old man next door peeking out the blinds at me. I quickly drop my head to my chin, my hair falling forward to hide part of my face. I hurry back inside and toss the mail on the living room coffee table, my heart pounding erratically until I'm back in the safety of my room. It's like I've reverted back to the girl I was when I first got here.

My eyes flick to my computer. Maybe I should respond to Brad Freeman's message. I could tell him I got my memory back and that I'm going to tell everyone the truth, once I tell my parents and we figure out the best way to proceed.

I log on to my email account and start to reply to his message, but I'm only a few words in when it hits me that this might be a bad idea. How do I know this message is even from the real Brad Freeman? It could be from a reporter, or some inquisitive Kadet who doesn't believe Freeman is guilty. Or even if it really is Freeman, what if he publishes my reply to him before I get a chance to talk to my dad?

Rachael knocks on the door to my bedroom. "Genevieve?"

Shutting my laptop, I grab a book and pretend to be reading. "Come in," I call.

She ducks into the room and shuts the door behind her. "I figured since it was just us girls tonight that maybe we could do something fun. St. George is having a Fourth of July carnival this week. They're supposed to have some awesome rides there."

The thought of carnival rides—of even just leaving the house—almost sends me running to the bathroom again. "I'm not sure I'm up to it," I tell her.

"You're still feeling sick?" She tilts her head to the side, her brow furrowing. It's easy to read her mind.

"Don't call my dad. There's nothing he can do from Salt Lake City and I don't want to worry him for no reason," I say. "I promise if I'm not feeling better by tomorrow I'll go to the doctor."

"All right," she says. "But you should at least try to eat something. I'll make you some chicken soup. How does that sound?"

My mom used to make me chicken soup when I was little—when I was sick, when I was cold, when I was sad. And somehow it made everything better. I don't even know if it was the soup or the loving way she prepared it, humming to herself as she sliced and diced bits of chicken and carrots, holding me up so I could watch the golden liquid bubble and boil. All I know is that growing up sucks because chicken soup might taste good, but it won't fix everything anymore.

"That would be cool," I say finally. "Thanks."

Rachael heads off to the kitchen and in a little while I join her. The soup is from a can, not fresh like my mom's, but it still makes me miss being a little kid again.

After dinner, Rachael invites me to watch a movie with her. I sit through the first half of it to be polite and then tell her I'm going to crash. I crawl into bed and try to fall asleep, but after an hour of tossing and turning I flick my light back on and decide to read instead.

I'm eight chapters into the latest James Patterson thriller

when my phone vibrates on my desk. I ignore it, but a few minutes later it vibrates again. I get up long enough to see the texts are from Elliott. I still can't bring myself to read them, let alone respond. Whatever there was between Elliott and me is going to be gone as soon as he finds out the truth.

My stomach twists into knots when I imagine his dark eyes filling with disgust. I remember the day I met him, how upset he was about the park volunteer who didn't show up. How is he going to feel about a girl who wrecked her boyfriend's car, killed him, and then let someone else take the blame?

"Hey," he says.

"Elliott?" Confused, I whirl around. My room is empty but I swear I heard his voice.

"Out here." There's a gentle tapping sound and I realize Elliott is standing outside my window. He gestures at the screen. "Can I come in?"

I glance toward my closed bedroom door and then toward the clock. It's after ten-thirty. If Rachael hears me talking, she's going to know I'm not on the phone.

I hold one finger to my lips and then quickly loosen the screws holding the screen on my window. Elliott vaults through the opening with catlike agility and lands on my floor without making a sound.

"What are you doing here?" I hiss.

"You weren't at work today. I wanted to make sure you were okay." He walks the perimeter of my bedroom, stopping to consider each of the photos of my dad and me on the wall. Then he sits on the edge of my bed and looks meaningfully at the spot next to him.

The image of the burning restaurant flickers at the edges of my mind. "I'm fine," I say tersely, ignoring his unspoken suggestion to sit. "I was feeling sick."

"Too sick to answer my texts?" With one finger, he traces the outside of a wild mustang on my quilt.

He's got me there. Ignoring the texts of someone who is worried about you is a bitch thing to do. "I slept most of the day," I mumble.

"Oh, good, then you're probably not tired right now."

"Not really," I say. "But if Rachael catches you in here, we're both going to be in trouble."

Elliott grins. "Rachael loves me. She'd believe it when I explained how I only sneaked in to check on you."

A rush of warmth courses through me at the thought. While I was ignoring his texts and hiding from the world, Elliott was thinking about me. Worrying about me. Part of me wants to go to him and wrap my arms around him. That feeling of comfort—of being connected to someone—is calling and I want it more than anything. I think about the way Elliott kissed me on the roof of the gym. It felt so freeing until guilt caught up with me, but only because kissing him was like an out-of-body experience. I would really like to be someone else right now, but it's not fair to use Elliott to escape the things I've done.

"Okay, and now you've checked, so . . ."

He slouches forward slightly. "You want me to leave?"

"I, no . . . I don't know." Pain knifes through my chest. Of course I don't want him to leave, but I know he's going to leave eventually, so better now than later.

"I have a question," he says.

"Okay," I say slowly.

"Am I just, like, total friend-zone material to you?"

"Uh . . . what?"

"I know you said you weren't ready, and I respect that. But I also know how you don't like to hurt people's feelings, so I've been wondering if maybe you just said that to be nice."

"Elliott. It's—"

"Not me, it's you?" he asks, a twinge of bitterness creeping into his playful tone.

"No." I sit next to him and punch him gently in the arm. "Well, it's definitely me, but it isn't that you're friend-zone material. I mean, you know you're hot, right?"

"Well, my dads are always saying I'm the handsome one in the family, but it's always nice to hear a girl say it, too. Especially if she's under fifty."

"You're hot," I assure him. "And more importantly, you've been incredible to me. Supportive. Kind. You've shown me so many things since I got here. And all I ever did was help you carry some lumber. So I guess whatever this is between us, I don't feel like I deserve it." My voice cracks. "It doesn't feel real to me."

Elliott reaches for my hand. "The way I feel is real." My fingers fall into the gaps between his. This small simple contact is an anchor, a tether to the real world, a way to keep my brain from spinning off into cyberspace where the hashtags are waiting for me.

"Don't let go," I whisper.

"I'm not letting go." Maintaining his grip on my hand, he reclines back on my bed, pulling me with him. He curls onto his side. Gently, he adjusts my body until our chests are touching, our legs intertwined. "But why doesn't this feel real to you?"

I consider his closeness, the constellation of freckles under his left eye, the way he smells, the angle of his jawline. Each of these tiny things is beautiful—its own kind of magic.

And I don't deserve any of it.

The hashtags blink on in my head: #HeartlessBitch, #Coward, #Liar, #Killer. Finally I can't take it anymore. "It doesn't feel real because you don't know anything about me," I blurt out. "I've been lying to everyone all summer. You don't even know my real name." I squeeze my eyes shut. I can't bear to see the look on his face.

Elliott drags one fingertip down the scar on my cheekbone. "You're wrong. I hope you're not mad, but I know who you are, Genevieve. I know what you've been going through."

My stomach lurches as my eyes flick open and I sit up. "What?" Elliott is the last person I expected to be following the Dallas Kade story. But he knows my name, so clearly he knows something. "How?"

"I overheard Rachael talking on the phone when you were in the hospital and they didn't think you were going to live. She didn't mention the accident to anyone, even when we could all tell something was wrong, so please don't be mad at her," Elliott says. "I was worried. So I eavesdropped. I heard her mention Dallas Kade and a car accident. I heard her telling your dad she loved him, and not to give up hope. Then I heard her breaking down into tears after she hung up."

Hearing about the way Rachael supported my dad makes me feel like even more of a bitch for the way I treated both of them. But that's not what hurts the most. Everything with Elliott makes sense now. "So I'm just a wounded bird to you or something? An innocent little animal who needs fixing?"

"What? No," Elliott says. "That's not what I mean."

"So you weren't attracted to me just because I needed . . . help?" It's a struggle to force out the last word.

"Maybe initially. Is that so terrible? That I saw someone hurting and wanted to help? But since then, no. I like all of you, Genevieve. At least all the pieces you've been willing to share with me."

My chest aches at the sound of my name—my real name—coming from his lips. My heart rises into my throat. "Are you still following the story?"

"No," Elliott says. "I never had any interest in *following the story*. I was just curious to know more about you after we worked together at the park. I tend not to believe anything on the internet, so once I knew the basic facts I dropped it. It explained why you were so sad."

"No, it didn't," I choke out. "You don't know half of it."

There's a noise outside my door and I freeze. I lie back down on the bed and Elliott scoots close to me. I pull the quilt up until it covers all of us. It's just Elliott, me, and a handful of horses hiding away in a cave made of fabric.

"So tell me," he says.

I swallow back a sob. "I want to tell you—God, it would feel so good to finally let it out—but if I do, you'll leave. Like my dad left, like Dallas left. Only this time it'll be worse because I'll deserve it."

Elliott squeezes the fingers of the hand that is still twined through his. "I promise you, I won't leave."

"How can you make that kind of promise?" I whisper.

"Because I'm not perfect. I don't expect my friends to be perfect either."

"But what if I did something terrible?"

He pets my hair. "Maybe you *did* do something terrible, but that doesn't make *you* terrible, okay? I've done bad things, but I don't think I'm a bad person."

It's hard to wrap my head around Perfect Park Guide Elliott doing anything wrong. "Like what?" I murmur into his T-shirt.

He shakes his head. "You first. It's clear whatever you've been hiding is eating away at you. You need to just let it all out, because otherwise you are going to destroy yourself."

I blink rapidly. Is he right? I've been so obsessed with the consequences of telling the truth, I never stopped to think about the consequences of hiding it.

"I always thought of myself as a good person," I say. "But

now I know the truth." My voice cracks. "I'm a liar, and a coward, and a *killer.*" And then, from the safe darkness beneath Grandma Larsen's quilt, the whole story pours out of me in a flash flood of tears and shame.

CHAPTER 31

Elliott waits until I finish. Then he says, "So even if Freeman's BAC *was* over the legal limit, he's not guilty of manslaughter, because his driving didn't cause the accident. Yours did."

"Thanks for pointing that out," I say tightly.

"I'm just trying to understand why you're hurting so badly."

"Because I *killed* Dallas." A new wave of tears starts to fall. "I took him away from millions of fans. I cut short what would have undoubtedly been this epic life. And then when I realized what I had done, I let someone else take the blame. Everything that has happened—Freeman being threatened, innocent people being harassed, a freaking building set on fire—is my fault."

Elliott wraps his free arm around me and pulls me in close. I bury my face in his chest, sobbing into the soft fabric of his T-shirt. He doesn't tell me it's okay. He doesn't tell me to stop crying. All he says is "I'm right here. I'm not leaving."

After I calm down, I tell him how my mom explained what happened in the hospital, but I didn't remember much about that night so I couldn't give the police any specific information. "It's not like I purposely implicated him." I wipe at my eyes. "But then I got online and started reading about the accident. And Shannon—that's my best friend—has been texting me stuff. That day by the Visitor Center restrooms was right after I finally pieced together what happened."

"So why didn't you tell the police then?"

"I don't know," I say miserably. "No, that's another lie. I didn't tell them because I was scared. I had read the things people were saying online about Brad Freeman and I didn't want that to be *me*. Do you know what it's like to see people reducing someone to a series of hashtags? Horrible ones like #Murderer and #HumanWaste?"

"Well, I doubt they would have been that cruel with you," Elliott says.

"Why? Because I'm a girl?"

"Because you weren't drinking and driving."

"Come on," I scoff. "If there's one thing I've learned from the internet, it's that people can always find a reason to judge someone. They were calling Freeman a murderer long before the toxicology reports went public." I shake my head bitterly. "I read the news articles published the day after the accident and the whole world had already made up its mind. No one gave a shit about the truth. They just wanted someone to blame." My voice wavers. "I didn't want to be that someone."

Elliott nods. "So does falling asleep driving make you legally responsible?"

"Not criminally," I say. "Not in Missouri, anyway. There are a couple of states where drowsy driving is a crime, but I think even those stipulate that the person behind the wheel has to have gone without sleep for twenty-four hours or something."

"So then it was just an accident, right?"

"I don't know. It doesn't *feel* like an accident. Accidents are things that are unpreventable. It feels like my fault. I should have known better. I should have known not to drive if I was tired. Especially not someone else's car. Especially not when it was dark and rainy." I sigh deeply. "If I wasn't so jealous and insecure, we never would have been on the road in the first place. The fact that falling asleep isn't an official crime in Missouri is just a technicality. It doesn't make me any less guilty."

"You couldn't have predicted what was going to happen." Elliott squeezes my hand.

"When the charges were dropped, I was relieved, you know? I figured people would leave Freeman alone finally. That they'd begin to make peace with the idea that Dallas was gone." I shake my head. "I was so wrong."

"Know what else you were wrong about?"

"What's that?"

"I'm still here," Elliott says.

"But why?" I bury my face in my pillow. "I'm the worst kind of liar, one who does something wrong and lets someone else take the blame."

"No. That might be what you did, but it's not who you are. You were in a horrible accident, and then you were scared and

everyone starting jumping to conclusions and issuing judg-
ments and threatening people. I understand why you didn't
want to tell the truth. Just like I can see how badly you want to
come clean now." He pulls the pillow away from my face. "So do
it. And I promise I'll still be here."

"I *do* want to tell the truth. I've wanted to since that day we
hiked Angels Landing. I felt moved up there; I felt guided." I
bite my lip. "But it's harder to feel God in my bedroom when
I'm reading endless hate on the internet, so then I got scared
again." I suck in a deep breath. "Yesterday I finally reached my
breaking point. I decided to tell my dad, but he's in Salt Lake
City for work until tomorrow."

"Are you going to tell him when he gets home?"

"Yeah." I pause. "If you've known who I was this whole time,
why didn't you say something?"

"Well, considering that you put a fake name on your name
tag and didn't mention anything, it seemed clear that you didn't
want anyone to know. I didn't want you to be uncomfortable
around me. I could see you were struggling, so I kept trying to
give you an opening to confide in me."

I think back to the way he called me Jennifer on the Angels
Landing trail, to the way he asked about my scar and joked that
meeting Garrett meant I knew someone famous now. He'd been
trying to get me to talk to him this whole time.

I tighten my grip on Elliott's hand. "I'm scared I won't be
able to handle it when everyone knows the truth. What if the
whole world hates me?"

"First of all, you're stronger than you think," Elliott says. "When you start to doubt yourself, remember the gym. You did better than you expected. Everyone is capable of more than they know. Second, the *whole world* is not going to hate you. Some people will understand why you remained quiet. Those people will respect you for coming forward."

"But other people are going to say horrible things about me for the rest of my life. I'll never escape this. What happens when I apply to med school, when I go to get a job? Hospitals will Google me and find out I'm the worst kind of liar. It's always going to be out there."

"If you're that scared, you could always tell people that you just got your memory back," Elliott suggests.

I mull the idea over in my head. It's tempting, but it would just be me earning all those hashtags that have been chasing me for the past couple of weeks. #Liar. #Coward. #Hypocrite. "No. I don't want to fix a lie with another lie."

"Well, I think people like deans and doctors will appreciate the fact you found the courage to do the right thing. Sure, maybe some of Dallas's rabid fans will hate you, but you don't have to give those people any bandwidth. Just block them."

"I canceled all my social media accounts, but it's impossible to insulate yourself from everything. Maybe some night I'll be feeling ashamed and go looking for what people are saying about me because I think I need a little extra punishment."

"You don't need more punishment," Elliott says. He strokes the scar on my cheek again. "You almost died. You ran away from your friends. You tormented yourself with guilt. Enough is enough." He turns my body around so that his chest is pressed against my back and his top arm is curled protectively over my waist. For a moment, I worry that he does feel differently after hearing my confession, that he's moved me so he doesn't have to look into my eyes. But then he lifts up just long enough to kiss me on the cheek. "I'm here," he says. "I'm not leaving."

"Thank you for not leaving." I relax back into the warmth of his body. It feels so comforting. But even that feels wrong. "Maybe you should leave," I whisper. "I don't deserve this."

"Shh," Elliott says. "Just rest."

A few more tears trickle down my cheeks, but these ones aren't from sadness. "Why are you so wonderful?" I ask. "Is this even real?"

Elliott pinches me gently on the arm. "This is real. My feelings are real." He brushes my hair back from my neck and presses his lips to my skin.

A tremor runs through me. "When you said you did bad things, were you just trying to make me feel better?"

Elliott shakes his head. "I've done multiple bad things, but the one thing I'll always regret has to do with my sister, Monica."

I roll back around so we're facing each other. "I didn't know you had a sister. Was she also adopted?"

"Yeah." Elliott blinks hard. "We grew up in Sacramento. When I was fifteen, Monica moved to New York to join a fancy ballet company. We kept in touch via email, and at first all her messages were happy and excited. She loved New York, she'd made new friends, she was doing well in the company. But after a few months, her messages started to get a lot more negative. She always seemed stressed out, like she worried constantly about getting kicked out of the company. She told me not to tell Garrett and Ezra because she didn't want them to know she wasn't happy, or to try to interfere on her behalf. Some of the stories she told me about her exercise requirements and dietary restrictions shocked me, but I figured maybe she was exaggerating—everyone likes to complain about their jobs, right? I told her I couldn't believe she would put herself through so much just to be a dancer, but that I admired her dedication and perseverance. Whenever she seemed discouraged, I just told her I was proud of her for chasing her dreams. We were all so proud of her."

"What happened?" I whisper.

"She collapsed during a performance. Her heart gave out. Something about massive electrolyte imbalance and muscle wasting from starving herself. She died. I wish I had listened, really listened, instead of just encouraging her to keep going. Then maybe I would have seen she was in actual trouble, that she was reaching out to me, not just griping about her job."

"Elliott," I say softly. "You were fifteen. You didn't know."

"Yeah," he says. "For the longest time, I didn't tell my dads about her emails. I was positive they would blame me for her death. My grades dropped. I quit sleeping. They thought it was depression from losing Monica. Eventually my birth mom convinced me to tell them that I was blaming myself, and although there was a lot of shock and pain that day, it was only then that the three of us started to heal."

"I am so sorry," I say. "And I know how inadequate those words are."

He nods. "Monica also loved to paint. She had never been to Zion, but a friend sent her a postcard once and she got kind of obsessed with the place. She used to paint it all the time in high school. Garrett and Ezra kept saying we were all going to go, but everyone was so busy that it never happened. After her funeral, the three of us came up here to spread her ashes. And we never left." He swallows back a lump in his throat. "I never planned on going to college in St. George. Eventually I'll have to transfer if I want to go to vet school, but it's . . . hard to leave my family. It's been over three years, but it still feels raw."

I twine my fingers through his. My turn to not let go. For a few minutes, neither of us speaks. Finally I say, "So you talk to your birth mom?"

Elliott toys with the pendant beneath his collar. "Yeah. It was an open adoption. She lives in Alaska, but we email a lot."

"So you're not mad at her for giving you away?"

"No. I mean, it hurts to think that my birth was scary and stressful for my own mom. But she had me when she was fifteen. She was living with her mom and they didn't have much money. Giving me up was the right thing for everyone. How could I possibly hold it against her when I'm nineteen and I'm being raised by two amazing parents with ample resources to support me, and I still can't imagine trying to be a dad right now."

"You are pretty lucky," I say. "What about your birth dad?"

"Not in the picture," Elliott says. "But like I said, I kind of hit the dad jackpot, so I don't need a third one."

"Have you ever met your mom or grandmother?"

He shakes his head. "My grandmother passed away, but my mom still lives in Anchorage. I definitely want to get up there to visit her someday and hopefully learn more about my Inuit heritage."

"Did she give you that?" I point at the deer pendant around his neck.

He nods. "It's a caribou. My great-grandmother carved it. It's one of the only things I have from my mom's side of the family."

"It's beautiful," I say, leaning in for a closer look. I swallow back a yawn.

Elliott yawns. "Sharing secrets is tiring, huh?"

"It sure is."

"But do you feel better?"

"I do." I feel depleted, dehydrated from shedding so many tears, but for once my chest has stopped hurting. I can breathe without pain. And muscles I've been holding tense for weeks are finally starting to relax.

"Me too." He leans over and kisses me on the forehead. "Do you want me to stay?"

I imagine what it would be like to spend the entire night

wrapped in Elliott's arms, to fall asleep not feeling afraid or ashamed for once. I want that, but I don't think I deserve it. Not until I tell everyone the truth. "Yes, but that might be pressing our luck with Rachael."

"What if I stay until you fall asleep, and then sneak out?"

I don't deserve that either, but I can't resist. "Okay."

As I lay my head on Elliott's chest and let my eyes fall shut, doing the right thing feels a little less scary. If he didn't condemn me, maybe there are other people out there who will understand why I didn't come forward. Maybe there are even other struggling people, ones who if they see me do the right thing might find the courage to do the right thing too. This is about more than me and Dallas and Brad Freeman. This is about not being afraid to speak up. This is about making my voice heard.

CHAPTER 32

When I wake up the next day, Elliott is gone but my phone is sitting on the other side of my bed, a single text on the screen: I'm still here. His caribou pendant lies next to my pillow. It's a sweet gesture, but there's no way I'm keeping it, not after he explained what it means to him. Still, looping the pendant around my neck does make me feel like Elliott is with me in spirit.

My dad is supposed to be home by early afternoon, but he calls Rachael to let her know he ended up staying late to monitor the patient's cardiac output for a few hours.

"He'll be home by dinnertime," Rachael promises me.

"How did the surgery go?" I ask.

"He said it was over twelve hours long, with different teams scrubbing in and out to tackle different areas of the tumor. He sounded exhausted."

"That's intense," I say. I hate that I'm going to dump my troubles on him after he's been working so hard, but the truth can't wait any longer. It shouldn't have waited this long.

I go for a run and then spend the rest of the day pacing back and forth in my room, replaying everything that's happened since the accident in my mind. Outside, a small parade moves down the main street of Springdale, people on floats throwing candy and waving tiny American flags.

Dinnertime comes and goes and Rachael calls Dad again, just to make sure he's okay. She talks to him for a few minutes and then hands the phone over to me.

"Hey, hon," he says. "Sorry I'm missing out on the entire holiday. I was hoping I'd be home in time for the parade."

"No big deal." I clear my throat. "I'm just glad you're okay."

"Is everything all right?" I can hear the concern in Dad's voice.

"Yeah, there's just something I wanted to talk to you about." My mouth goes dry.

"Well, this traffic doesn't seem as if it's going to be thinning out anytime soon, so you might as well go for it."

"Uh, no. That's okay. I'll wait and talk to you when you get home." I don't want to distract my dad while he's driving.

"Okay. If you're sure," he says. "I didn't schedule any surgeries for tomorrow just in case I got stuck in Salt Lake City, so I'll reserve my whole morning for you . . . unless you'd rather stay up and wait for me. They've apparently closed the highway due to some kind of oil tanker spill, so I'm not sure how long it'll be before they get the road moving again."

"Tomorrow is fine." There's no point in canceling on Halley

and Elliott just to ambush my dad when he's exhausted. I'm sure we'll have to talk to a lawyer before I can make any kind of public statement, and it's not like we'll be able to get ahold of one in the middle of the night. I feel a tiny bit of relief that this whole mess is almost over. Soon I'll be able to tell everyone. Then the Kades can cancel their wrongful death lawsuit. Then I can finally answer that email from Brad Freeman. After tomorrow, we'll all be able to get on with our lives.

Elliott picks me up at nine p.m.

"Tell me again why Halley wants to go to this party so badly?" I ask. I slide into the passenger seat of his truck, checking my hair and makeup in the reverse camera on my phone. I'm still wearing a headband every day. My hair has started to grow back in around my scar, but it's still only about a half inch long.

The scar along my cheekbone has faded from a red line to a pink one, and all it takes is a bit of concealer to hide it almost completely. The only thing standing out as unusual about my appearance is the emergence of blond roots at the crown of my scalp. I meant to re-dye my hair, but I haven't gotten around to it. Hopefully no one will notice them in the dark.

"I think because her parents are so protective of her they don't let her go out much. But she's worked at the park for so long that they don't mind letting her go to anything that's an official Zion function."

I snort. "A party back by some dark river is an official function?"

"Hell no," Elliott says. "But I'm guessing Halley doesn't get too specific with them when it comes to the logistics."

"I get it," I say. "I'm just nervous because this will be the first time all summer that I've been around lots of people."

"Everything is going to be fine. Trust me when I say they're going to be more interested in drinking and fooling around than in trying to figure out who you are." Elliott pats me on the leg as he turns into the parking lot for the Springdale Family Kitchen. He pulls into an empty spot, grabs his phone from the center console, and taps out a quick text.

A couple of minutes later, Halley ducks out the front door of the restaurant. She's wearing a floral sundress that hangs just past her knees, a thin pink cardigan, and her trademark cowboy boots. Her blond hair is braided into two pigtails as usual. She opens the door and hops into the cab next to me. "Ready to party?"

I force a smile. "Let's do this."

Elliott pulls back out onto the main street of Springdale. A few minutes later, he drives through the entrance to Zion. "I'm surprised you'd want to go to something like this," I tell Halley. "Won't there be a lot of people drinking?"

"Yes, but that doesn't mean I have to drink. And there will also be a lot of people listening to music and eating snacks and wading in the river, all things I like to do."

"And Nephi will be there, right?" Elliott glances past me to Halley.

Halley blushes. "His sister said he was hoping to make it. He just got back from his mission last week."

"Well, then he'll definitely be looking for a little fun. Mormon missions are really strict," Elliott explains to me. "The missionaries have about a million rules they have to follow."

"It's not that bad," Halley says. "I want to do it someday, but not until I've completed a couple years of college."

Elliott stays on Zion Canyon Scenic Drive until it ends at a parking area with a shuttle stop marked: #9 Temple of Sinawava.

"So who's Nephi?" I nudge her in the ribs as Elliott parks the truck in a spot at the edge of the parking lot.

"He's Tazmyn's older brother. I know him from her house and also from church," Halley says. "But it isn't like that." She shoots Elliott a glare.

He snickers. "Sure it isn't. Halley and I started out in the gift shop here together and Nephi was a park guide. Her eyes turned to cartoon hearts whenever he came around."

"That was like three years ago, Elliott." She sticks her tongue out at him. "I've grown up a little since then."

"Is this guy hot?" I tease.

"He is sooo dreamy." Elliott smirks.

"Quiet, you." Halley reaches across me to punch him in the leg.

Elliott grimaces. He cuts the engine to the truck and removes the keys from the ignition. "Let's go so you can see for yourself, Jen."

We follow a group of boys who look a few years older than us down a dark but paved trail that leads out to the Virgin River. The area is partially illuminated by a string of lanterns along the shore. Cottonwood trees cast eerie shadows over the surface of the water.

The boys in front of us point at a soft glow coming from around a bend in the river. "Over there," one of them says. They wade into the water, exchanging exclamations about how cold it is.

"Can you get those boots wet?" I ask Halley.

"Yep. These old things have been through it all. They're indestructible." She points at a pile of thick tree branches near the end of the trail. "Grab a walking stick. It makes it easier to move around in the water."

We each take one of the sturdy branches and then wade into the river. The temperature difference between the warm air and the frigid water is enough to make my heart stutter. The water laps gently at my knees, just deep enough to cover the scar on my calf. I pick my way carefully, the bottoms of my tennis shoes slippery against the riverbed's mossy stones.

Halley squeals. "Something touched my leg," she hisses.

"Probably just a cattail or some kind of weed," Elliott says. "Or a snake."

"What?" I say, freezing mid-step. "There are snakes in here?"

Elliott laughs. "Just kidding." He rests one hand on my lower back.

"The park has a few snakes, but none of them are swimmers," Halley assures me.

Ahead of us, one boy is holding his cell phone out in front of him, using the light of his screen to navigate the dark water.

"Almost forgot." Elliott pulls a flashlight out of his pocket and directs the beam down at the surface of the water. "See. No snakes."

Halley points at the glow from around the bend, which is getting brighter. "We're almost there."

When we come around the bend, I hear music playing. There's a clearing off to one side of the water—a small beach of smooth pebbles and cast-ashore driftwood. Beyond it, a wall of rock partially covered with moss rises high into the sky. A tinny dance tune emanates from the speaker of a portable music player set safely back from the water. A line of lanterns placed along the edge of the rock wall illuminates a couple of large coolers and about thirty kids standing in small clusters or sitting on various logs. The river continues forward, disappearing into a narrow slot canyon, the red rock cliffs rising hundreds of feet in the air.

I scan the group of kids. I recognize a few of them—there's a girl who works the cash register in the Zion Lodge Gift Shop, and two girls I'm pretty sure work the hotel front desk. Away from the main group, three boys stand in a semicircle, their forms all in shadow except for the glow from the end of their cigarettes.

Halley's eyes are drawn to a couple of kids sitting on a wide log at the edge of the gathering. "It's Tazmyn and Nephi," she says, unable to keep the excitement from her voice. "I'll be right back." She drops her walking stick on the ground and picks her way across the overlapping rocks.

The two girls hug and Nephi gives Halley a big smile. He scoots over so she can sit down too. She twirls one of her braids around her index finger as she looks up at him.

"She's not coming back, is she?" I ask.

Elliott grins. "Probably not."

He takes my hand and leads me over to the coolers. One of them is filled with soda and water, the other with beer. We each take a can of soda and find an empty spot to sit down on one of the pieces of driftwood. I watch as Nephi pulls a box of sparklers and a book of matches out of his back pocket. Tazmyn and Halley each take one of the sparklers and giggle with delight as Nephi lights them. The girls spin around, the fireworks cutting sharp lines in the darkness.

"I set my phone alarm for eleven-thirty so we can be sure to get her home by midnight," Elliott says.

Halley's sparkler burns out and Nephi offers her another one. "So what do we do in the meantime?" I ask.

"I mean, it's no Ninja Warrior gym, but we can just hang out or wade in the water or walk farther up the river if you want. It's amazing how dark it gets inside the slot canyons at night."

I start to tell Elliott a walk sounds good, but then Halley bounces over with Tazmyn in tow. "Come meet my new friend, Jennifer," she says.

I try not to wince at the incorrect name. Elliott stands so the two girls can sit. Tazmyn and Halley squish into the spot he vacated, with Tazmyn ending up next to me. My eyes are drawn to the piano key bracelet on her wrist. I swallow hard. "Nice to meet you," I say.

"Halley says you just graduated from high school, too," Tazmyn chirps. "Are you starting college in the fall?"

"Yeah. I'm going to . . ." I have to think for a second to remember what I told Halley back when I first met her. "Northwestern."

Tazmyn cocks her head to the side. "You look familiar. Where did you go to high school?"

My heart starts pounding and I resist the urge to get up from the log and run away. I look down at my lap. "I went to a school in Illinois," I say. "A small town. You've probably never heard of it."

She snorts. "Doesn't get much smaller than this. I thought maybe we played you in tennis or something." She leans in close to me for a better look.

I plaster a smile on my face. "Nope. I'm not much of an athlete."

"Tazmyn played doubles for Hurricane High," Halley says. "She and her partner went to State."

"Where we got creamed in the first round by some girls from Salt Lake City," Tazmyn says.

"You know, you don't always have to add that part," Halley says with a grin.

A new song starts playing. Someone cranks the volume extra high.

"Woo." Halley jumps up from her seat. "Let's get this party started."

She grabs Tazmyn's hand and the two of them scamper across the rocks and start dancing with each other right in front of the music player. I exhale a sigh of relief.

"Come on." Elliott grabs my hand and at first I think he wants me to dance with him, but then he leads me toward the river.

I glance over my shoulder. "What about the walking sticks?"

"I won't let you fall."

I grip his hand tightly as we make our way into the water. Once again, the chilly temperature makes me gasp. "Where are we going?"

Elliott points upstream. The river disappears between two impossibly high walls of rock. "In there," he says.

We follow the river into the dark crevasse. He's right. I can't see anything in here. Craning my neck, I look up at the sky. It's just a ribbon of navy blue against the blackness of the cliffs.

"This is amazing," I say.

"I wanted to get you alone so I could tell you I'm proud of you." Elliott reaches out and takes my other hand too.

"Don't be proud of me. I should've told the truth a long time ago."

"I don't care. I'm still proud of you."

I turn to face him. "Thank you for not judging me," I say softly, pulling him into a hug.

"You did the wrong thing," Elliott says. "But now you're

doing the right thing. We can't define people by their worst actions, you know?"

"Yeah," I say. I do know that. It's why I forgave Dallas, why I forgave my dad. But does the rest of the world know that? I'm not so sure.

Elliott and I stand there, our bodies tight against each other while the water laps at our legs. Neither of us seems to want to let go. Finally he pulls back and kisses me on the forehead. "I'm glad I got to know you this summer. Even if you didn't want to be stupid with me."

I've still got both arms wrapped around his waist. "Trust me, I wanted to. I just didn't want you to regret things after you found out who I really was."

"And now that I know who you really are . . . ?" Elliott trails off.

My face gets hot. "I guess I thought the moment had passed, you know? That it was too late."

Elliott laughs lightly. "It's never too late to be stupid." He presses his lips to my forehead again and I feel his mouth curl into a grin.

I laugh. For the first time all summer, I feel *happy*. I'm going to do the right thing, even though it's hard. It's terrifying to think about, but it's also freeing. "Good to know," I say.

His lips move from my forehead to my cheek and then the crook of my neck. "So is that a yes?" he murmurs. His mouth drags hot across my exposed collarbone.

My knees buckle and I almost end up in the river. I tighten

my arms around him. "It would seem so," I say.

Elliott presses my body back against the rock wall for support. He rests one hand on my waist and the other on the side of my face. His lips brush gently against mine. "I've missed you," he says.

I reach up in the darkness and trace the contours of his face, my fingertips making their way from his chin, to his jaw, and then up into his hair. "I've missed you too."

Emotions I've been working hard to hold back all summer start to spill out of me and I pull Elliott's mouth toward my own. I'm so eager and impatient that our noses bump and teeth knock together before our lips slide into place. The frigid water is still lapping at my legs, but I can't feel it anymore. My entire body is flush with heat, with desire. If it weren't for the faintest hint of dance music from the clearing, I'd think that the two of us were completely alone.

I wish the two of us were completely alone.

I coax his mouth open with my tongue. It doesn't take much coaxing. Elliott pins one of my hands back against the rock, his other hand tracing the waistband of my shorts, his fingertips hot against my skin. I close my fist around a handful of his hair and arch my back against the canyon wall. I forget everything but the feel of Elliott's lips on mine, the feel of his hands caressing me.

And then there's a flash of light.

I freeze, confused, disoriented. I'm temporarily blinded by the flash. I realize the music has changed from dance music to something slower. My stomach drops low as I realize what song it is, the second single from Dallas's album. The love song he wrote for me.

Elliott doesn't seem to recognize it. "What are you guys doing?" he asks.

My vision has returned to normal. Tazmyn and Halley stand at the opening of the slot canyon. Tazmyn has her phone out, pointed at Elliott and me. She clears her throat. "I remember why you look familiar now, *Jennifer.*"

CHAPTER 33

Halley is staring at me, her face a mixture of confusion and betrayal. "You're Genevieve Grace?" she asks.

I can barely look her in the eye. "I was going to tell you tomorrow. I swear."

"She was." Elliott rests one hand on the small of my back.

"I don't understand," Tazmyn says. "How can you be here kissing some other guy? Didn't Dallas Kade write this song for you? I mean, it's been less than two months since he *died*. What's wrong with you?"

Halley turns away from the opening in the rock. I push past Tazmyn and go after her, with Elliott right behind me. "I didn't mean to lie to you, Halley," I say. "I came here to get away from everything that happened, but the day we met I saw your brace-let and I figured you were a fan and . . ."

Halley spins around so fast she nearly falls in the water. "And what? Did you think I would gossip about it? Now I get why you've been so quiet all summer. You know, I could've *helped* you if I had known."

"Looks like she found help from someone else," Tazmyn says coolly.

"Enough." Elliott's voice carries through the night. A couple of people by the coolers stop talking and look over at us. "You don't know Genevieve," he continues. "You don't know what she's gone through."

"Clearly, she's suffering greatly." Tazmyn's eyes drop to the level of my waist, with Elliott's arm hooked protectively around it.

"She's right. I shouldn't—I'm sorry—I have to go—" I pull away from Elliott and hurry across the river, almost falling twice on the slippery rocks.

"Do not post that photo," I hear Elliott saying as I reach the paved trail that leads back to the parking area. And then, "Genevieve, wait!"

I don't wait.

I don't turn around.

I hit the parking lot and keep going. When I reach Zion Canyon Scenic Drive, I accelerate into a sprint as best I can in my soggy tennis shoes. The road is completely black, with only the faint outline of cottonwood trees illuminated by the moon. I'm miles away from the entrance to the park, but I don't care. My breath catches in my throat as I push onward. How could I have been so stupid? How could I have thought going to a party with a bunch of kids my own age with Elliott was a good idea? I should've known something like this would happen.

All the hashtags I've been running from flash through my head: #Hypocrite, #Coward, #Liar, #ControlFreak, #JealousBitch, #Killer. My brain adds one more to the list: #Slut. My shoes rub against my heels, chafing my skin to the point where I have to slow down. I peek over my shoulder, but all I see is darkness. In front of me, something moves in the roadway—a porcupine. Yellow eyes glow as it stares me down for a moment before scurrying across the road and down into the underbrush.

I can just barely see the entrance to the Grotto Picnic Area ahead when I hear the sound of a vehicle. Elliott pulls up next to me and flashes his lights. He pulls over alongside the dark road and gets out.

"What are you doing?" I ask. "You should go back to the party. You're Halley's ride home."

"Halley is fine," he says. "She can catch a ride with Tazmyn and Nephi."

"I'm fine too," I say. "Really. I don't mind walking home."

"Do you realize how long of a walk it is? It'd take you over an hour."

"It's not like I have anywhere to be."

"Well, I'm not letting you walk. It's dark and you're not even wearing light clothes. You could get hit."

"Maybe I should get hit," I say. "Maybe that's what I deserve."

"Why? Because you made a mistake? Because you kept something secret? Because you kissed me?"

I shrug. *All of the above?*

"No one deserves to get hit," Elliott says. "Get in the truck, Genevieve."

"I'm fine," I say again.

"Get in the truck or I'm calling Rachael," he says firmly.

"You're going to narc me out to my stepmom? Some friend."

"Some friend is right." Elliott opens the passenger door.

I don't want to be around anyone right now, but I'd rather deal with Elliott than stress out Dad or Rachael, who may or may not decide my distraught state and disheveled appearance warrant a late-night call to my mother.

"Fine." I step up into the truck and Elliott shuts the door behind me. I wrap my arms around my middle and turn away from him as he slides into the driver's seat and heads down the road. I don't say anything until the park's exit comes into view. Then I sigh. "I'm sorry I ran off. I just couldn't deal with it. Tazmyn's probably right, you know? Maybe it is horrible of me to have feelings for you so soon after Dallas died."

"You can't control how you feel," Elliott says. "Though if you don't want to act on your feelings, I totally respect that. But don't let some friend of Halley's, or the internet, make that decision for you, okay? You decide what's right."

I bite back tears. "You're one of the only things that has felt right all summer."

Elliott reaches out for my hand and wraps his fingers around it. "Then don't let strangers take that feeling away from you. You don't have to be miserable for the rest of your life just because you survived. Or because you fell asleep. Or because you lied."

When I don't respond he continues. "Sorry it took me so long to catch up with you. I was talking to Halley. She's trying to convince Tazmyn not to post that picture."

"Why? It's the truth."

"It's *our* truth," Elliott says. "Maybe you have things that the public deserves to know, but they don't need to know about you and me. They don't have any claim to your personal relationship with Dallas. That's your business, just like we're our business."

"I don't even care," I say. "It's such a tiny thing compared to the other stuff I've done. Let her post it if she wants to." And I mean it. It'll just be a preview of things to come. "Does Halley hate me for lying to her?"

"No," Elliott says. "She doesn't understand why you would keep everything a secret, but that's because she doesn't know the things that I know."

"I really was going to tell her tomorrow. First my dad, then everyone else."

"I know." Elliott turns off the main road onto the street where Dad and Rachael live. He pulls up across from the house. "I think you're going to feel a lot better after you talk to your dad."

"Maybe." Right now the word "better" seems very far away. A mirage. An illusion. An impossibility. "Thanks for the ride." I slide out of the truck and head across the street.

Elliott follows me to the door. "Genevieve, wait. I don't want to leave you like this."

I reach up to touch the caribou pendant hanging in the

hollow of my throat. "Thank you for loaning me this." I start to pull the black cord over my neck.

Elliott grabs my hand. "Keep it," he says firmly.

"I can't ke—"

"At least until you've dealt with stuff. That pendant has given me a lot of strength over the past few years. Maybe it'll work for you too."

Tears hover on my eyelashes. All I can do is nod.

Elliott pulls me into a hug. The two of us stand on the porch for what feels like forever. His arms are tight around my back and my head is tucked firmly under his chin. He smells like hair product and river water, a hint of smoke from the party clinging to his shirt. I wish I could melt right into him. I wish I didn't have to let him go.

He pulls back and grabs my hand, lacing his fingers through mine. "You want me to come over tomorrow, be with you while you talk to your dad?"

I shake my head. "I can handle it."

"Okay. But remember I'll be here." He touches the pendant around my neck. Then he pulls his phone out of his pocket. "And here. Call me anytime."

I squeeze his hand. "I will. I know. And thanks."

Elliott brushes his lips against my forehead and gives me one last look before he turns away from me.

I watch him walk down the driveway and hop back into his truck. Then I turn and open the front door to the house, stepping quietly inside so as not to wake Dad or Rachael. Turns out

I needn't have bothered. The lights are all off, but Dad is sitting on the sofa, staring at the television. He blinks sleepily when he sees me.

"I can't believe you're still awake," I say. "I thought you'd be exhausted after your trip."

"You haven't heard, have you?"

"Heard what?" My muscles go weak at the sound in my dad's voice. I reach out for the edge of the sofa to steady myself. I lower my body to the cushion next to him. "Is it Rachael? Mom? Did something happen?"

"I know you've been worried about the possibility of having to testify in a wrongful death lawsuit," Dad says quietly.

"Oh. I've actually kind of come to terms with that. What I wanted to talk to you about—" My words fade away as Dad holds up a hand.

"Glen Kade left me a message earlier tonight," he says. "There isn't going to be a lawsuit. You won't have to testify."

"Okay." I pause. "Well, I think that's good. I know the Kades don't want to profit off Dallas's death. I'm sure they only considered it because drinking and driving groups and crazy Kadets were pressuring them."

"Yes," Dad says. But it's as if he didn't even hear me. He's staring past me at the television, which is on mute.

I spin around, my heart sinking into my gut when I see the headline splashed in red across the bottom of the screen: "Dallas Kade Fandom Responds to Brad Freeman Suicide Attempt."

CHAPTER 34

My chest starts to burn. I realize I haven't taken a breath in a few seconds, so I inhale sharply. "Suicide attempt? Is he okay?"

"I'm not sure," Dad says. "But I wanted to be the one who told you. I know you feel like the whole world has been coming down on him really hard."

"I don't understand," I whisper. "Was it because of the lawsuit?"

"No one knows the exact details yet," Dad says. "According to the news, Freeman got into a physical altercation with some men at a park today and he got charged with assault. He left his ex-wife a strange apology message saying he was going to do the one thing that would make everything go back to normal. It concerned her enough that she sent the police over to check on him. He was alive but unresponsive when cops arrived. He had tried to hang himself."

I perch on the edge of the sofa as a video clip begins to play on the TV. It's wobbly and washed out, like the one of the Eight

Ball Bar & Grill being vandalized. Someone's cell phone, I realize. I recognize the setting—a popular St. Louis water park that Shannon's family used to take us to when we were little.

I watch as Brad Freeman strolls past the end of the wave pool carrying two large sodas. A younger guy in royal blue swim trunks looks up from his lounge as Freeman passes and says something. The TV is still on mute, so I can't hear the words, but whatever he says is enough to make Freeman pause. The younger guy hops up from the lounge and pushes Freeman. One of the sodas falls to the pavement. Freeman says something in response and suddenly more people enter the frame. You can't tell who throws the first punch, but it doesn't matter. About thirty seconds later both Freeman and the guy in the blue trunks are being restrained by security guards.

My eyes flood with tears. Dallas is dead, and Brad Freeman tried to kill himself, and both of those things are on *me*. Maybe Dallas was an accident—I didn't mean to fall asleep behind the wheel—but Freeman . . . I should've known, I *must have* known that the constant accusations and threats could lead to this. After all, that's the major reason why I've stayed silent for so long—because I didn't want that bullying directed at me. What if he dies? The hashtag #Murderer blinks on in the back of my brain again.

"Genevieve," Dad says. "Are you all right? I know how hard all this has been on you."

"I'm all—" I can't bring myself to finish the lie. I'm not all right. I will never be all right. I didn't put a noose around Brad

Freeman's neck, but my inaction, my silence, let things escalate to that point. All he wanted was for people to believe him. All he wanted was for people to accept the decision made by a judge who had more facts than anyone else.

But instead we took everything away from him—the idea of safety, his friends, his job, his sense of self-worth. Some people did it with harsh words and accusations. I did it by saying nothing. He reached out to me for help and I ignored him.

"I don't know." I struggle to keep my voice level. "I just want Brad Freeman to be okay."

"Me too." Dad nods soberly. "Do you want to talk about it? I could make us both some coffee."

I shake my head. My dad looks like he's about to fall asleep and I can't talk now anyway. My mind is full of horrible images of Brad Freeman trying to hang himself. I wonder what *he* was thinking about, how hopeless and alone he must have felt to try to take his own life. *Because of you.* Yes, because of me.

I feel dead inside, like someone scraped out my guts and replaced them with rocks. I can't believe this is happening. A few hours ago I was laughing, I was happy.

"I'm really tired," I say woodenly. "I think I'm going to go to sleep. We can talk tomorrow."

"Okay," Dad says. "But please remember that Rachael and I are here for you. And your mom is just a phone call away. Or if you need to talk to a professional, I can get a referral from someone at work."

"Sure," I say, but I barely hear him.

As I close the door to my room behind me, my phone buzzes with a text.

Halley: I just want you to know I'm not mad. I'm trying to convince Tazmyn to delete the picture.

Me: It doesn't matter, but thanks.

I think of the stupid disagreement at the party, how less than an hour ago I was worried about the fact that Tazmyn took my picture with Elliott. I was afraid of being judged, of being called a #Slut.

But now someone else might die.

Suddenly being called a slut doesn't seem very important anymore.

I lie down and pull the horse quilt up to my chin, but it's pointless. I'm not going to be able to sleep until I know whether Brad Freeman will be okay. My laptop sits on the desk across the room, calling out to me. I stare at it for a few minutes, caught between a desperate need to know and the fear of actually finding out. Finally, I crawl out of bed and Google his name, holding my breath as the search results appear. All of the articles that pop up are at least a couple of hours old, and there's no update on his condition. Hoping maybe Carly Freeman posted something, I check her blog, but there is only the single post setting the record straight about the alleged restraining order.

I switch over to Twitter to see if there is any up-to-the-minute news there. I wonder what people are saying, what they're thinking. Do they feel guilty like I do? Like their rush to judge and punish a stranger contributed to yet another tragedy? I search the #BradFreeman hashtag and scan the last few tweets.

Patrick S @pxs1228 • 41s

I hope #BradFreeman doesn't make it. Another drunk driver off the roads and we won't even have to clog up the court system to make it happen.

Quite Contrary Mary @manikmari • 2m

I know I should probably feel sad #BradFreeman attempted suicide, but I don't. He made a choice #DallasKade didn't get to.

Suicide Prevention @afspnational • 3m

There is always hope. You are never alone. We're here. #StopSuicide #BradFreeman

YOUNITY FOREVER @laf0387x • 5m

Hey #BradFreeman. Burn in hell, you piece of shit murderer.

Monkey Man @boxxofmonkees • 5m

Oh look! Even #BradFreeman realized the district attorney screwed up.

The tweets go on and on, most of them dismissive or cruel. Occasionally there's a message in support of Brad, or one reminding people that this isn't what Dallas would have wanted, but those people are quickly ridiculed and ignored. I never realized that the number of retweets someone gets seems directly proportional to how mean their original tweet is.

I always assumed I'd go back to the internet after everything quieted down. I mean, I can't imagine going through college without social media accounts. I'll probably need them for some of my classes. But seeing this steady stream of hate—even now, after Brad Freeman tried to kill himself—sickens me. How can people be this hurtful?

I'm just about to log off when I notice a tweet that agrees with me:

Megz @glittergirl13 • 4m

@pxs1228 How can you say horrible things about #BradFreeman when he might not even live?

Good question, Glitter Girl. I click to expand their conversation.

Patrick S @pxs1228 • 3m

@glittergirl13 Because #BradFreeman is a low-life, alcoholic wife-beater who killed a music superstar and deserves to die.

Megz @glittergirl13 • 3m

@pxs1228 He NEVER hit his wife.

Patrick S @pxs1228 • 3m

@glittergirl13 How do you know?

Megz @glittergirl13 • 2m

@pxs1228 Because that's my mother you're talking about.

Patrick S @pxs1228 • 1m

@glittergirl13 You're Freeman's kid? Sucks to be you. I'd kill myself if he was my dad.

Megz @glittergirl13 • 1m

@pxs1228 Oh yeah? Well I'd kill myself if YOU were my dad.

Patrick S @pxs1228 • 31s

@glittergirl13 Good thing I'm not interested in raising any white trash little brats then, isn't it?

Megz @glittergirl13 • 11s

@pxs1228 You're an asshole. And you're also blocked. Buh-
bye.

I click on @glittergirl13's profile. It reads: *Megan F. 13. I like
horses, books, and glitter.*

I open another search box and type in "Megan Freeman."
The name is way too common and over a million hits come back.
I try searching for an overlap of Megan and Brad Freeman and
sure enough, a couple of articles appear that were written about
the accident. Brad Freeman has a thirteen-year-old daughter.
One who likes horses and books, just like I do.

One who is now being picked on by strangers.

Something snaps inside me and all the fear and sadness and
shame I've been drowning in is replaced by a new feeling—
clarity.

I know what I have to do.

CHAPTER 35

The door to Dad and Rachael's room is shut tightly.

I take in a deep breath, let it out, remind myself that this is the right thing. Then I knock gently. "Dad? Are you still awake?"

My dad comes to the door a couple of minutes later wearing scrub pants and a wrinkled T-shirt. "Gen?" He rubs his eyes as if maybe he thinks I'm a mirage. "What's wrong? Are you okay?"

"I have to talk to you. It's about . . . Brad Freeman."

Dad swallows back a yawn. "Sure. Of course."

Rachael appears at his shoulder, a V of worry etched between her brows. "Is everything all right?"

"I've got it," he says. "Go back to sleep."

They exchange a light kiss and then Dad follows me into the living room. I glance at the sofa and then turn toward the kitchen, taking a seat at the table.

"A dinner table convo, huh?" He slides into the seat across

from me and drums his fingertips on the edge of his chair.

I realize my hands are shaking. I bury them in my lap. "It has to do with the accident," I start. And then, once more, everything comes spilling out.

Just like Elliott, Dad doesn't interrupt me. When I'm finally finished, he rubs at his temples for a few seconds. "I don't understand," he says. "You never lied, not even as a little kid. I remember that time you broke your mom's vase. You could have hid the evidence or made up a story, but instead you came to find us in the backyard to confess what you'd done. So why—how, even—could you keep something this important a secret?"

"I was scared," I admit. "By the time I got my memory back, things had already escalated. And then the charges got dropped, so I thought maybe things would settle down on their own. I know that doesn't make it okay. But at least I can tell the truth now and try to keep from making things any worse."

Dad rakes his hands through his hair. "Oh, Gen. Things are going to get plenty worse, for you at least. You withheld information from the police. You could be charged with a crime, and that's even before we get to your responsibility for the car accident or . . . anything else that's happened." He shakes his head. "Your mom and I were so angry at this man . . ."

I lower my chin. "I really messed up. I'm sorry."

"I'm not the one you need to apologize to." Dad swears under his breath. "When you asked me about how I managed to confess to your mother, I knew *something* was going on. I should have pressed you to talk to me."

"You couldn't have known, Dad," I say. "This isn't your fault. I didn't lie because you lied. I made my own bad choices."

He nods slowly, his expression heavy. "I understand more than most people how fear can push you into bad decisions. We just have to figure out how we can do the right thing and keep you protected—"

I pull my feet up onto the chair and wrap my arms around my legs. "I don't want to be protected. I want to take responsibility, whatever that entails. I want people to know that Brad Freeman wasn't responsible for the accident. I want to tell the whole truth."

"To the police?"

"To *everyone*."

"Okay. I think you're doing the right thing." He clears his throat. "We do need to speak to your mother before you tell anyone, though."

"She's going to tell me not to do it."

"Probably," Dad says. "But if you're brave enough to admit what you did to the whole world, you're brave enough to stand up to your mom."

"I should probably go back to St. Louis so I can tell everyone in person." When I think about facing Dallas's parents and Brad Freeman's family, I start to second-guess my decision again. I have no idea how I'll be able to get the words out. And what about Freeman himself? How am I supposed to look him in the eye after I ignored his email message? Assuming he recovers and I even get that chance.

"We can probably get a flight out tomorrow and take care of everything Thursday and Friday. Then you can stay or you can come back here with me, if you want."

"But what about your cases?"

"I can reschedule them and get one of the other guys to cover my clinic hours."

"Thank you," I say hoarsely.

Dad nods. "I'll go book us a flight and then call your mom and fill her in. You should try to get at least a couple hours of sleep."

"I love you, Dad."

"I love you too," he says, but I get no comfort from the words. I'll never forget the look on his face right now, a mix of worry, disappointment, and shame.

CHAPTER 36

We've started our descent into St. Louis by the time I figure out exactly how I want to tell the truth. Dad recommended reaching out to one of the major newspapers across the country, but almost all of them ran articles vilifying Brad Freeman at one time or another. I don't want to give one of those papers my exclusive.

"I think I want to tell Chris Reale the truth," I say. "From *Reale News Now.*"

"I don't know that one," Dad says.

"He's a smaller St. Louis news blogger, one of the only people who didn't presume Freeman was guilty from the beginning." I don't remember Chris's exact words, but I know he was one of the few online voices who withheld judgment.

"Sounds like a smart choice."

"But I want to tell the Kades and the Freemans before I talk to any of the news people."

Dad exhales deeply. "I don't envy you, honey. The world is

different now than it was when I was growing up. Back then if you lied about something or you caused an accident that killed someone—even someone famous—you didn't have to see what everyone was saying about you. Now the whole world thinks they deserve to be part of your punishment. It's scary."

"I am scared," I admit. "I feel like everyone is going to hate me."

Dad pats me on the leg. "I know one guy who isn't going to hate you," he says. "And I suspect there will be other people who respect you for coming forward."

I nod. It's basically the same thing Elliott said to me. I sent him a quick text this morning to let him know I was heading back to St. Louis to deal with things. He responded right away to tell me he'd be thinking of me and to call anytime. I reach up to touch the caribou pendant hanging around my neck. I'm glad to be taking a piece of him with me. Thinking of the way he listened to my story without condemning me gives me strength. Of course, things are worse now. The morning news said that Freeman had regained consciousness and was expected to make a full recovery, but I blink back tears as I realize a second person almost died because of me.

When the intercom crackles and the flight attendants ask us to stow our tray tables and return our seatbacks to their full upright positions in preparation for landing, my stomach drops lower and lower with the plane.

When Dad and I pass through the central security area and I see my mom waiting, I'm even more terrified. Mom is a pale, elongated version of me and today she looks paler and taller than usual.

I'm expecting a lecture, but she rushes up to me and wraps me in a hug. "Genevieve, I'm so glad you're okay." When she pulls back from the embrace, her cheeks are wet.

Dad pats her awkwardly on the back. "How about I grab the luggage and you two get the car. I'll meet you in the passenger pickup area?"

Mom nods at him. "Thank you, Greg."

Dad heads for the baggage claim and Mom and I split off toward the parking garage. She wipes furiously at her cheeks as a young couple turns to watch us pass.

"Mom, why are you crying?" I ask.

"I'm sorry. I just—I should have listened to you. You tried to tell me and I ignored your concerns. I could have prevented this."

I link my arm through hers. "You were just trying to protect me, and besides, you didn't have all the information. I should have told you or Dad everything as soon as I remembered."

"Yes, you should have," Mom says fiercely. She digs a tissue out of her purse and blots at her eyes.

We fall into silence as we exit the brightly lit airport into the dim garage. I follow Mom, surprised to find the car in section Yellow P. My dad came up with that idea when I was little, so we'd never forget where we parked. I remember giggling and shouting "yellow pee!" over and over. My mom told my dad he was gross, and a bad influence on me.

"Yellow P, huh?" I say.

Mom's expression softens slightly. "I try not to discount a good idea just because I'm not so fond of the source."

Back at the house, the conversation about coming forward continues. Mom has reverted into "all business" mode, her tears replaced by a steely expression.

"I appreciate that you're trying to do the right thing here, Genevieve." She paces back and forth across the floor of our family room. "I'm just worried about how this will affect your future—med school, residency, applying for jobs. I don't want it to ruin your life."

"Trust me, I've been thinking about that for weeks. But at least I still have a life to ruin," I say quietly. "And there are a lot of people who deserve an apology from me. I watched Brad Freeman's daughter get bullied on Twitter last night, and it was one more terrible thing that I caused. If anyone deserves to be bullied, it's me."

"No one deserves to be bullied." My mom's lips harden into a thin line. "What if we reached out to this family, told them the truth, and then offered them monetary compensation to keep the information confidential? The newspapers made it sound like Mr. Freeman has been struggling financially. I'm sure your father and I could both contribute—"

"No. I mean, it's great if we can cover his medical bills and stuff, but I don't want to buy them off. I know you're just trying to protect me," I continue before Mom can interrupt, "but keeping this secret has been eating away at me. I might never forgive myself for not coming forward sooner. At least this way I won't have to hate myself for anything else. And this way maybe other people will see my story and do better than I did."

Mom's eyes water. She nods grimly. "Well, if you're determined to do this, let me at least speak to Vince first and see what the possible consequences will be for us as a family." She pulls her cell phone out of her pocket.

"Elena. Do you need to call your lawyer right—"

"Yes, Greg. I do," Mom barks. "We need to find out if what Genevieve has done constitutes a crime. And if there's the possibility of a lawsuit, then I would like to be prepared."

My dad scoffs. "She didn't cause this. If anyone needs to be sued it's the men who assaulted him. Or those idiots online telling him he should just go die. The bullies who harassed his family and got him fired from his job."

"I don't mean for Freeman," my mom says. "I mean for Dallas."

Crap. I didn't even think about that. Just because falling asleep driving isn't a crime, doesn't mean it can't be used in a wrongful death lawsuit.

"Glen and Nora weren't even going to file against Freeman until all the shit hit the fan," Dad says. "They're our friends. Do you honestly think they would go after us because our daughter fell asleep driving their son's car while he sat intoxicated in the passenger seat?"

"We can't be sure," my mom says.

"He wasn't totally wasted or anything," I say.

"But he'd been drinking," my dad says. "And you offered to drive because you thought it was the safer choice. Let me talk to them."

I shake my head. "I can do it." I hate that coming forward means making them relive Dallas's death one more time, but they would want the world to know the truth.

Wednesday night, I practice my confession on one more person —Shannon. I call her to let her know that I'm in town and the two of us meet up at Dallas's grave site.

We sit cross-legged on the grass in front of the stone as I catch her up on everything that's happened. She curls the end of her dark braid around the palm of her hand as I speak. When I'm finished, she doesn't respond right away.

"Your hair seems longer," I say to fill the silence.

"Extensions, duh." She kicks at the toe of my sparkly flip-flop with the edge of a strappy gold sandal. The movement causes a small stuffed bunny to roll down from the top of the pile of things people have left for Dallas.

"Look at all this stuff," I say. The pile makes the haul of gifts and cards from my hospital room seem like a droplet in an ocean. There are tons of handwritten notes, T-shirts, stuffed animals, and flower arrangements in various states of decay. I reach down and pick up what I think is a stuffed Toothless from the movie *How to Train Your Dragon*. It's missing one of its plastic eyes and the brutal St. Louis weather has bleached the black coat gray. There's a handmade bracelet wrapped about its neck, tiny beads spelling out: I LOVE YOU.

"I don't understand," Shannon says finally. "Why didn't you tell me? Did you seriously think I wouldn't support you?"

"It was just hard," I say. "I felt bad not telling you Dallas cheated on me. But I was afraid you would respect me less for staying with him. Then after I realized what I had done, I was so ashamed of myself. I didn't want you to think of me as a liar and a bad person. I didn't want to lose you too."

"Gen. If I were the kind of person who would respect you less for making your own choices, or the kind of person who would judge you for struggling with an impossible situation, then I wouldn't deserve you."

"I know. I think when my dad left, it hurt me a lot more than I realized. I don't have very many people in this world that I'm close to, so the thought of losing any of them is terrifying." I set the stuffed dragon back on the top of the pile of items. "I think I felt like—feel like, maybe—I have to earn the love of people around me. So I hide a lot of my imperfections."

A tear rolls down Shannon's cheek. "Well, you earned my love back when we were six, remember?"

I do remember. Mom and I were coming home from dance class and I saw Shannon sitting on the porch. She'd moved in a couple of weeks earlier but I hadn't officially met her yet because she wasn't outside much. That day her parents were arguing so loud we could hear it in the yard. "Can I invite her over to play?" I asked my mom.

"I think that would be an excellent idea," Mom said brightly. "Why don't you show her your room and I'll speak to her parents and see if she can have dinner with us."

Shannon was only too happy to escape to the quiet sanctuary of my bedroom. And from that day forward, anytime she needed to get away from her parents fighting, she knew she had a place with me.

"And you gave me all that love right back when it was my parents' turn to get a divorce." I shake my head. "I don't know what's wrong with me. I've had a lot of uncomfortable revelations about myself lately."

"You were so weird once you went to Utah. I should've known something wasn't right. I wish I could've been there for you." Shannon plays with the end of her braid again.

"You've been there for me almost my whole life. I never would've made it through the day I came back to school if it wasn't for you."

"As I recall, you only made it through half the day," Shannon says.

I smile. "Because I had to leave you to go to class."

Shannon nibbles on one of her pinkie nails. "So, like, are you going to be in trouble with the police?"

"Apparently not. My mom's lawyer said not coming forward about the accident isn't a crime because I didn't directly lie to the police in order to implicate Brad Freeman."

"Well, that's a relief."

I rest my head in my hands. "Nothing is a relief to me. I just want everything to be out in the open."

I tried to object when Mom told me I didn't even need to speak to the police. "I should set the record straight," I insisted. I felt like Detectives Blake and Reed were two more people who deserved an apology.

"There is no record," Mom said. "The case is closed. I can have Vince give them a call just to pass on your message if you like, but the police are busy, honey. You don't want to take up their time just so you'll feel better about things."

"Speaking of everything," Shannon says teasingly. She pulls out her phone and taps at the screen.

My neck muscles go rigid. I haven't touched my laptop since two days ago when I saw Brad Freeman's daughter being bullied. "I'm not sure I want to get online right now."

Shannon shakes her head. "You don't have to get online. I was just wondering who this is."

She holds out the picture of Elliott and me kissing that Tazmyn took on the Fourth of July.

"Oh. His name is Elliott. He works at the park with Rachael. I didn't mean to keep him a secret either. I wasn't really sure where it was going."

"It kinda looks like it's going to the bedroom." Shannon grins.

"Ugh. I can only imagine what people are saying."

"People are idiots," she says. "You're almost eighteen. You and Dallas weren't married. You don't have to stay faithful to his memory, no matter what a bunch of stupid Kadets think."

"I know. I just hate that I dragged Elliott into this mess too."
I pick at a fraying thread on my jean shorts. "He's actually the
first person I told about all this."

"Oh, great. Another boy I'm going to be jealous of."

I reach out for Shannon's hand and give it a squeeze. "You're
always going to be my first love, you know that?"

"Same. Best friends forever, okay?" she says. "No matter
where we end up. No matter what we do."

"Deal." I hold out my pinkie finger.

She loops her finger around mine and we shake on it.

Pinkie swear, huh? Dallas says from somewhere inside my
brain. *Serious business.*

CHAPTER 37

Thursday is one long, exhausting series of confessing, over and over. We start with Dallas's parents. It's just my dad and me because my mother has three surgeries to perform today. She tried to rearrange her schedule, but one of her patients came all the way from Tulsa, so she couldn't reschedule.

Nora Kade grows paler and paler as I tell her and Glen the whole story. "Were you really going to let us sue that man?" she asks.

I shake my head. "I knew I had to come forward. I guess I was just working up the nerve."

Glen Kade shakes his head. "I hate the fact that Nora and I are probably part of the reason Brad Freeman tried to take his own life. Maybe if we hadn't pursued the lawsuit . . ."

I think of the email from Brad—the one I never found the courage to answer. "This isn't on you guys," I say. "You made the best decisions you could with the information you had. You trusted me and I let you down."

Nora starts crying, big racking sobs that remind me my actions hurt a lot more people besides Dallas and Brad Freeman.

"If there's ever anything I can do," I say softly.

Glen nods. "I'm glad you found the courage to finally come forward."

"Me too," I say. "I just wish it hadn't taken me this long."

According to the morning news, Brad Freeman is at the same hospital where I was cared for after the accident. To protect him from reporters, the staff isn't giving out his room number, but my mom has one of his attending doctors pass him a message and he agrees to meet with us.

His door is open and as Dad and I approach I can see that his room is empty and he's sitting up in bed reading a book. He looks just like the picture from *Reale News Now*, except he's got a couple of days worth of dark beard stubble. I pause for a moment outside the door and then reach out to knock on the doorframe. He looks up from his book, his smile fading slightly when he doesn't immediately recognize us.

I swallow hard. "Mr. Freeman? I'm, uh, Genevieve. Genevieve Grace. And this is my dad. Can we come in?"

"Oh. Sure." He sets his book down on the bed and gestures at a couple of chairs along the side of the room. "Grab a chair. And call me Brad, please."

Dad and I enter the room, and I start to pull the door closed behind us.

"Actually that has to stay open," Brad says. "The nurses need to be able to . . . keep an eye on me."

"Oh, sorry," I say awkwardly.

"I'm Dr. Greg Larsen." Dad slides two chairs closer to the bed. "Sorry to bother you like this."

"It's no bother." Brad's eyes skim over me. "I'm glad you're doing so well. I didn't recognize you because of your hair."

"Right," I say, touching my head. "I dyed it."

I lower myself into the chair that's farther away from Brad. I try not to stare at his neck, at the white gauze bandages wrapped around it. My eyes drop to the cover of his book. He's reading the latest James Patterson thriller, the same one I was reading in Utah. "I started that the other day." I point at the book.

"It's good so far." He looks back and forth from me to my father, his brow furrowing. "For some reason I thought you had left St. Louis."

"I did." I thread and unthread my fingers together in my lap. "I went to Utah. But I came back . . . to tell the truth. And to apologize to you." My lower lip trembles. Tears pool in my eyes. I look away for a second and then back toward him. "I—I fell asleep," I say hoarsely.

And then the tears fall, hot against my skin. My breath sticks in my throat. Dad presses a tissue into my hand. "I'm sorry. I shouldn't—" I start to apologize for crying. But then I hear Elliott in my head, telling me not to hide my emotions, so I crumple the tissue in my palm and let the tears fall. "I fell asleep and I'm the reason for the accident. I'm the one who killed Dallas Kade, and I'm so sorry for the way you've been treated, for the way *I've* treated you."

Brad blinks hard and then looks toward the far wall. Dad hands him a box of tissues. He blots at his eyes and swallows hard before he speaks. "You came all the way back here to tell me that?"

"I came back here to tell everyone," I say. "You, the Kades, the media. I want the world to know what really happened." I swallow back a sob. "I'm so sorry I didn't answer your email. I started to, but then I got scared."

"I figured maybe you hadn't remembered anything, or that your parents had told you not to interact with me," he says.

I shake my head. "I got my full memory back right about the time the charges against you were dropped. I kept telling myself that it was over, that nothing bad would happen. But bad stuff was happening every day. For a while, I stayed offline so I could avoid seeing it. But when you sent me that message, I couldn't pretend anymore. I realized I had to tell my dad, but he was out of town."

"I got back late the night of the fourth," Dad says soberly.

Brad clears his throat. "Well, I appreciate you coming forward like this. I don't know—"

"Are you serious?" a high-pitched voice asks from behind me.

I spin around. Megan Freeman and a woman I presume is her mom, Carly, stand in the doorway to the room. Megan looks exactly like her Twitter picture except that her face is contorted in rage.

"I appreciate you coming forward? That's bullshit, Dad." She storms into the room and skids to a stop next to my chair. Turning her attention to me she says, "I can't believe you knew and you're just now saying something. He could have died because of you." Her eyes fill with tears "You bitch! How could you run away and keep everything a secret and leave my dad here to be harassed and assaulted?"

"Megan, you need to calm down," Carly says quietly. "Maybe we should take a walk."

"Let her stay," I say. "I'm sorry," I tell Megan. "I know how badly I messed up."

Brad clears his throat. "Hey, Megz. Some of the blame is mine, all right? I'm the one who . . . let things get so bad. I should have gotten help."

Megan is still focused on me. I'm not even sure she heard her dad speak.

"Do you know what it's like to go to the water park for Fourth of July and watch your dad get *arrested*? Or what it's like to watch random strangers beat him up for something he didn't even do?"

I shake my head.

"Megan." Brad tries again. "Genevieve is trying to do the right thing and this situation isn't easy for her."

"Good." Megan turns toward her father. "Because it hasn't been easy for me either. And clearly it wasn't easy for you." She turns back to me. "You know what? The whole time my dad gave you the one thing no one gave *him*—the benefit of the doubt. He was positive that one day you would remember what happened and clear his name."

"And it seems like that's what she's doing." Carly places her hands on her daughter's shoulders. I'm not sure if the gesture is meant to be comforting or restraining.

"A little late, Mom," Megan says bitterly.

Next to me, Dad doesn't say anything, but he rubs me gently on the back. The tiny gesture is enough to let loose another wave of tears. If the EMTs had been even a few minutes later, Megan wouldn't have a dad to sit next to her and support her.

I swallow hard. "I know there's nothing I can do to fix this, but I am going to tell everyone the truth so they'll know that the accident was my fault. I'm going to speak to Chris Reale this afternoon. He's a reporter who always gave your dad the benefit of the doubt."

"Chris Reale seems like a decent man," Carly says.

"I trust him to report the actual truth. He'll clear your dad's name, Megan." My voice cracks. "I—I hope one day you can forgive me."

Megan's eyes narrow. "Are you kidding me? I will *never* forgive you, for as long as I live. I hate you. I wish you had died in the accident."

"Megan!" Carly inhales a sharp breath. "You take that back right now."

Megan shakes her head. "Sorry, Mom. Some things you just can't take back." She spins on her heel and storms out of the hospital room, slamming the door behind her. Carly gives us all an apologetic look and turns to go after her daughter.

A nurse pops her head into the room. "Everything okay in here, Mr. Freeman?" Her mouth puckers up as she takes in all the red-rimmed eyes. "You're supposed to be taking it easy, remember?"

"We're fine," Brad says. "Thank you for checking."

"We're getting ready to leave," my dad adds.

I keep replaying Megan's words in my head. *I will never forgive you, for as long as I live.* There's a knot of pain in my chest. My whole body is trembling.

Brad turns his attention back to me. "She's an emotional kid. She didn't mean that."

"It's okay," I say softly. "If she's going to hate anyone, it should be me."

Dad rubs my back again.

"Thank you for telling us before the media." Brad reaches out for a cell phone on his nightstand. I can't help but notice it's a model from a few years ago and the screen has a crack in it. "I'll have Carly make sure Megan doesn't get on that phone of hers before you can speak to Chris."

I nod. "I appreciate it." I fidget in the chair. "That's all I came to say, unless you have any questions for me." I want him to tell me he forgives me, but I know that's expecting an awful lot. I should probably just be glad he didn't swear at me the way his daughter did.

Brad shakes his head. "I'm a little overwhelmed at the moment."

"There's one other thing," my dad says. "Genevieve's mother and I would like to offer you some money. I know your truck was totaled in the accident and—"

"Oh, there's no need for that." Brad holds up his hand. "Your coming forward means more than finances. I'll get by."

"You deserve to do more than get by," my dad says. "At least let us cover the cost of your medical bills."

Brad is silent for a few seconds and I can tell he's wrestling with the idea. Finally he says, "I appreciate the offer, but I should be okay. Carly and Megan actually started one of those online funding sites to help with expenses, and I've got other family I can reach out to if needed until I get back on my feet."

"Okay," Dad says. "But please let us know if you or Megan ever need anything." He sets one of his business cards on Brad's nightstand.

We turn to leave, but I pause at the doorway. "Mr. Freeman—Brad," I start. "I really am sorry."

He nods, his expression unreadable. "I know you are."

Dad and I head out into the hallway. As we navigate the bright white corridors back to the bank of elevators I say, "Do you think we can find that fundraising site and make an anonymous donation?"

Dad squeezes my shoulder. "I think we can definitely do that."

It's not much, but it's a start.

CHAPTER 38

Our next stop is a meeting with Chris Reale. I don't know why, but I'm expecting him to be this squinty-eyed judgmental asshole who lectures me about responsibility. Instead he turns out to be a laid-back guy in his thirties who shows up to our meeting in jeans and a T-shirt. Dad and I meet him at a local Italian restaurant because apparently he works out of his home.

We stand in the foyer for a few minutes while the hostess goes to inquire about our seating arrangement. I glance around at the other people, worried about being recognized, worried about them overhearing things.

"Relax," Chris says. "John said we could use his private banquet room to talk since it's not booked today. He hooks me up on a regular basis and you can expect total discretion from the staff."

A server returns and leads us through the dining area to a back room. Even though I'm wearing sunglasses, I keep my eyes trained on the floor. Chris, Dad, and I take a seat at a table set with napkins and silverware. A waiter brings us three menus.

"Order whatever you want," Chris says. "It's on me."

Dad starts to object. "Oh, you don't need to—"

Chris cuts him off. "Are you kidding me? This is the first interview Genevieve has given to anyone, right? This is a big deal for me. I can afford to spring for some Italian food."

I look up from my menu just long enough to make eye contact with him. "Thank you."

"Not that it's all about me and my career," Chris adds quickly. "I'm about the same age as Brad Freeman and I've empathized with him throughout this ordeal because I could see myself in his position, you know? I'm glad to get a chance to set the record straight about his involvement."

"And mine," I say.

Chris rests his elbows on the table. "Look, Genevieve. I want you to know I'm on your side, too. You're here, helping get the truth out into the world. That's admirable, and I won't throw you to the wolves, no matter what you tell me. You can strike anything you say off the record if you want."

"That's very understanding of you," Dad says. "My main concern is protecting my daughter's personal information so that she isn't harassed by internet nut jobs."

"Understandable," Chris says. "And do both you and your ex-wife have unlisted phone numbers and addresses?"

"I do," Dad says. "And Genevieve will be staying with me for a bit. Isn't that right, hon?"

I nod. I came back here to clear the air and take responsibility for the things I did, but that doesn't mean I have to hang out and let strangers throw rocks at me. I'll miss Shannon and my mom, but I feel like I have unfinished business in Springdale. I want to help with the displays for the Zion Canyon Touch Trail and watch kids use it after it's completely finished. I want to get to know Rachael better, and spend more time with my dad. And then of course there's Elliott. I'm not ready to let him go yet either.

The waiter reappears with three glasses of water and takes our order.

After he leaves, Chris turns on a tape recorder and I start to tell the story again. He lets me get all the way through, redirecting me a couple of times when I wander off topic.

"What made you originally want to tell the truth?" he asks.

"My conscience, I guess. I've always believed in telling the truth. Going through every day having to face the fact that an innocent man was being blamed for something I did forced me to realize I was being a bad person."

The waiter arrives with our food. I pick at my toasted ravioli, dipping a deep-fried square into the marinara sauce until it's almost saturated. I nibble at a soggy corner.

Chris samples his fettuccine and then takes a big drink of water. "Was there one moment that pushed you over the edge?"

"The first person I told was this guy I met in Utah. And instead of condemning me, he encouraged me to tell the truth." I pause. "Before that I had talked to my dad about a time when he had to come forward about something. The two of them helped me see that although everyone might not forgive me, the people who care about me would at least try to understand why I did what I did."

"So this guy you talked to—is it the guy I've seen pictures of you with?"

"Probably," I say. "I haven't been online in a couple of days."

"So you're dating again?" Reale arches an eyebrow.

I clear my throat. "Yes. I know a lot of people aren't going to understand, but I don't have to defend my feelings. I loved Dallas—I will always love him—but in the months preceding the accident, we'd starting growing apart, heading in separate directions. We were fighting that night, in fact. I was pretty insecure when it came to him being a celebrity."

"If you hadn't been fighting, do you think it would have changed how the rest of that night played out?"

"Probably. I'm trying not to go down those 'what if?' rabbit holes anymore, because they're long and dark and they never end. I made a decision that we had to go home; I made a decision to drive. Those choices had horrible consequences, but I can't go back in time, you know?"

"I do," Chris says. "More than you know." He asks me a few more questions and has me and my dad sign a few release forms. As we're heading back to the entrance of the restaurant, Chris touches me lightly on the arm. "How scared are you about the public response to this?"

"I'm not looking forward to it," I admit. "But the pain of public outrage doesn't compare to the pain of realizing a second person almost died because of me."

Chris nods. "I hope you're getting some help for that."

"I have an appointment with a therapist back in Utah."

"Good. What's the best way to reach you in case I have any follow-up questions?"

"You can email me," I tell Chris. "Or call me. I don't have a problem answering follow-up questions. Just know that I probably won't read the article because I don't want to read the comments."

"I'll read the article." Dad wraps a protective arm around my shoulders. "And maybe we can read the comments together."

We head back to Utah on Friday and the article goes live the next morning. I'm back in my room at Dad's house and I don't even log on to look. Instead I get up early with Rachael and head to Zion. I'm greeted by a smile from Elliott and a warm hug from Halley.

"Good to see you back," Elliott says. "Did everything go okay?"

"I guess. I'm avoiding the internet so I won't have to read all the horrible comments."

"There aren't any," Elliott says. "Chris turned the comments off on his article. He said it was a short factual piece to set the record straight and that the truth should speak for itself. He said he'll be doing a follow-up opinion piece later in the week and that people so inclined can comment on that."

"That was nice of him," I say. "But I'm sure there are plenty of comments in other places."

I'm right, of course, and after I get home from work my dad skims through a bunch of them. "They're not as bad as you expected," he says. "It's mostly just a bunch of people criticizing you for not telling the truth. But hey, there are a few votes of support mixed in with all the rage. Some people think you're pretty brave. And look, your hashtag is trending."

"Fabulous. What every girl dreams of." I dare to peek over my dad's shoulder. "Wait, go back," I say, as he skims through the #JusticeForDallas and #GenevieveGrace threads on Twitter. "Did someone just tweet that I killed Dallas on purpose because he was about to break up with me?"

Dad scrolls back up and taps the screen to expand a conversation. Sure enough, there's a stream of tweets that reads:

Lila Alice Ferrier @Lila_Roxx • 4m

I know someone who was at the Try This at Home release party and she saw #GenevieveGrace and #DallasKade fighting.

Lila Alice Ferrier @Lila_Roxx • 4m

I bet #GenevieveGrace swerved into the other car on purpose because #DallasKade dumped her for @RealAnnikaLux.

Patrick S @pxs1228 • 3m

@Lila_Roxx Wouldn't be the first time a teen girl went psycho when she got dumped. #GenevieveGrace

Marco T @marcoplayspolo • 2m

@pxs1228 @Lila_Roxx How are we just now hearing about this? Are the cops going to open a new investigation into #GenevieveGrace?

"People are idiots," my dad says.

"They are angry, anyway," I say. "What's funny is that some of these people are the same ones who were tweeting me messages of support and speculating that I was carrying Dallas's baby a few weeks ago."

"Some people just want to be part of the story, even if it's a story that's completely fabricated," Dad says. "But look—we read them and you survived."

"I guess." There was a time when a bunch of comments calling me a murderous psycho bitch would have really upset me. To be honest, they *do* upset me.

But I won't let them destroy me.

EPILOGUE

AUGUST 15

"I never wanted to be a hashtag," I say, forcing my eyes to remain up and facing the crowd. Halley is sitting four rows back and on the middle aisle, because she insisted that I could look at her the whole time if I needed to and it would seem like I was addressing the entire group. This presentation for her Mormon youth group is the first of at least thirty public speaking events I plan to do over the next year.

I couldn't get over the fact that nothing I did was technically illegal, so with the help of my therapist I reached out to organizations focused on internet bullying and drowsy driving, offering my services as a speaker or volunteer. I had a lot of takers, so many that I've decided to take a gap year before I start college so I can focus on helping other people avoid the mistakes I made.

Halley clears her throat and I realize I've lapsed into silence. "Sorry, this is hard." I pause for a second to take a sip of water from the bottle clutched tightly in my hands. "Once I had a teacher ask the whole class to pick five hashtags we would apply to ourselves. It was just an updated version of that 'What five words best describe you?' interview question. I picked things like #BlondAmbition and #PreMed and #NeverSayQuit. I thought I was such a good person back then. Lately, people have been hashtagging me with things like #Coward and #Selfish and #Liar. The worst part is, they're right."

I swallow hard. "I did a lot of things wrong the night of the accident. And then I continued to mess up, for weeks afterward. How does someone who once tweeted, 'Where there is truth, there is trust. And with trust, you can survive anything,' become a #Liar?" I raise my chin and look straight at the crowd. "This is how it happened."

And so I give them the whole story: the party, the accident, the horrible sick feeling in my stomach when I realized I was responsible. I tell them about hiding, about running away, about trying to start over, but repeatedly being drawn back into the internet drama.

I clutch a balled-up tissue in my hand. I had no idea how many times I would break down crying while telling this story in front of a group of other teens, but surprisingly I'm holding it together. Maybe that means I'm starting to accept my role in all this, or maybe I'm just out of tears.

After I take responsibility for what I did and caution people about drowsy driving, I return to the idea of the internet. "It's funny," I say. "Maybe you think you're just one person. What you do doesn't really matter. You can read a few tweets or blog posts and then publicly render your judgment of a total stranger. Who cares? You're just one tiny voice in a huge ocean. But the thing about tiny voices is that when they band together they can be incredibly loud. Uncomfortably loud. Sometimes that's a good thing—a strong thing. A group of voices can wake people up to the truth. But a group of voices can be a bad thing too, because we're not always right." I pause. "Or even when we *are* right, sometimes the things we do to each other still aren't okay."

Halley gives me an encouraging nod. "Keep going," she mouths. "You got this."

I inhale deeply. "Sometimes we bandwagon, we jump to conclusions, we point fingers at people, because it seems fun or makes us feel like part of something. Maybe we do it because we feel angry or powerless and it gives us the illusion of control. But we don't think about how it feels to be on the other side of those fingers. We don't think about what it's like when you just need a few minutes of peace and everywhere you look people are judging you." I pause again. "We don't think about what it would be like if you just needed a reason to keep going and instead you got a bunch of reasons why you should go die."

I look from one side of the room to the other. "Brad Freeman made the decision to try to end his own life, but he had a lot of encouragement. You have more power than you think. Be careful what you do with it."

Halley congratulates me after the speech and tells me I did amazing. Several of her friends come up to me to say they were moved. I make small talk and answer their questions for about twenty minutes, but the truth is, I'm dying to get out of here. After the crowd has died down, I give Halley a hug and tell her I'm taking off.

"Going to see Elliott?" she asks, a gleam in her eyes.

I smile. "Maybe." This is Elliott's last week of work at the park before he packs up and moves back to St. George for the school year. I know we'll only be about forty minutes apart and will still get to see each other when I'm not doing presentations, but I still don't want to waste the time we have left.

I slide into my dad's Prius and start the engine. Once I got back from St. Louis, Rachael and Dad encouraged me to start driving again. It was scary at first, but Dad said if I was brave enough to tell the truth, I was brave enough to get back behind the wheel. He and Rachael took turns riding along with me as I worked my way up from the streets of Springdale to nearby two-lane highways and eventually back onto the interstate. I'm grateful to them for pushing me. It'll make traveling to my presentations and seeing Elliott a lot easier.

A lot of other things have happened in the past few weeks too. I've been called basically every name there is on the internet and turned into a few unfortunate memes about lying, but I've also received some nice messages of support too. Brad Freeman did a TV interview where he publicly forgave me and told the world that what they were doing to me wasn't any better than what people had done to him. Last I heard he had quit drinking completely and was working with a lawyer to try to get his paramedic license reinstated. I hope that works out for him. Tyrell James emailed me to say he's writing a song in honor of Dallas and other performers who have died in car accidents. He plans to use the proceeds to raise awareness for driving safety. Tyrell is another person who I figured might hate me, but if he does, he's keeping it to himself.

Clint is in the entry booth as I pull into Zion. He gives me a little wave. I park in the lot by the Visitor Center and take the Zion Park Shuttle to the lodge. Officially the Zion Canyon Touch Trail doesn't open for three more weeks, but once everything was completed we pulled down the caution tape and let people try it out. When I see a man my dad's age walking along it with two little girls, my eyes start to water.

I take the short trail from the lodge to the Grotto Picnic Area. I know exactly where Elliott is because he's doing nature talks all day. Right now he's up at Scout Lookout, giving a talk about the peregrine falcons that nest on the cliff.

When I make it up to where he's presenting, the crowd is just starting to dissipate, some people heading toward the series of Walter's Wiggles that will zigzag them down the side of the cliff, others moving toward the safety chains that lead out to Angels Landing. The first time I stood in this spot, part of me didn't care if I lived or died. I'm glad I survived those moments.

"Thank you," I murmur into the ether, just in case someone is listening.

"Talking to God again?" Elliott has sneaked up behind me.

"Maybe," I say.

"You know, Ezra and Garrett go to this nondenominational church in St. George every Sunday. I join them sometimes. You could come along too."

I smile. "I'll think about it." I wouldn't say that I've found faith or anything this summer, but like my dad said back in St. Louis, I'm more open to the possibilities now.

"I've been thinking about you all day," Elliott says. "How did it go?"

"Not bad, actually," I say. "No one spit on me or cussed me out."

"Mormons are good like that," he says with a wink. "I'm sorry I couldn't make it." He pauses. "So what's up?"

"Nothing," I say. "I just wanted to see you."

"I'm glad." Elliott points at a wide flat rock across the clearing. We make our way over to it and sit down, just a couple of feet from the edge of the cliff. A curious chipmunk comes to investigate us.

"Shoo," I tell it. "There are no handouts here."

Elliott watches the chipmunk disappear into a clump of sagebrush. "I wish I wasn't moving next week. I can't believe you're not going home."

I lean my head against his shoulder. "I can't believe this place is starting to feel like home."

"Do you have any hesitations? About not starting college?"

I shake my head. "I can take some online courses to complete a few gen-ed requirements if I want, but doing these presentations feels more important, you know?"

"And your mom is okay with it?"

"Yeah. She's being really supportive of the decision," I say. "I know she's going to miss having me close, but I plan on visiting her a lot. She even said she might come out here for a long weekend sometime so I can show her the trail we made."

"Awesome. Of course you'll have to help me with my hair and outfit before I meet her." Elliott grins. "I want her to like me."

I laugh. "I think she's actually changed a lot over the past couple months. You'll probably be okay."

"If not, we'll just bring her to the gym and I can wow her with my mad ninja skills." He winks.

"Sounds like a plan."

We sit holding hands, looking out at the view—red cliffs banded with pink and white stretching out into the distance, the sinewy twists of the Virgin River and the park's scenic drive below us. The sun is beginning to set and I know that soon we'll have to start back, but I want to enjoy this moment while I can.

"You been online lately?" Elliott asks. We both know I can't avoid the internet forever.

"Not much. I peeked at Twitter yesterday. Megan Freeman had tweeted a couple of things about me—like she wondered how I could sleep at night and she thought her dad was wrong to forgive me."

"You're going to have to see her again soon, right?"

"Yeah, in October." A film student working on a documentary about internet shaming culture had reached out to both

Brad Freeman and me, asking us if we'd be willing to talk on camera. As far as I know, Carly and Megan are also going to be part of the interview.

I wonder if Megan will ever forgive me.

I wonder if I'll forgive myself.

"Hey." Elliott yanks a small pair of binoculars out of the side pocket of his uniform pants and holds them up to his face.

"What is it?" I ask.

"Look." He hands me the binoculars and points off into the distance, at the top of the next cliff.

"Holy crap," I breathe. A mountain lion is moving along the edge of the summit. "That's the most beautiful thing I've ever seen."

Elliott laughs lightly. He strokes the side of my face, where beneath my makeup a scar from the accident still lingers. "It's definitely in my top five."

I am enthralled by the cat, by the way its thick tail hovers just below the ground, by the powerful and purposeful feel of each of its strides. "Should we make a lot of noise to protect ourselves?" My lips curl into a grin. "A wise man once told me that was the proper protocol."

Elliott wraps an arm around me. "I think we're safe."

I smile as I lean into his body, but the truth is, I don't know if I'll ever feel safe again. Our "protective bubbles"—our houses, our cars, our friends, our online identities—might make us feel secure, but most of it's just an illusion. It's easy to get hurt, just like it's easy to hurt other people. That's part of why I'm doing these presentations. At first it was about penance—I thought they might take away some of the guilt. Now I'm hoping my story can help protect people by keeping others from making the same mistakes I did.

It's a daunting task and part of me worries the whole next year will end up being a disaster—that I'll be booed off stage, or no one will listen to me and nothing will change. It's probably impossible to make a real difference.

But I know a lot of people who have accomplished some pretty incredible things—my mom raising me mostly on her own while maintaining a research lab and busy surgical practice, Elliott's dad making it to the third stage of the *American Ninja Warrior* finals, Dallas turning a hobby into a major recording contract.

With practice and dedication and hope, other people have redefined what's possible. If they can do it, maybe I can too. It won't be easy and there are no guarantees, but I'm going to try anyway.

ACKNOWLEDGMENTS

First and foremost, a huge thank-you to my readers, for choosing this book from among countless others, and for being willing to genre hop with me as I write twisty mysteries, fluffy romances, and more serious contemporary novels. I hope to keep surprising you for many years to come.

Thank you to my friends and family, both immediate and extended, many of whom do not even know about this novel yet because I wrote it so quickly. I am so lucky to have you in my corner. Thank you for pep talks, music recommendations, boxes of edible things, and endless panda pictures.

My gratitude goes out to the amazing industry professionals I am fortunate enough to work with. Thanks to Jennifer Laughran, for both general and agent-related awesomeness, and for finding the time to read this manuscript quickly when I was really struggling; Karen Chaplin, for your always excellent editorial suggestions, and for knowing when to guide me and when to let me find my way; Olivia Swomley, for your stealth editorial contributions, and for heading up the *GATU* book-signing all-star team; Rosemary Brosnan, for supporting my work, letting me switch book ideas at the last minute, and for being the nicest person I've ever met in a public bathroom; and to my copy editors and proofreaders, for being so thorough and informative and kind. It might not always seem like it, but I swear I learn from your copious corrections. Thanks also to everyone else at HarperTeen who had a part in producing and/ or supporting this story. I am so lucky to be part of your team!

Thanks to my beta-readers and experts: Lynn Doiron; Philip Siegel; Cathy Castelli; Marcy Beller Paul; Hannah Taylor; María Pilar Albárran Ruiz; Christina Ahn Hickey, MD; and Ranger Larry Walter. As always, thanks to the Apocalypsies, the YA Valentines, and all the super-awesome book bloggers who manage to balance being supportive with keeping it real. I love you guys.

For all the *American Ninja Warrior* contestants: whether you fall off the first obstacle or hit all the buzzers, please know that you are inspirations to countless people. Whenever I think something is impossible, I watch *ANW* and remember just how powerful hard work and tenacity can be.

Last but not least, thank you to the targets of online shaming. I have read many of your stories, and I admire the grace and courage you summoned in the face of adversity. You, too, are my inspirations.

AUTHOR'S NOTE

This book is the intersection of two things I love (*American Ninja Warrior* and Zion National Park) and two causes I feel strongly about (online shaming and drowsy driving). Here are two major questions I contemplated while writing *This Is How It Happened*:

1. Is the prevalence of online shaming contributing to an internet culture where moderate voices are unwelcome and honest people who want to confess or come forward remain silent due to fear of excessive retribution?

2. Is drowsy driving as dangerous as drinking and driving? And if so, why is it so much easier for people to drive tired than to drive drunk?

My interest in online shaming dates back to 2005 when I was teaching English in South Korea. While I was there, a college student gained online notoriety after her dog defecated on a subway train and she refused to clean it up. An outraged passenger with a camera phone snapped pictures of the girl and posted them online. Within days, the girl's name, address, and current university were made public by "netizens" seeking justice. The girl and several family members were mocked and harassed, the university's server crashed from people posting angry messages, and the girl responded online to apologize for her actions and say the backlash had driven her to the point of contemplating suicide. She ended up dropping out of college and moving away from Seoul to escape the public scorn. Some of the people I was teaching English with thought this story was hilarious, total poetic justice. But I couldn't help wondering, did the punishment really fit the crime?

I researched and reviewed more than thirty instances of online shaming while writing this novel. Some of the targets had done something embarrassing, some had engaged in activities people found offensive, and others had been accused of crimes. Almost all of the targets I read about struggled with feelings of isolation, despair, and hopelessness during and after their shamings. Many said they contemplated suicide. I know there are some people who will say whatever they want whenever they want to say it regardless of the consequences, and that's their right. But I also know there are people who might rethink a comment or tweet if they knew it would push a struggling person closer to the edge, or cause harm to innocent bystanders. I don't believe in censorship but I do believe that when we say something online we are publishing ourselves and we need to own our words—not just in that moment but forever, because once it's on the internet it might never go away.

The National Highway Traffic Safety Administration (NHTSA) estimates that drowsy driving was responsible for 72,000 crashes in 2013. In a study done by the National Sleep Foundation, 37% of the people polled admitted they had fallen asleep while driving at least once. Within my own family, there have been multiple fatigue-related car accidents, and I remember doing road trips in college where I drove to the point of hallucinating before I felt the need to pull over and get some rest.

Maybe it is our "it won't happen to me" mentality or our incorrect belief that we can control our bodies that makes people so willing to drive while fatigued, but there's no way to predict exactly when sleep will overtake us. And even if a driver doesn't fall asleep, excessive fatigue slows reaction times, reduces the ability to focus, and impairs the ability to make good decisions. The TV show *Mythbusters* tested the idea that sleep-deprived drivers are as impaired as drunk drivers and not only confirmed it as true, but found in some cases that the sleep-deprived drivers performed worse than those driving under the influence of alcohol.

Drowsy driving often doesn't receive the same attention and publicity as drinking and driving or texting and driving, but it's still a serious issue with potentially lethal consequences, especially for seniors, night-shift workers, and younger drivers. According to the NHTSA, teen drivers who sleep less than eight hours nightly are one-third more likely to crash than those who sleep eight or more hours nightly. If you are planning to drive a long distance, consider planning out ahead of time places where you can stop and rest. If you become fatigued while driving, switch drivers if possible, or look for a safe place to pull over for a short nap. If that's not feasible, call a parent, friend, or transportation service. It might seem like a hassle or an expense you don't want to deal with, but it also might be the thing that saves your life.

Speaking of saving lives, the Twitter address for the American Foundation for Suicide Prevention listed in this book is real. You can follow them at @afspnational or reach them at 1-800-273-8255 if you or someone you know needs help.